Land Beyond the Wave

Paul Cuddihy is the editor of *Celtic View*, the official magazine of The Celtic Football Club. In 2009 he wrote the best-selling biography *Tommy Burns: A Supporter Who Got Lucky*. He also co-wrote *Century Bhoys: A History of Celtic's Greatest Goalscorers* (2010) and *The Best of the Celtic View* (2007), while he also edited a number of books for the club. In 2004 he was one of the prizewinners of the inaugural Scotsman Orange Short Story Competition. In 2010 he wrote his first novel, *Saints and Sinners* followed by *The Hunted* in 2011. He was born in 1966 and lives in Glasgow with his wife and three children.

Land Beyond the Wave

Paul Cuddihy

First published by Capercaillie Books Limited in 2012.

Registered office 1 Rutland Court, Edinburgh

Printed by Antony Rowe, Chippenham

Set in Galliard by 3btype.com, Edinburgh

A catalogue record of this book is available from the British Library.

ISBN 978-1-906220-68-6

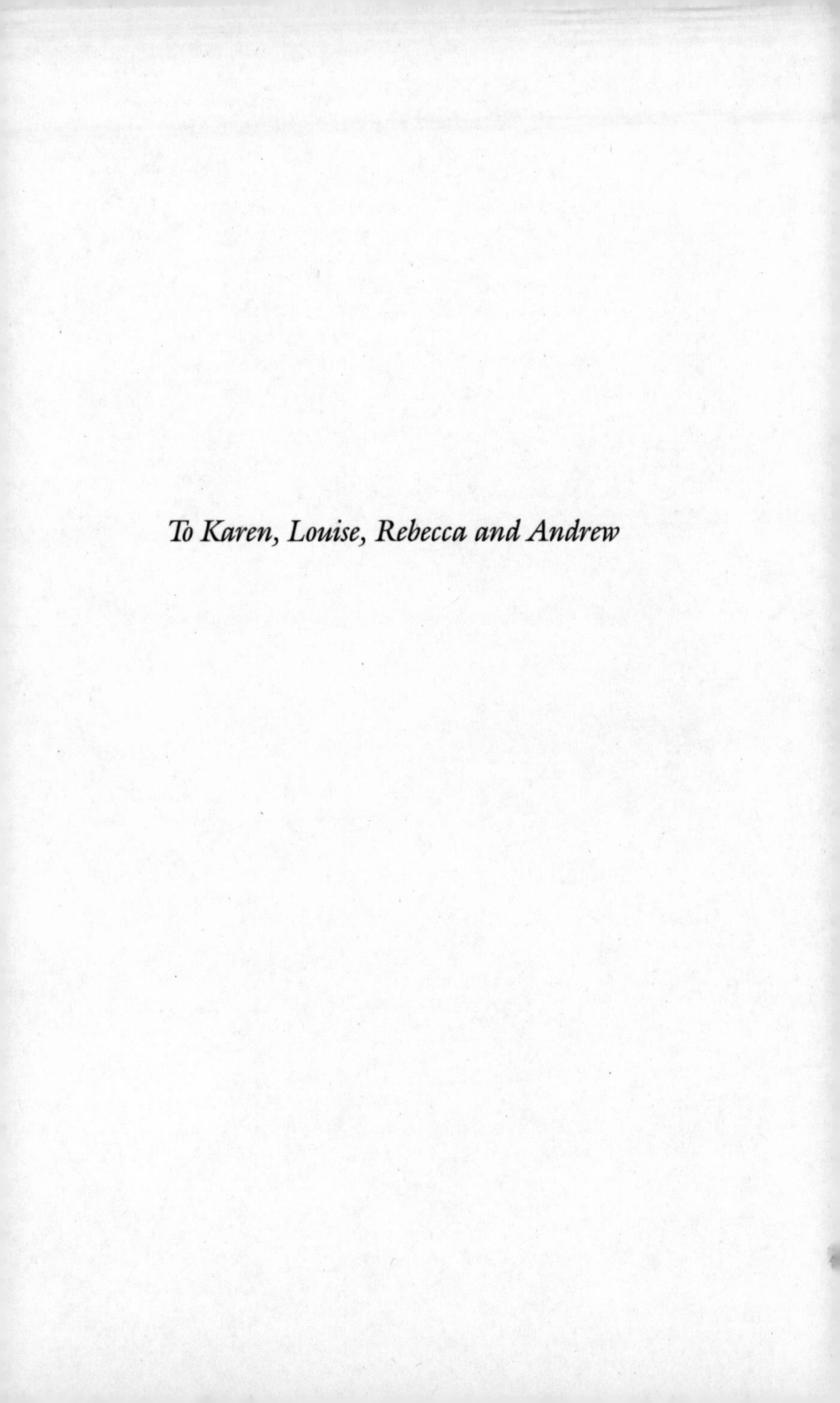

To Karen, Louise, Rebecca and Andrew

The Wearing of the Green

March 17, 1922

The little girl was dancing up and down on the spot like she needed to go to the bathroom.

'Stand at peace, Kathleen,' her mother said, clutching a hairbrush and sweeping it through her daughter's brown hair, smoothing it against her back. Kathleen sighed impatiently. She could hear voices out in the hallway, laughing and shouting and cursing, and she was desperate to join them. Every time she turned her head, even a fraction, towards the noise, her mother pushed it back so that she was staring at the small picture of Our Lady which hung on the plain wall. Our Lady had brown hair too, most of it hidden behind a white veil, and Kathleen wondered if she had to stand while her mother brushed her hair. The little girl joined her hands together like she did at Mass every Sunday, imitating Our Lady's pose.

'What are you doing?' her mother asked.

'Nothing,' she said, letting her arms hang at her side again.

Her mother took the green ribbon which was draped across her knee and tied it round the brown tresses of hair she'd gathered in her hands, singing the words of a song that Kathleen had heard many times before.

'The wearing of the green. Oh, the wearing of the green. They're hanging men and women for the wearing of the green . . .'

Kathleen started humming the tune too as her mother turned her round so they faced each other.

'Let me see you,' her mother said. She leant forward and kissed her daughter gently on her forehead. 'A beautiful little Irish girl for Saint Patrick's Day,' she said, smiling, and Kathleen beamed.

'Now can I go?' she said, starting to move away before a firm hand gripped her shoulder.

'Just one more thing,' her mother said. She moistened a handful of her cardigan sleeve in her mouth before rubbing it roughly across Kathleen's face.

'Mommy!' the little girl cried, trying to move away from the improvised cloth.

'A nice clean face,' her mother said, with a final nod of approval. 'Now you're a princess. My Irish princess.'

She hugged her daughter tightly, even as the little girl tried to squirm out of her grasp, desperate to join the other children she knew were waiting impatiently outside the apartment. Kathleen didn't want the rest of them to leave without her. She knew if they weren't there, her mother wouldn't let her go to the parade. It had taken a lot of pleading and pouting the previous night before her mother had relented. She'd heard the other children talking about the Saint Patrick's Day parade and she wanted to join them.

'You're too young, darling,' her mother had said when Kathleen told her where she was going. She hadn't even thought to ask permission.

'But everyone's going,' she said, throwing herself down on the chair and folding her arms.

'Don't be pulling faces like that, little lady,' her mother said. 'You're five, not fifteen.'

'But it's Patrick's day parade.'

'Saint Patrick,' her mother corrected.

'There's music and marching and fireworks too. And Mary Maguire says you can buy the biggest ice-cream in the whole of New York. It's this big,' she said, stretching her arms as wide apart as they could go.

Her mother laughed. 'That's a big ice-cream.'

'So can I go?'

'No.'

'Please!'

'When you're older.'

'But everyone's going.'

'I don't care if the whole of the city will be there. You're not going.'

'You could take me.'

'Kathleen, darling. I couldn't stand on my feet for that long. Besides, it's too far away for me to walk.'

Kathleen sat and sulked, throwing occasional sullen glances at her mother which were either ignored or laughed at. In the end, her mother relented. There were lots of other children going to the parade, just about everyone in the building for starters, and plenty of adults too, more than enough to keep a watchful eye out for her. Kathleen rhymed off all the names she could think of who would be there, some now in the hallway waiting impatiently for her.

'She'll be fine, Theresa,' her father had said, peering through the cloud of smoke hovering above the chair where he sat. His boots were sitting by the fire, wet socks draped over them, and his bare feet rested on another chair he'd brought from the kitchen. A saucer was balanced precariously on his stomach, filled with ash and cigarette ends. Her mother shrugged, defeated by superior numbers. Kathleen smiled gratefully at her father, though he'd closed his eyes. She knew he wasn't sleeping.

He hadn't always lived with them – he hadn't always been her father – but even though it had only been since she was four, Kathleen found it hard to imagine him not living here in the apartment. There was also going to be a new baby in the family soon and it would be a brother or sister for her. When her mother told her, she also suggested it was a good idea to call him 'Daddy', since that's what the new baby would call him. She nodded because it was a good idea, and when he had smiled the first time she'd said it, she guessed he thought it was a good idea too. He had left for work early that morning, long before Kathleen had woken up excitedly, but she was sure he would want to hear all about the parade when he came home.

When her mother opened the door, everyone in the hall turned round. Some of them cheered, while others took it as a cue to race noisily down the stairs, their shoes and boots clattering on the wooden floor until they reached the bottom and burst out of the building into the March morning, which offered a chilly welcome none of them noticed.

A handful of the children remained on the landing, and Kathleen's mother eyed them all, looking for the most suitable candidate to keep a watchful eye on her daughter. The task fell to Joseph Tierney. He stayed directly above them. He was older – Kathleen thought he was about eleven – and her mother gave him his final instructions as she stood at the doorway, reluctant to let go of her daughter's hand.

'You two stay together,' she said. 'There will be loads of people there, thousands, so it would be easy to get lost. Kathleen, you make sure you hold Joseph's hand all the time.'

Kathleen nodded, even though she didn't imagine Joseph would want to do that once they'd reached the next block and were out of sight of her mother's anxious gaze. She was sure she could see the older boy rolling his eyes, though her mother didn't appear to notice.

'And once the parade's passed by and all the marchers have left, come straight back home.'

'Yes, missus,' Joseph said, nodding solemnly.

There was one final hug and kiss for Kathleen before, reluctantly, her mother let go of her and, holding Joseph's hand, she ran down the stairs with the rest of the children, just as excited and thrilled as they were to be heading towards the parade.

Joseph held on to the little girl's hand, even as they weaved their way through the crowds. Many of the people were no doubt heading to the same destination as they were. The Saint Patrick's Day Parade which was marching all the way up Fifth Avenue until it stopped at the Cathedral. Joseph had figured that would be the busiest place, so he'd suggested standing further down the route, a few blocks from the Cathedral. The others had agreed, so they were all heading for the corner where West and East 28th Street met, hoping to get a good vantage point to see everyone marching by. After that, they could make their way up Fifth or, if that was too busy, cut down on to Sixth and head towards Central Park, where there would be stalls and shows and rides and ice-cream sellers and countless other places to spend the few cents jangling in their pockets. They would be able to stay there a while before having to head home. He'd make sure it wasn't so long that the adults would start worrying.

He didn't let go of Kathleen's hand. He saw the look in her mother's eyes when she'd instructed them to stick together, and realised it was more than his life's worth to let the little girl run along the streets herself and risk losing her in the throng of people. He wasn't bothered anyway. He just pretended she was his little sister, and no-one else had teased or tormented him either.

She didn't stop talking. That was his one complaint. She had a thousand questions and spotted a million different things on the way. The smell of a hot dog vendor; the rumble of a passing motor car; the pretty dresses some of the women wore; the blue sky; buildings that reached up towards it and towered over them. They'd walked down Tenth Avenue and then headed along West 42nd Street. It seemed like everyone had the same idea so Frank Devlin suggested cutting down Ninth Avenue, claiming it was quicker, and quieter. No-one disagreed, so they all began traipsing along the street, with Joseph and Kathleen lagging behind slightly. The little girl's pace had slowed. She was puffed out.

'Stop a minute,' Joseph said, halting and going down on one knee to tie one of his bootlaces. It hadn't been loose, but he figured if he suggested they stop because she was tired, Kathleen would have refused. She stood watching him as he slowly finished with one boot and then, swapping on to his other knee he loosened the lace of his left boot and began re-tying it.

'Are we nearly there yet?' Kathleen asked. The rest of the children were lingering at the end of the block, having belatedly noticed that Joseph and Kathleen had stopped. It wouldn't have bothered Joseph if they'd gone on ahead. He knew where they were heading and he would find them eventually.

'It won't be long,' he said to Kathleen, standing up. 'Just another few blocks.'

The little girl nodded, automatically slipping her hand in to his as they started walking again. The other children, seeing them on the move, resumed their journey, and they disappeared round the corner at West 34th out of sight. There was no point speeding up, Joseph thought, and he stopped again, this time outside a convenience store.

'Are you thirsty?' he asked Kathleen, who nodded. 'Come on,' he said, tugging her hand and they walked into the store, which was dark and misty, a million tiny specs of dust floating in the air obscuring their vision. Joseph felt like waving his hand through it all to get a better view.

'Do you want a soda?' he asked. Kathleen nodded again.

They walked over to the counter, where an old woman sat on a chair. Her blue eyes watched the children approach while her mouth continued chewing. Joseph would catch an occasional glimpse of something dark, and he wondered if it was tobacco? His grandfather had the same habit.

'Two bottles of soda, please?' he asked the woman, who

slowly pushed herself up off her chair and shuffled down the counter to where all the drinks were kept.

'This do you?' she said, holding up two bottles containing a dark liquid. Coca Cola.

'Thanks,' he said with a nod, while Kathleen's face broke out in a beaming smile. He handed over the four nickels to the woman, who slipped them into the pocket of her faded cardigan rather than in the money box that sat on a shelf behind the chair where she'd been sitting. Joseph could hear the coins rattling with others in the pocket as the woman shuffled back to her seat.

Standing on the sidewalk, they stood and drank quickly until the bottles were just about clear again. They swapped burps, and Kathleen giggled guiltily.

'Wait here,' he said, taking the bottle off her and running back into the shop, reappearing quickly enough to stop the sudden alarmed look on the little girl's face become a permanent one. He wasn't giving up the two nickels he'd paid as a deposit for the bottles. Joseph burped again and Kathleen laughed. She was skipping along the road now, almost dragging him along in her wake as he held her hand loosely and quickened his pace to keep up with her. Still the questions continued.

'Will there be lots of people at Patrick's parade?'

'Loads.'

'How many?'

'Thousands . . . millions maybe.'

'Is everyone Irish?'

'In the world?'

'In New York?'

'Not everyone.'

'My mommy says that all the best people are Irish.'

'She's right.'

'I hope I get a baby sister. A girl's better than a boy, sure it is?'

'I'm a boy.'

'But you're big . . . You're not a baby. My daddy wants a boy. He tells my mummy the bump is a boy. But I think a girl would be better. She'll be my baby sister.'

They passed lampposts with green bunting tied to them and stretched across the street. Some of it hung too low and was broken by trucks driving by, and there were stray bits lying on the road. Irish flags hung out of windows. The *Tricolour* and the *Green Harp*. There was even one Starry Plough flapping in the breeze. He liked the Tricolour best, its green, white and orange making it stand out. It was so different from the American flag, with its stars and stripes. One of them stood at the front of his classroom, propped against the wall behind the teacher's desk and every morning, before lessons started, they had to say the *Pledge of Allegiance*.

Shop windows were decorated in the appropriate colours. Some of them were closed, with the owners obviously heading out to see the parade as well, but the shrewd ones stayed open, ready to make a few extra dollars on this day.

A few people staggered up and down stairs which led to basements that Joseph knew sold liquor. He could hear blasts of music drifting up from these places whenever a door was opened to welcome in someone or spew out another drunk on to the streets, songs he recognised from when his father would sing them on a Saturday night for the whole family. Joseph's favourite was *Dear Old Skibbereen*.

When he was younger, he would climb on to his mother's knee and snuggle in, letting her wrap her arms round him so that he could feel himself instantly heat up, and he'd listen to his dad singing.

My son, I loved my native land with energy and pride . . .
Till a blight came over all my crops and my sheep and cattle died.
The rents and taxes were to pay and I could not them redeem . . .
And that's the cruel reason why I left old Skibbereen.

They had reached the corner of West 34th and Seventh when they heard the first firecracker. Kathleen squealed and began dancing on the spot.

'We're nearly there. We're nearly there,' she said loudly, almost singing the words in her excitement.

Joseph smiled, glad the little girl hadn't noticed him jump when he heard the noise. He'd got a fright but he would be better prepared for the next one. They weren't too far away now. He'd lost sight of the others, but since they'd already agreed on a rendezvous point, he'd be able to meet up with them soon enough. He wondered where the firecrackers were coming from. They were still far from Central Park so the noise couldn't have carried from there. It might just be someone in the street, or perhaps on top of a building, shooting them off into the sky. It might even be someone following the parade, though he couldn't hear the music coming from that yet.

They stood waiting on the edge of the kerb, Kathleen's hand still clutching his tightly, unable to venture across the road until there was a break in the traffic. There was another firecracker, and Kathleen squealed again, though this one was quickly followed by the screech of tyres. Joseph glanced at the little girl, who didn't appear to have registered the other noise, and then he looked up and down the street.

A car suddenly appeared round the corner, speeding wildly across the road and slamming into a parked car. There was a bang, like a clap of thunder, and the sound of breaking glass. The car's engine roared angrily as the driver tried to reverse, and then there were more snapping noises, though this time Joseph knew exactly what it was. The car managed to trundle backwards and then, with a loud groan, it shuddered and began moving forward just as another car appeared round the same corner. Now the air was full of noise as gun shots rattled back and forth between the two cars. The first one, with its bashed front, was desperately trying to escape along the street. The driver clutched the steering wheel while another leant out the passenger door and fired a machine gun at the pursuing car, which returned fire.

People were shouting and screaming. Some dived to the ground, hiding behind parked cars or scrambling on their knees towards doorways for shelter, as car windows and shop fronts caved in as stray bullets hit the glass, shattering it instantly. Joseph had been momentarily frozen to the spot. It was happening so quickly, but he found himself beginning to tug Kathleen, pulling her away from the kerb. As he began to move, he saw the chasing car move to the far side of the road, and then screeched back into the middle so that it rammed the slower vehicle, sending it spinning out of control towards another parked car. A man leant out and fired his gun, spraying bullets over the crashed car, his body shaking with the venom of the weapon.

Joseph moved again, trying to pull Kathleen with him, but it seemed like she was resisting his efforts to drag her to safety. He couldn't understand why. Surely she must realise the danger too? He tugged again, and now he was struggling to hold on to her hand. It was slipping out of his grasp. He pulled and snatched and tried to hold on to her but it was like trying to clutch a bar of soap. Suddenly her hand had gone and he stumbled forward, no longer struggling to drag a heavy weight.

He looked back and couldn't see her at first. Where had she gone? Then his eyes looked down and she was there, lying face down on the ground, the green ribbon in her head dazzling in the daylight, her brown hair all shiny and smooth.

'Kathleen?' he mumbled, not sure at first if she'd simply stumbled into the road, but sinking to his knees as he heard the screams of a woman behind him. The scream was repetitive, like an alarm, getting louder as more people ventured nearer to see what had happened. Joseph saw the car race away down the street and round a corner, the gunman having disappeared back inside, but his eyes kept returning to the body on the ground as his hand continued snatching at fresh air in the hope that he might be able to grasp on to her tiny hand again.

Commandments

When they had started working, it seemed like the whole barn was filled with crates, but it didn't take long to transfer them to the three trucks parked outside. It helped that there were a few of them working on the task – four men to each truck – and everyone was keen to get it done quickly so they could return to the city and enjoy what was left of Saint Patrick's Day. There wasn't much talking between the men. Jimmy Healy sat on an empty, upturned crate on the dirt track at the side of the vehicles, smoking and occasionally shouting instructions or words of warning to be careful, but for the most part the only sound that could be heard was the birds in the trees, serenading them as they worked.

'Do you think they know the *Foggy Dew*?' Pat Hanlon said during a rare break for a smoke. No-one could see the birds. They were hidden high in the branches of the giant fir trees towering over them like living, breathing skyscrapers. Everything seemed bigger here, the buildings, streets, trees, birds, noise. Ireland was a million miles away now, a fading memory like the pages of an old newspaper left out in the sunshine for too long.

'Back to work, you lazy Micks,' Jimmy said, standing up to stretch and then sitting back down. His Dublin accent was still as thick and polluted as the Liffey, and thirty years in New York hadn't diluted it at all. It was as if he'd just stumbled off the boat yesterday. If you closed your eyes, you could almost believe you were back in O'Connell Street, with the hustle and bustle of daily Dublin life, the ruined buildings and shattered lives a visible reminder of what the city and the country had gone through and was still going through, a cloud of tension hanging in the air, invisible yet still tangible, ready to burst at any moment. There wasn't a man who wasn't glad he was now standing in the mid-day sunshine of the New York countryside. The chaos that was the big city was less than an hour's drive away, yet it felt like they were in the middle of nowhere.

If anything, it made Tommy think of Donegal, with its sprawling fields that stretched as far as the eye could see. It seemed like a lifetime ago that he'd been there. It was still home, at least in his head, and his heart too, but America was where his life was now. Something hit his face and he jumped, the cigarette falling from his mouth and on to the ground. There was laughter as he bent down to pick up the still-smouldering cigarette which lay beside the ball of straw that had struck him.

'Wake up, Tommy boy,' Jimmy said. 'You were dreaming.'

'Leave him alone, Jimmy,' said Pat. 'He was just dreaming about riding that woman of his. Is that not right, Tommy?'

'No, I was dreaming about riding your missus,' Tommy said, and the rest of the men started laughing as they all trudged slowly back to the barn, though Pat didn't join in.

Tommy thought of Theresa sitting at home, or fussing in the kitchen, preparing dinner. She'd promised him something special 'for a special day'. She was still sleeping when he'd left the apartment this morning. It was dark in the bedroom, though his eyes began to adjust to their surroundings after a few minutes, helped by the slivers of silver moonlight that peeked in shyly through gaps in the curtain thrown across the window.

He tried to be quiet as he pulled his trousers on, slipping the braces over his shirt. He stepped into his boots, glancing round at the bed. Theresa looked so peaceful as she slept, almost as if she was a picture. His gaze moved to her belly, starting to swell with the baby that would soon be theirs together. He was tempted to undress and slip back in beside her, pressing against her until he could feel her body heat seeping into him. Maybe he'd fall asleep, warm and contented, or maybe he'd be wide awake, his hand running up and down the inside of her thighs until she either slapped them away forcefully or, still half-asleep, turned to face him, kiss him, caress him, let him enter her as she lay on her side, careful to make sure the bump – the baby – was comfortable.

He leant over the bed and kissed the small bump, gently, so as not to wake her. He wanted to stay but he had to go. A job was a job and he'd promised Jimmy he would be there. The Dublin man was waiting for him, the truck parked at the corner of West 47th Street and Eighth Avenue as they'd arranged. Jimmy would be standing on the sidewalk, cigarette in his mouth, cup of coffee in his hand – he always seemed to be able to acquire a coffee, no matter where they were or what time of day or night it was – as the black New York sky slowly began metamorphosing into deep shades of blue, the March sun slowly waking up in line with the inhabitants of the city. Some of them would already be up and on the move, either going to work or returning home from a night of work or pleasure, their weary tread or swaggering gait giving each away.

Many more would be watching the parade, either giving up the prospect of work for the day or skipping off so that they could enjoy the festivities, which included the very thing they were now loading up on to the trucks. The men kept working, carrying crates from the barn, though they had broken the back of the job, and most of the consignment now resided in the vehicles. Apart from the birdsong, it was only the occasional clunk of bottles which broke the silence. Those ones hadn't been packed properly, and they were always guaranteed a few breakages on a job like this. As long as the leakages weren't spotted while they were loading or unloading the crates, then it was someone else's problem. They all knew what was in the crates, liquor to quench a thousand thirsty mouths or more.

Speakeasies in the city had to be stocked up; restaurants and cafes were grateful for some backroom stock; individuals paid good money for a bottle or two. No-one asked any questions. Certainly, Tommy and his colleagues weren't interested in anything beyond the money they would get at the end of the day, but there seemed to be a never-ending stream of willing customers.

It wasn't dangerous work, not when Tommy thought about some of the things he'd had to do back in Ireland when it seemed, at times, like it was kill or be killed. This was still illegal, though, and that's why Jimmy wanted men like him – men who were handy with their fists and handy with a gun, too, if necessary. Not that Tommy had needed to use a weapon so far. He was glad of that. It was something he was reluctant to do now. That was part of his past, but it was still there – the gun – in his pocket. Jimmy supplied the weapons and redeemed them at the end of the job. They all understood, and accepted, that they might have to use them at some point. There was always the chance the police would disrupt their operation, though guns would be the last resort in those instances. If it was a rival gang, however, that would be a different matter.

Where Jimmy got the guns from, no-one asked, just as no-one wondered where they went when they were returned. Jimmy was their boss. He recruited them, but while Tommy suspected that Bill Dwyer was the man in charge, it was better not to ask any unnecessary questions. Jimmy didn't like questions, or the person who asked them.

In less than an hour, the barn was empty and the trucks were full, each with a variety of destinations to visit so that, come the end of the day, they would be as empty as they had been at the start. Tommy looked at the crates, crammed in so there was barely an inch of space, before the tarpaulin cover was pulled over and attached securely to the wood panel which ran halfway up the back of the truck. There was a lot of liquor in those crates, which meant there was a lot of money. Only a fraction would end up in his pocket.

Four of them crammed in to the front of one of the trucks alongside Jimmy, who was driving. Artie Reilly ended up sitting on Pat's knee, though he was still pressed up against the passenger door.

'Why do I always end up on someone's knee?' he asked.

'Because you like it,' Pat said.

'No, I don't.'

'Look, Artie. We're moving,' Pat laughed. 'Are you excited now?'

Artie glared at Pat, muttering curses under his breath, but he didn't know what he could say out loud. He was the youngest in the group – probably not even eighteen yet, Tommy guessed, so there was wariness, if not deference, to the older men.

'To hell with you,' Artie eventually muttered and the rest of the men laughed. He was the only one of them with a New York accent, and sometimes they would talk the Gaelic just to annoy the boy. Tommy often thought of telling Pat not to push Artie too far. The boy might only be just that, but his arms were solid and he was capable of flattening any of them with a single punch if he wanted, or was provoked enough.

Jimmy was whistling now – *Hail Glorious Saint Patrick* – and Tommy smiled, closing his eyes with a yawn as the truck slowly made its way towards the main highway which would take them back to the city. He knew there were a few stops along the way, but he figured he'd be able to snatch twenty minutes' sleep at least before their first delivery.

He didn't remember any lavish celebrations for Saint Patrick back home. There might have been a glass raised or a prayer offered, but there was no bunting or flags or parades. It seemed like the further they were from home, the more Irish people became. He'd talked Theresa into letting Kathleen go to the parade the night before. There would be plenty of children there to look after her, and Theresa could do with the rest. She always looked tired, which was only to be expected with the baby on its way. A day without having to look after a five-year-old would do her good.

Not that Kathleen was any trouble. He liked the little girl. He supposed he probably loved her, even if she wasn't his. She called him 'daddy' now, which sounded nice – strange, but nice – and with another on the way, it would soon be a little family for him. He hadn't expected to find that when he arrived in New York. He didn't know what he'd find. He wasn't expecting anything. He was running away from everything, and a wife – they weren't yet married, but they would be soon enough – and a daughter was the last thing he would have predicted.

New York had seemed so big and noisy and scary – yes, he'd been scared when the ship first docked. He could see the buildings in the distance, all in a race to reach the sky while struggling to avoid slipping off the edge of the island and into the water. It seemed like he had stumbled into a different world. He had seen tall buildings in Dublin, elsewhere too, but nothing like this.

The first port of call for everyone was Ellis Island. A sea of bodies seemed to swell in every room, people of all shapes and sizes, some of them talking in a language he understood, but many of them speaking in tongues he didn't recognise. It was the noise of a million voices – excited, nervous, agitated, angry – all crammed together, waiting to be allowed into this new country and across the short stretch of water to the big city, all of them saying the same thing but no-one realising it.

'Help me. I'm scared.'

That had been almost two years ago now. Sometimes, when he thought about it, Tommy smiled, trying to imagine that feeling of uneasiness and fear which had gripped him as he sat in line, shuffling along the wooden benches until he reached the front of the queue. This was his city now, even if Ireland was his home, and roots were being established that would keep him here forever. That had been the plan when he made the journey across the Atlantic Ocean.

The drive back towards New York had been smooth for some time now. Tommy had presumed it meant they were on the highway, though he didn't bother to check, but suddenly there was a jolt. He opened his eyes as he heard some of the crates banging together in the back of the truck.

'Where are we going, Jimmy?' Neil McCallum asked. It was the first time Tommy had heard him speak all day.

'Just got to pick up something for the boss,' said Jimmy. 'I'll only be a few minutes.'

The truck bumped slowly down a dirt road that weaved its way through thick woodland. It took at least ten minutes from the main road until they turned a final corner. A small wooden hut sat on its own in a clearing, isolated in this forest. Jimmy stopped the truck, the brakes creaking as the vehicle shuddered to a halt a few yards further on.

'You can get out and stretch your legs,' he said, opening his door and jumping down to the ground, immediately striding over to the hut. Tommy had rarely seen him move so fast.

There were grunts and groans, but mainly sighs of relief, as the four men clambered out of the truck. All of them started moving as soon as they could, only a few paces back and forth, but enough to cajole some life back into their limbs. Cigarettes were offered round and lit, and the four of them stood smoking in silence. Pat drifted over to the bushes.

'Good idea,' said Tommy, and soon the only sound to be heard in the clearing was of urine crashing off the foliage.

'I needed that,' Pat said with a sigh of relief. 'It's a nightmare with his bony arse on my knee.'

'Well, how do you think I feel?' Artie said, buttoning up his trousers, a cigarette hanging out his mouth.

'I know how you feel,' said Pat. 'Excited.'

Artie shook his head, flicking the finger to Pat, who was still laughing. As they shuffled back towards the truck, Jimmy appeared at the door of the hut, waving a bottle in the air.

'Time for a wee refreshment,' he shouted over to them.

'That sounds like a plan,' Pat said, surging towards the hut ahead of the other three. Neil shrugged and trudged forward as well. Tommy wasn't bothered either way, while he could tell Artie was nervous, not used to drinking as much as the older men.

'We'll just have the one,' said Tommy, patting the younger man on the shoulder, and the two of them headed over to the hut. When they walked inside, Pat was face down on the floor and a man Tommy didn't recognise was kicking him as Pat tried to protect his head from the blows.

'What the hell's going on?' Tommy said, stepping forward. A hand on his shoulder stopped him.

'Leave it, Tommy,' Jimmy said quietly, and Tommy knew instinctively to remain where he was. Neil stood to Tommy's left, staring in disbelief, the same expression on Artie's face.

'That's enough,' a voice in the shadows said, and the

man immediately stopped his assault. 'Get him up,' the voice said.

A tall man, smartly dressed in a dark suit emerged in front of them. Another man appeared from behind him with a wooden chair which he placed in the middle of the room, and he helped his colleague pick the injured man up and drop him on the chair. Pat immediately flopped forward and the two men held his shoulders to keep him on the chair. Blood was streaming down Pat's cheek, and it was like a dark shadow covering half his face. The man in the suit now stood in front of Pat.

'This is Mister Gorevin,' Jimmy said by way of introduction, and the man glanced round, giving them all a brief nod of acknowledgement. This was who they were working for, Tommy realised. He knew who Gorevin was. He was linked to the biggest bootlegging racket in Manhattan. Jimmy, normally so confident and secure with his authority, instinctively took a step back into the shadows, and Tommy followed suit.

Gorevin's hair was blond and seemed to glow in the dimness of the hut, like there was a halo shadowing his every move. It was slick and shiny and clung to his skull. He was taller than the doorway of the hut, Tommy guessed, picturing the man having to stoop to enter. When he'd glanced round, there was a glimpse of his profile. His nose was crooked, a ridge protruding from it, evidence of war wounds from the past. The suit was smarter than anything Tommy had ever owned, or was ever likely to, and the black shoes peeking out from the bottom of the trousers shone so much that Tommy was sure he'd have been able to see his face in them.

'Get his attention, Jimmy,' Gorevin said, and Jimmy stepped forward, pouring some of the bottle over Pat's head. Pat screamed and sat bolt upright as the alcohol stung his wound.

'Do you know your commandments?' Gorevin asked.

Pat stared at him, puzzled.

'The seventh commandment . . . thou shalt not steal.'

Pat continued looking at Gorevin, occasionally flinching whenever the alcohol stung him.

'You broke the seventh commandment, Mr Hanlon, and now you must accept your penance.'

Pat shook his head violently, even though it must have hurt, whispering 'No,' over and over again.

'Do you honour your mother and your father?' Gorevin asked.

Pat stared, bemused.

'The fourth commandment . . . Honour them now by telling the truth, by admitting that you have stolen and that you are truly sorry for what you've done.'

'I don't . . . I don't . . .'

'The truth, Mr Hanlon . . . I am the way, the truth and the light, Mr Hanlon. No-one comes to the Father except through me.'

'I don't know,' Pat said, starting to cry. Gorevin nodded to one of the men holding Pat's shoulders. He produced a small knife from his pocket and drove it firmly into Pat's thigh.

He screamed and the other men in the hut – Tommy, Artie, Neil and Jimmy – all jumped, stepping even further back towards the door. The man pulled the knife roughly out of Pat's leg, eliciting another scream, and blood immediately started spurting out of the wound. The man wiped the blade on Pat's sleeve. The grip on him was tighter now as his body fought to collapse to the ground in pain.

'Why, Mr Hanlon? That's all I want to know. Do we not pay you enough?'

Pat was crying now, sobbing uncontrollably, his shoulders visibly shaking even as the two men gripped them. He was mumbling and shaking his head but Tommy couldn't make out what he was trying to say.

'What you did was wrong, Mr Hanlon. You know that. You just need to confess now.'

'I didn't do anything,' Pat spluttered, shaking his head again as he mustered up every ounce of strength in his body to speak.

Gorevin nodded and the man plunged the knife into Pat's other thigh. The scream was shorter this time, more exhausted, or traumatised, and it seemed like Pat passed out for a few moments.

'Get some water for him,' Gorevin said and Jimmy disappeared out the hut. As the door opened, a streak of sunlight raced into the dim proceedings. Jimmy returned with a bucket of water, which he threw over Pat. The cold liquid seemed to bring him to his senses and he sat up, at first with a look of bemusement on his face like he'd just woken up and wasn't sure where he was, but that was quickly replaced by terror when he saw Gorevin standing before him.

'This can be easy or it can be hard, Mr Hanlon. It's up to you.'

Pat's head was shaking, though Tommy wasn't sure whether he was refusing Gorevin's request or if he just couldn't control his neck.

'I'm a reasonable man, but I'm not a patient man, so I won't ask you again.'

Pat started crying, slowly at first, but soon he was sobbing loudly, tears and snot gathering on his face. Tommy looked away, not wanting to see a grown man cry. Jimmy nudged him and gestured for him to keep his eyes on Pat. This was also for their benefit.

Gorevin sighed. 'So how is your good lady?'

Pat looked up, trying to peer through the tears at the man who stood before him.

'How long have you been married now?'

Pat mumbled something that none of them could make out.

'For richer, for poorer,' said Gorevin. 'In sickness and in health. 'Till death do us part . . .'

The man with the knife handed something to Gorevin, and he held it up above his head so that the traces of sunlight which managed to invade the hut caught it in their sights. It was a ring.

'Do you recognise this, Mr Hanlon?' Gorevin said, waving the ring in front of Pat's face. 'She put up a good fight to keep it. She's got spirit has your Mary, I'll say that for her.'

A sudden burst of strength surged through Pat's body and he tried to throw himself at Gorevin, though he was immediately restrained by the other two men, one of whom delivered a couple of punches to Pat's face, his head rocking back and forth.

'In fact,' said Gorevin, 'we ended up having to take this as well.'

He threw something on to Pat's lap, and everyone

strained to see what it was. Pat started screaming, loudly, frantically moving his legs to try and get rid of what was on his lap as Gorevin smiled and the two men laughed. The object dropped to the ground as Pat kept screaming, and Tommy looked down. A bloodied finger lay on the dirty floor at Pat's feet. Pat leant over and threw up, covering the digit with vomit. Tommy swallowed hard to keep down the bile that was threatening to burst out his mouth too.

'Why did you do it, Mr Hanlon? Patrick?' Gorevin said gently, almost in a whisper.

Pat mumbled, shaking his head.

'I can't hear you.'

'I'm sorry,' Pat said. 'I'm sorry. I'm sorry.'

'It's okay,' Gorevin said with a heavy sigh. 'It's okay.'

'Not Mary,' Pat mumbled. 'She did nothing. It's not her fault.'

Gorevin glanced round at Jimmy and nodded, a sign that they were all to leave the hut. None of them needed a second invitation, and they quickly stumbled out into the daylight behind Jimmy, gasping for air like they'd just resurfaced after being held under water. They all made their way to the truck, desperate to get back in the vehicle and drive away before there was any chance Gorevin might change his mind and bring them back inside. They all froze, though only momentarily, as a scream burst out of the hut, before they quickened their pace until they were back in the truck. There was more room inside the cabin now, but none of them acknowledged that fact as they drove back up the dirt track towards the highway, the scream continuing to resonate in their ears long after they left the clearing behind and were heading towards the city.

A Taste of Home

The truck, now emptied of its contents, stopped at the same corner of West 56th Street and Ninth Avenue where Jimmy had picked them up many hours ago, when it was dark and quiet and much of the city slept, oblivious to any activity, legal or otherwise, going on outside their building, on their streets, in their neighbourhoods.

Tommy stepped down slowly on to the sidewalk, which was teeming with a steady stream of people flowing in all directions. The roads were clogged too, mainly with cars and trucks, driving and stopping, sounding horns angrily at every delay, before they began moving again. Voices were, by and large, indistinct, merely adding to the volume of noise that swirled about in the air, bouncing off the buildings which rose up either side of the street and then colliding again in the middle in a crescendo that would startle any newcomer to the city. It had done so with Tommy when he had begun trawling through the streets, though it soon became a background noise that was easy to ignore. Occasionally, a voice would manage to make itself heard above the cacophony, usually selling something – a newspaper, a hot dog, fruit, vegetables, flowers, a shoe-shine.

The noise was apparent only because the journey back to the city had been so quiet. No-one spoke. Jimmy never sang or whistled a tune from the old country, which he would normally have done. He stared at the road ahead, hands gripped on the steering wheel, their journey slowing as they approached the city. The truck crawled across Brooklyn Bridge and then it was a long and faltering trip through Manhattan, stopping at a number of places to make quick and discreet deliveries before resuming their journey across the island until their reached their final destination.

Crates were hastily deposited in dimly-lit cellars, or bundled into store-rooms, with covers pulled over them before the door was padlocked again. Everyone in the neighbourhood knew what was happening; many of them would be customers, already looking forward to sampling down the contents of the crates later on that evening.

While they worked, Tommy and his colleagues still kept a wary eye out for any sign of the police, or any other potential threat. Thankfully, it had been an incident-free delivery day. Tommy almost laughed out loud. It was only incident-free if they ignored the fact their colleague had been tortured in front of them. He hoped it was all over for Pat now, though the thought still made him shiver. He'd wanted to bless himself, or even touch the holy medals he always wore for comfort, and although he was sure Jimmy wouldn't have said anything to him, he didn't want to run the risk of letting Jimmy see him appear superstitious. Trust no-one. That had always served him well in the past, and in this city, it would serve him still.

The truck pulled out from the kerb, ignoring the horn sounding from the car behind which had been forced to break suddenly to avoid a collision where it would almost certainly have come off second-best. Tommy watched the vehicle merge into the general traffic mêlée of the street, barely acknowledging Artie and Neil as they grunted goodbye before heading in the opposite direction. Jimmy hadn't said anything either. What was there to say? Tommy knew the Dublin man had only been obeying orders. Wasn't that what 'soldiers' did? Hadn't he once done the same thing, even though it had nearly cost him his life, and it had cost the life of someone he cared about?

He shook his head, trying to dispel the image of a face he could never forget. The past was . . . well, in the past, and he couldn't do anything to change it. He could only look to the future, and that's where Theresa took over, her image replacing that of someone else he had once known, and maybe even loved.

He had twenty-five dollars in his pocket. It was good money for a day's work. More than good, it was great, more than he'd earn in a week labouring. He'd done work like that when he'd first arrived, anything to earn a few dollars, but this was better. It was still labouring, for the main part, though it wasn't legal like working on a building site, but it paid more, even if the risks were somewhat higher. He tried not to think about that too much.

Occasionally he might have to work at a speakeasy, operating the door, or standing inside, keeping an eye on things and ensuring there was no trouble, even as the amount of alcohol consumption increased. That's how Jimmy had spotted him in the first place. He'd been watching one of the tougher looking customers for a couple of hours; as the man tossed down one drink after another he'd become more aggressive and when he slapped his female companion Tommy stepped in. The girl was still rubbing her cheek which was already red and stinging when Tommy told the man it was time to leave. He wasn't surprised there was an objection, and he delivered a short, sharp punch to the man's throat, leaving the man gasping for breath. In the same instant, he grabbed him and dragged him out of his seat and across the dance floor.

There was a policy of dumping unwanted guests out the back door rather than the front – it was bad for business if people saw them – so the man was dumped in an alleyway at the back of the building, still gasping for air. As he sat on the damp ground, Tommy stepped up and swung a baseball bat, breaking the man's jaw and leaving him unconscious on the cobbled surface. That would teach him to hit a woman. As he put the baseball bat back in its place, just inside the door, he heard a match strike and turned round, alert and on edge for an attack. It was Jimmy.

He liked what he'd seen, he told Tommy as they stood smoking at the doorway, the unconscious body just a few feet away. Tommy was happy enough to accept the offer of work from Jimmy, though he did express his preference for less confrontational tasks. He'd spilt enough blood for Ireland, more than enough in anyone's lifetime, and he had no desire to start doing so again, particularly when the only cause was making money.

The notes felt like a lead weight in his pocket, slowing him down. Guilt was a heavy burden to bear. They were all due twenty dollars. That's what had been agreed beforehand, but Pat had forfeited his share, which was split four ways, including Jimmy. The extra five dollars was not unwelcome, particularly with a new baby on its way, but it was money steeped in the blood of their colleague. Their friend.

Every step he took nearer to his own apartment, the louder Pat's screams seemed to reverberate in his ears, and he knew the sound would haunt his dreams for weeks to come. He had seen and done some bad things in his life. Men had dropped dead at his feet as a result of his actions, but there had always been a reason for it. A cause. Even when that cause had been personal – he had settled a family score while on a mission to Glasgow three years ago – he still felt the end justified the means. But Pat's death . . .

Maybe it was the suddenness of it which unnerved him, or the fact he had managed to detach himself, by and large, from the bloody reality of such a world and such a life, but he had been scared in that hut, and that wasn't a criticism generally levelled at him. He shuddered again as he thought of what he had witnessed, and shivered as he imagined what would have happened after they left the hut. No-one spoke in the truck because no-one knew what to say.

Tommy had shot men. He had knifed them. He once sliced a man's throat open and had barely paused to give it a thought. That had been in Glasgow and the man deserved it. He had murdered Tommy's father, even as Tommy grew, unannounced, in his mother's belly. That wasn't why he was in the city, however. He'd been there to kill a British general for the IRA, but it hadn't quite gone to plan. The general had survived, even if his father's killer hadn't, and given what had happened since in Ireland, it was better that he was here in America. No-one knew he was here. That wasn't quite true. There was one man who had helped him reach this promised land – his uncle – but he was dead now and had taken that secret with him to the grave. There was another man who had helped, but

Tommy's trust in his continuing silence was absolute. He was safe here, so long as he didn't steal any alcohol, of course.

He thought again of Theresa lying in bed this morning when he left, and of her belly, which he had kissed so tenderly. Kathleen called him 'daddy', but he wanted his own child – flesh of his flesh and blood of his blood. He hadn't thought too much about it before, about becoming a father, not even when he fell in love during his time in Glasgow. That had been different, anyway. They were both in the middle of a war which could have claimed their lives at any moment. Plans for the future beyond where they were sleeping that night would have been foolish and futile. Now, though, he had a ready-made family that was soon to expand. He wanted a son, someone to carry on the family name. He felt it was a boy growing inside Theresa. He told her that.

'Just wait and see,' she said, laughing.

His son would be called Michael, named after his own father, the man that neither son nor grandson had ever known. He hadn't told Theresa that yet. He'd wait until his son was born and then he'd tell her. He knew she wouldn't object.

He crossed 51st Street, hands plunged in pockets, keeping a grip of the money. It might be blood money, and he felt guilty about it, but it was still twenty-five extra dollars, and it was better in his pocket than in anyone else's. He stopped outside a row of shops and smiled. It reminded him of a rhyme learned on his mother's knee so many years ago . . . of the butcher, the baker, the candle-stick maker.

There was only a bakery in the row, but it seemed like he could buy anything in this city. Fancy clothes that people wore when they were out, and not just on a Sunday. Electric lamps that brightened their apartment better than any candle. Curtains that were made to cover windows, rather than old blankets thrown over the glass. Vacuum cleaners to scoop up every crumb he spilled on the floor. Refrigerators that kept their food cold and fresh. A hair dryer that resembled a gun a child might draw in a picture. He never used that, though Theresa often did, for her and Kathleen. Food that he'd only imagined was eaten by kings and queens.

The bakery was drawing him in. Green bunting adorned the frame of the window and the window bore the message 'HAPPY ST PAT ICKS DAY' in white icing. The 'R' in Patrick had obviously crumbled, or perhaps someone had hungrily nibbled at it until it disappeared.

He would have bought a bag of doughnuts if there had been any left. He loved them, especially when they were freshly baked and coated in sugar. Each bite, washed down with a gulp of coffee reminded him of his new surroundings. It was the taste of New York. Theresa preferred oatcakes. 'A little taste of Monaghan,' she said whenever she nibbled on them. She had never been to Ireland, but it's what her mother always used to say, she had told him. He'd surprise her with a bag of them, a special treat for Saint Patrick's Day. There wasn't much left in the shop – it was late afternoon – but two oatcakes sat, almost forlorn, on the bottom shelf. Tommy's face lit up when he saw them.

'Don't worry about it,' the baker said when Tommy went to pay, waving the money away. 'I'd just have tossed them out.'

'Thanks,' said Tommy, touching his cap

'I'll be closing up soon anyway.'

'Busy day then?'

'Run off my feet. If only every day could be Saint Patrick's Day, I'd be a rich man by now . . . . Here you go,' he said, handing the brown paper bag to Tommy.

'A little taste of Monaghan,' Tommy said automatically.

'Monaghan? We're practically neighbours then. I'm a Louth man. Dundalk.'

Tommy frowned.

'I know what you're thinking . . . the accent. My parents were from there. Came over back in the seventies.'

Tommy nodded. He didn't want to explain that he wasn't from Monaghan.

'Have a good day,' the baker said in a pure, unadulterated New York accent.

'You too,' said Tommy as he walked out the shop, colliding with a man who staggered into him.

'Woah! Watch yourself there,' the man said. He had been drinking – Tommy could smell the fumes wafting out of his mouth – and he swayed on the sidewalk like a solitary palm tree in a windy desert, even though it was a calm, if cold day. Tommy turned and began walking down the street. He was only a couple of blocks from home now and suddenly he was desperate for the warmth of the apartment, and Theresa. He wanted to see her face when he gave her the oatcakes. Maybe Kathleen would be back from the parade and he'd hear every excited detail from the little girl.

A hand tugged his sleeve, halting his progress. It was the drunk man. Tommy glanced at the hand, and then at the man, raising his eyebrow. At one time, that would have been enough to encourage anyone to loosen their grip. The man didn't take the hint.

'Will you have a drink for Saint Patrick?' he said, clumsily pulling a small bottle of whiskey from his jacket pocket.

'I'm fine, thanks,' Tommy said.

'Just the one. Go on. One drink won't kill you.'

The man tried to thrust the bottle into Tommy's hand, but he pushed it away gently, shaking his head.

'Nothing for me.'

'Come on, fella. A drink to Saint Patrick, and to Ireland. God bless Ireland!' he shouted, raising the bottle in the air. A few passers-by glanced round at the man, but most kept their heads down, not wanting to get dragged into this impromptu drinking session. Besides, the sight of a drunken Irishman on these streets was hardly a rare one, even after Prohibition had apparently drained the land of alcohol. The man loosened the lid and held the bottle up again.

'To Ireland, united and free. And death to the traitor, Michael Collins.'

He spat the name out venomously before taking a gulp from the bottle. Tommy could feel his free hand ball into a fist. The man had cursed his former leader, his comrade-in-arms. His friend. Michael Collins was the man who had fought the British to a standstill. He'd signed a treaty with the Brits that had freed most of Ireland, but not the north, six counties of it at least, and because of that, some saw him as a traitor, and the country was now mired in a civil war. They had fought the British and now they were fighting each other.

Tommy had seen all this unfolding from afar. His fighting days were over, though he wondered what side he would have chosen had he still been in Ireland. He knew the answer to that question, really. In his heart. He would have been on Michael Collins' side. Always. He was Mick. The Big Fella. Their leader. He would have done anything for the Big Fella, even died for him. He nearly had when Collins had sent him on that mission to Glasgow.

He delivered a swift but barely noticeable punch to the drunk man's stomach, enough to knock the wind out of him, and the man slumped to his knees, coughing and spluttering and gasping for breath like a drowning man, though, like every seasoned drunk, he still managed to keep hold of his bottle without spilling a drop.

Tommy stepped round the man and strode away, not bothering to check whether he was back on his feet or not. Anyone seeing him would just presume he'd lost his balance. A policeman passing by might have a word, even though it was unlikely there would be an arrest. The cells of New York's police stations would be full enough without arresting every drunken Irishman on every street corner.

He was nearly home now, and he could picture Theresa in the kitchen, either leaning against the sink for a rest or sitting at the table enjoying a cigarette while Kathleen stood at the window keeping watch for a sight of him approaching. He was hoping it would be stew and potatoes for dinner. That had been Theresa's treat when she'd made a special dinner before, and he was sure it would be again today. On this day for the Irish, it would remind him of home.

He didn't think about Ireland all the time any more, not since he'd settled into life in this new city, and he thought of Michael Collins only when he heard his name in conversations. That happened more than he would have liked, certainly since the Treaty was signed and the civil war had started. Just as it had divided the country, it also split the Irish in New York. He tried to avoid becoming involved in any debate on the issue since, when all the talking was done and every argument was exhausted, he still remained a Michael Collins man. That would never change.

He hoped the Big Fella was fine. He knew his heart would be breaking over the civil war, putting brother against brother, father against son, Irishman against Irishman. That's not what Collins had fought for; it's not what any of them had fought for, and Tommy would never have imagined it could have come to this. He had escaped to America because he wanted to leave the fighting behind him. He'd had more than his fill of it, and a new life on the other side of the world was the only way he could see of escaping it. It hadn't been easy, but it was worth it. He told himself that every night when he rolled over in bed and found himself pressing against Theresa's warm body. He'd snuggle in closer, wrapping his arm around her so that he was also cuddling her bump. His baby.

He was smiling as he thought of the son he would soon hold in his arms when he turned the corner at the end of the block and into 45th Street, his own building less than a hundred yards away. There were people everywhere, a crowd large enough for him to think that a politician must have arrived to address them, or Babe Ruth had made the trip down from Upper Manhattan for an unexpected visit.

The crowd covered the road so that no traffic could pass, though there were no vehicles attempting to get up or down the street. There were people on the parked cars, mainly youngsters who had clambered up on them to sit on the bonnet or roof. The sea of bodies had washed up on to the pavement and was also lapping the stoop at the front of the tenement. He knew they were at his building, instinctively. They were glancing up towards the apartment or along the street as if they were keeping watch for someone. For something.

Suddenly a scream burst out of the building, like the shriek of a banshee on a stormy Donegal night and he stared up towards his apartment. A Tricolour hung limply from the fire escape on the front of the building. Tommy still held the bag of oatcakes in his hand, though he realised he had suddenly lost his appetite.

Endless Tears

Everyone standing outside the building looked up to the third floor window where the scream had escaped from and then, almost in the same instant, they seemed to turn *en masse* towards him, almost as if the sound which pierced the Manhattan air was heralding his arrival. He stared back at them, holding the gaze of each person, or so it seemed to them as their eyes focused on him. His legs were moving. He could feel them propelling him forward, closer to the crowd, yet it seemed like they were moving heavily, weighed down and trudging through an invisible muddy field that continued to hinder his progress.

He still reached them soon enough, pushing through bodies like he was swimming against the tide. People tried to get out his way. He felt hands patting his back; was it possible to tell the difference between a sympathetic gesture and a congratulatory one? He hadn't done anything of note that he could think of, and when he saw faces turn away from him, or eyes quickly averted from his gaze, he feared the worst.

He took the stairs two at a time, the staircase lined with more people who pressed against the wall to let him pass. The heavy thud of his boots as they propelled him towards the apartment echoed through the otherwise hushed building. The apartment door was open and he sprinted towards it like he was racing to catch a trolley car before the door closed and it moved on to the next stop. When he got to the door, his way was barred. Father Michael Murphy stood before him.

'What's happened, Father?' he blurted out as the priest took a step closer to him. 'What the hell's going on? All these people?'

'Tommy, there's been a terrible accident.'

'Theresa!'

He shouted her name, glancing beyond the priest at the sea of bodies filling up his house. Some of them looked towards the door, others looked away. There were a few sobs, and one or two women buried their faces in handkerchiefs, shoulders shaking. A hand firmly gripped his shoulder and he stared at the priest, at eyes swelling up with tears.

'Tommy,' he whispered. 'I'm so sorry.'

'What's happened to her?' he shouted, shrugging free of the priest's grip and barging past him. 'Theresa!' he shouted again, then stopped and looked round. 'The baby. Is it the baby?'

The priest shook his head and moved towards him again, trying to grab his shoulder, but Tommy pushed his hand away.

'Just tell me, Mike. For God's sake.'

'Tommy . . .'

There was another scream and both men turned round. Tommy stumbled forward, nearly crashing into a wall before staggering into the bedroom. The bed was surrounded by people, some of them standing, while others knelt in prayer. They were blocking his view but he caught a glimpse of legs through the human barrier.

'Theresa,' he managed to whisper as the bodies shuffled apart to create a gap at the foot of the bed which he quickly filled.

Theresa was lying on her side. A woman he recognised as Alice Payne from downstairs, sat at the side of the bed, holding Theresa's hand and stroking her hair like a mother with a sick child. Theresa's eyes were closed, her face drenched in tears, and every few minutes her face seemed to screw up as if in pain. The bump was still there, Tommy noticed.

'Theresa,' he whispered again, dropping to his knees and shuffling along the floor until he was beside her head. Alice moved back to give him room, though when she stopped caressing her hair, Theresa groaned.

'Theresa,' he said, louder this time, but it didn't seem like she'd heard him.

'Tommy, it's Kathleen.'

He looked round at Father Mike standing in the doorway.

'She's gone, Tommy . . . Kathleen's dead.'

Tommy almost burst out laughing. It sounded absurd. It was absurd. Kathleen couldn't be dead. She was only five. She was just a little girl. She was five. She couldn't be dead. Five.

He shook his head as Father Mike nodded, and then the room filled up with another scream, a howl from the bed that was like a bolt of lighting surging through a body. Alice instinctively sprung forward, her hand stroking Theresa's hair. Her lips pressed close to Theresa's ear and whispering futile words of comfort. If Theresa heard her, and Tommy doubted that, there were no words yet invented which could bring any sort of solace. He shook his head again and turned round to look at Theresa, at her face, the bump, her body which would occasionally spasm as she lay sprawled across the top of the bed. He felt a hand rest on his shoulder, giving him a squeeze. He wasn't sure if it was Father Mike or not, but he didn't look round.

'Kathleen,' he whispered. 'Kathleen . . . Kathleen . . . Kathleen.'

Theresa heard him and her wailing, building in volume, seemed to accompany his whispers in a macabre, musical arrangement that sparked tears in the apartment and beyond; on the landing, down the stairs, outside on the stoop, the sidewalk, among people spilling on to the road and sitting on the fenders of parked cars. It felt like everyone was crying now.

'Kathleen,' he whispered. 'Kathleen . . . Kathleen . . . Kathleen.'

Father Mike handed him a cup of coffee and a lit cigarette, both of which he gratefully took. The priest sat facing him at the table and Tommy glanced up and beyond his shoulder.

'I've cleared them all out. Alice is still in there with Theresa and a couple of the neighbours too, but that's all.'

'Thanks.'

'They mean well,' Father Mike said, lighting up his own cigarette. 'Well, most of them do. There are a few who just want to be where the gossip is. I chased them away for sure.'

A cloud of smoke quickly formed at the kitchen table, like the mist rolling off the Hudson River and ambling up through Hell's Kitchen on a winter's morning. Tommy was grateful for the camouflage it offered.

'The police want to speak to you,' Father Mike said.

Tommy nodded. He couldn't hear Theresa any more. She was sleeping, restless and mournful, but the doctor who'd been summoned had administered something which had, at least temporarily, numbed the pain and dampened down the shock. That would only last until she woke up and remembered what had happened, and then he was sure the screams would start all over again.

What had happened? He wasn't exactly sure himself. There had been chaos when he arrived home, and what he really needed was calmness so that he could register the facts properly. This much he had been told. She had been shot. Kathleen. A bullet hit her as she stood at the kerb, waiting to cross the road when it was safe to do so. She was dead. Kathleen. Shot through the heart. Theresa's daughter. Her little girl . . . Their little girl. Kathleen. He closed his eyes and a few stray tears escaped down his cheeks.

'It's okay to cry, Tommy,' Father Mike said softly, but Tommy shook his head. He needed to keep a clear head, to try and understand what had happened, how it could have happened. She was five-years-old. Just a child. Almost still a baby.

She wanted to see the parade, like thousands of others in the city, to watch the bands marching up Fifth Avenue, playing songs of Ireland as green bunting hung from lamp-posts and windows, Tricolours too. Boys with green dye through their hair, girls wearing green ribbons; a thousand voices singing and shouting, some of them Irish, most of them in their new American tongue, native New

Yorkers now but always Irish too. Jugglers throwing wooden bottles in the air – two, three, four at a time. Men standing at street corners, penny whistles at their lips, caps at their feet in the hope they'd fill up with coins. Green and white and yellow balloons everywhere; children holding them and losing them and mourning them. Others had ice-cream smeared across their mouths, which they were trying unsuccessfully to lick off. Vendors selling hot dogs, hamburgers, freshly-baked biscuits that sizzled on the hot plate as they cooked; the aromas attacking the senses, reminding passers-by of Dublin, Derry, Donegal . . . and they would all stop, eager for a little taste of home.

Drunk men staggered through the crowd, brown paper bags clutched to their hearts and constantly pressed to their lips; a modern miracle in the midst of Prohibition, or just the luck of the Irish. Women sashayed and swayed along the sidewalks, dressed in their Sunday Mass finery, hoping to catch a complimentary eye or casting a scornful glance at their rivals.

The parade continued to pour along the avenue that was wide enough to sail a ship down it, past shops and restaurants and hotels and cafés that all seemed to be Irish for the day; a never-ending stream of bands and marchers, the music a litany of songs learnt on their mammy's knee; *The Boys of Wexford. The Ballad of Dan Foley. A Nation Once Again*. Sometimes the sheer volume of numbers – the newspapers would later report at least fifty thousand had marched along New York's streets – would force them to halt their forward progress. The marchers used it as an opportunity to rest legs they hadn't realised up to that moment were weary, while bands stomped up and down on the spot. It was then that the national anthem might be played, their song of freedom, the song of the republic hopefully soon to be. *The Soldier's Song*.

'Soldiers are we, whose lives are pledged to Ireland. Some have come, from the land beyond the wave . . .'

The music, and the words, in the Gaelic, of course, rose up towards the rooftops of skyscrapers forming a concrete guard of honour for the Irish celebration. The sidewalks, packed with thousands of spectators, provided a voluble choir, and they would sing with gusto and pride. They were celebrating their saint, not just as Irish men and women but as Irish-Americans, and many a smile could be seen bobbing about in this sea of happy faces.

None of them would have heard the shots or the screams or the screeching of cars fleeing the scene, or police sirens echoing through the streets as cars raced from nearby stations, alerted by a phone-call or a frantic passer-by who'd burst into the station, or both. There were no songs at the corner of West 34th and Seventh. No marchers or bands or balloons or biscuits. Just a little girl lying face down in the road, the green ribbon still tied firmly to her brown hair, as a dark patch of thick liquid slowly spread out from under her body.

Tommy was suddenly aware of a stinging sensation in his fingers and his eyes re-focused on what remained of his cigarette. It had burnt down to a tiny fragment and was now burning his flesh. He dropped it on the table, oblivious to the pain.

'Do you want another one?' Father Mike said.

'Please.'

This time the priest handed him the pack of Camels

and Tommy took one out for himself, gratefully accepting the book of matches the priest gave him too. He sparked up a light and then inhaled deeply, allowing the nicotine to settle in his lungs before allowing any of it to escape.

'What am I going to do?' he muttered.

Father Mike shook his head. Tommy looked at him, almost pleadingly, looking for an answer, any answer, but there was nothing the priest could offer him. He stood up and walked over to the sink, pouring the coffee, which was now cold, down the drain, turning on the tap and filling the mug with water. He took a long drink, gulping down the cold liquid.

'The police want to speak to you,' Father Mike said.

'When?'

'They're in the other room.'

'What, now?'

The priest nodded

'Do they know who did this? Have they caught them yet?'

'I don't know, Tommy. They just said they'd wait here until you were ready to speak to them.

'I'm ready now,' Tommy said, walking towards the door.

'Tommy!'

He stopped.

'They might not have all the answers, or at least the ones you want to hear.'

Tommy frowned.

'Here,' said Father Mike, throwing the packet of cigarettes towards Tommy, who caught it. 'You'll probably need these.'

'Are you not staying?'

'I'll look in on Theresa and then I need to be getting

back. We've got a Mass at six o'clock for all the workers who couldn't make it this morning.'

'Okay,' said Tommy. 'Well, thanks . . .'

'I'll be back in the morning to discuss, you know . . . the service.'

Tommy nodded.

'But it can wait until tomorrow,' the priest said.

There were two policemen in the front room. One of them, who wore a uniform, stood looking out the window. Tommy wondered if there was still a crowd milling about outside or whether they'd all drifted home, dissipating like an early-morning mist, all of them with hushed voices, whispering words of disbelief at the news which had spread through the neighbourhood, up and down every staircase of every tenement in Hell's Kitchen like a vicious gust of wind. They were taking that news home with them, spreading it further afield until it would seem like the whole West Side was talking about it. The papers would carry the news too, just a few lines, but it would be there in black and white for everyone to read and digest.

The other policeman wore a dark suit with a matching waist-coat. His white shirt was almost dazzling in the dim light of the room. The sun found it difficult to push its way into the buildings crammed together on the multitude of streets springing off the long avenues which stretched up and down the island, instead content to spread its warmth on the streets and anyone walking along them.

The policeman – Tommy guessed he was a detective –

stood up as he walked into the room. His overcoat was draped over the back of the chair and he placed his fedora delicately on top of it.

'Mister Delaney, I'm sorry for your loss,' he said. The uniformed officer took his hat off too and nodded in agreement.

'Thank-you,' Tommy said. It still sounded funny when he was called Delaney. That was Theresa's name. Kathleen's too.

'Do you want to sit down?'

The detective gestured to the chair facing the one he'd been on and Tommy nodded, sitting down as the detective did the same. It was almost as if it was his house and Tommy was the guest.

'I'm Detective John Lincoln,' he said, holding out his hand which Tommy shook unthinkingly. 'And this is Officer Dolan.'

The uniform nodded again.

'How is your wife?'

'I don't know. Sleeping.'

'It's a terrible business,' Lincoln said. 'I just want to assure you that we'll do everything we can to catch who did this.'

'Do you know who did it?'

'We're still making enquiries, Mister Delaney. Taking statements. Trying to find witnesses. That's not always easy, as you might appreciate.'

Tommy stared at Lincoln. Was he making a reference to his connections? Would he know what he did? Who he worked for? Did he know where he had been today?

'But I'm sure that we'll find some answers. People are shocked by this, Mister Delaney. Truly shocked.'

Tommy took out a cigarette, putting it in his mouth and holding out the packet. Lincoln took one with a nod but Officer Dolan shook his head. Tommy studied the detective as they both started smoking. He guessed they were both about the same age. Thirty-years-old. Lincoln's hair was brown but already there were strong flashes of grey running through it. It was cut short and tidy, and he'd obviously run wax through it. His moustache was darker, almost ginger in shade, and drooped down both sides of his mouth, and Lincoln would touch either edge with the tip of his tongue. Tommy wasn't sure if the detective even realised he was doing it. There was a gold band on his finger, so Tommy presumed there was a Mrs Lincoln.

'We've still to speak to the boy,' Lincoln said. 'Hopefully he might tell us something which will help.'

'The boy?'

'Yes . . .'

'Joseph Tierney,' Officer Dolan said, reading from his notebook again.

'Joseph was with your daughter – Kathleen – when it happened.'

'She called me daddy.'

'Sorry?'

'Kathleen . . . That's what she called me.' Tommy looked at the detective, shaking his head.

'We can talk later, Mister Delaney. I can come back.' Lincoln started to stand up.

'What did Joseph see?' Tommy asked.

'I don't know. We haven't had a chance to speak to him yet. That's where we're heading next.'

Joseph lived in the apartment directly above. Tommy

couldn't really picture him but he knew the boy's parents, at least who they were. His father was a labourer, and Tommy would sometimes meet him leaving for work in the morning or coming home at the end of a long day. They never exchanged more than a passing nod or 'Hello' at most, but that was enough for both of them. He only knew the other man as 'Tierney'. There were no first names exchanged. Mrs Tierney – Clare – had flaming red hair that looked as though it was permanently on fire. Six children had taken their toll on her, though there were still signs that she'd been a fine-looking girl in her day. Sometimes, if Tommy caught sight of her hair as she shuffled along the street, it would take his breath away, reminding him of someone from his past whose red hair he had once held and smelt.

'I want to catch the man who did this,' Lincoln said, looking round for somewhere to stub out his cigarette. There was a glass lying on the floor at the side of the couch with a tiny drop of dark liquid in it, abandoned by one of the mourners who'd cluttered the house. When Tommy picked it up he could smell right away that it was rum. He still held it out for Lincoln, though, who dropped the cigarette into the glass without mention of its contents, the cigarette sizzling briefly as it hit the liquid before it died.

'So do I,' said Tommy.

Lincoln glanced at him.

'I want to catch him too,' said Tommy.

'It's a matter of gathering evidence and that will take us to him.'

Tommy shrugged his shoulders, even though his instinct was to shake his head. It wouldn't be as easy as Lincoln was trying to make out. People didn't readily talk in these neighbourhoods, not to the police, regardless of what had happened.

'I'll ask around as well,' he said. 'See if anybody knows anything or has heard anything.'

'It might be better if you leave the detective work for us,' said Lincoln.

'She was my – Kathleen.'

'I know, Mister Delaney, and I can appreciate how you feel right now.'

'Can you, Detective Lincoln? Can you really?'

Lincoln stood up, snatching his hat, followed by his overcoat. 'It's best you let us do our job.'

Tommy stood up as well.

'It might be that the people involved won't take kindly to someone poking their noses into things. We're the police. That's expected. It's our job.'

'I want to find who did this.'

'I want that too, Mister Delaney. We all do.'

Officer Dolan nodded as if to confirm that this was, indeed, the case.

'Look after Kathleen's mother,' Lincoln said, nodding towards the bedroom. 'She needs you now. Let us catch the bad guys.'

'Just make sure you do then.'

Tommy stood aside to let the two policemen past and they walked to the front door. Lincoln turned round as Dolan opened the door. Tommy stood in the door frame of the front room.

'If you hear anything, Mister Delaney, let me know. I'm at the 26th Precinct up on 47th Street.'

Tommy nodded.

'And don't go doing anything stupid.'

Tommy said nothing, his mind already racing with the names of people he could ask. Someone was bound to know something.

'We will catch him,' Lincoln said, as the two policemen disappeared down the hallway, Dolan silently closing the door.

Tommy stood on the same spot for ten minutes at least; thoughts of how he would conduct his own investigation running through his head while, at the same time, he was in two minds over whether to go into the bedroom to check on Theresa, worried at what he might find, but knowing that Lincoln was right about one thing at least. He would need to look after Theresa now.

Agony of the Cross

Jesus was looking at him, a mournful expression on his face like he knew and felt the pain of everyone in the church. He was nailed to a cross, of course, so that might have something to do with his own agony, which had been lovingly carved by his creator before being sold and shipped out to churches, not just in New York, but all over the world.

The crucified Christ used to fascinate Tommy as a child, sitting beside his mother every Sunday morning at Mass. He would stare at the cross while the priest spoke or turned his back on them and muttered words in a language Tommy never understood. His mother would nudge him or tug on his sleeve when it was time to stand or sit or kneel, or give his head a jolt so that he bowed it at the appropriate time rather than continuing to stare at Jesus.

He always believed Jesus was staring back at him. His head seemed heavy and he was struggling to hold it up as he hung on the cross, but his eyes followed Tommy. He also believed Jesus knew what he was thinking, and he tried desperately to make sure his mind was clear of any impure thoughts, as the priest always called them before asking him to recount and recant them in confession.

That had been a long time ago. His mother hadn't been particularly religious. He guessed later that God hadn't always dealt her a fair hand in life, and she carried that resentment with her. Certainly, she always seemed wary, almost hostile, to the priest whenever he would occasionally visit. It was a small village in Donegal, however, and attendance at Sunday Mass was just about mandatory, but that was the only time they went, and when the priest was casting his net at school, looking for new altar boys to recruit, Tommy wasn't among their number.

He wasn't religious either, despite the holy medals which hung round his neck. One was of St Michael the Archangel, helping to protect him against the wiles of the evil one, or so it was claimed. It had belonged to his father, a man he had never seen, who had died even before he was born. His mother had given it to him on her own death-bed. The other medal belonged to his cousin, Danny, shot dead by a British bullet on a wet hillside in Donegal. Tommy had been there – it had only been three years ago – and he often thought of Danny, more than he ever did of the father he never knew. The medal was of Our Lady, the Blessed Mother, who gazed down on and looked after all her children on earth. He touched the medals now through the stiff, starched white shirt which pressed itself uncomfortably on his skin, and it was as if they were white hot, like rivets on a building site, burning his fingers. He let them go quickly. Where was Our Lady when Kathleen needed looking after?

Tommy heard a bell and could feel people near him standing up, the noisy clatter of kneelers being scraped across the stone floor as people made more room for their feet, and he followed suit. He glanced at Theresa, sitting to his right. The constant movement – stand up, sit down, kneel down, sit up – would have been too much for her anyway, and it was more important that she rest her tired legs. He was glad, too, because he was worried that, if she stood up, she might immediately topple over.

A black veil covered her face. She seemed to be looking straight ahead, though he couldn't tell if her eyes were open or closed. Occasionally, he would touch her arm delicately, worried that she was so fragile he might break her, but more worried because there didn't seem to be any sign of life from her and he needed reassurance she was still alive. She would stir whenever he did touch her, though she never looked round. He knew why. Kathleen's coffin would be in her eye-line then, and that was an object too unbearable to see more than was absolutely necessary.

The small brown box sat on top of a set of wooden legs that had been hastily assembled by the undertaker as the coffin was being carried into the church. A white sheet was draped over it as it sat, centre-stage, at the steps in front of the altar, whose gates were closed, only to be re-opened at the end of the ceremony when the priest led the mourners, and the coffin, out of Holy Cross Church.

It was where Theresa went every Sunday with Kathleen. Occasionally he accompanied them, but most times he'd either be working or he'd just decline the invitation. He wore his medals, and if he was ever forced to admit it, then he would say that he did believe in God and that, sometimes, he did pray. He didn't like churches, however, and despite the fact his escape to New York required the help of a priest, it hadn't made him a more faithful or fanatical Catholic.

The red brick façade of the church made it a distinctive presence on 42nd Street, and it seemed so familiar to Tommy as they walked towards it, even though he rarely stepped inside. After today he doubted he would ever venture back.

The coffin looked small and light enough that he could carry it himself, but he knew that would have been difficult, even if he had wanted to. He could see the strain on the faces of the pallbearers as they carried it on their shoulders, a mixture of emotion and effort. He couldn't do it, even being one of six to carry it. He didn't want to carry her, this little girl who had called him 'Daddy . . .' A lump caught in his throat and he swallowed hard, determined to remain strong.

He tried to picture Kathleen in the apartment, laughing or crying or talking or eating, anything to block out the image implanted in his mind. It was Father Mike who'd explained that someone would have to go and see Kathleen, to identify her and sign for her release from the mortuary so that she could be brought home and buried. When he said someone, he meant Tommy. The priest had gone with him. They walked to the mortuary, a nondescript building in the middle of a row of shops and offices on 26th Street. He'd offered to drive but Tommy had wanted to walk, hoping that the fresh air might clear his mind or at least allow him to gather up his thoughts.

He had seen dead bodies before. He'd stood over men as they bled to death in front of him, as a result of his actions. Sometimes those faces, in their final moments of wretched agony, still haunted his dreams, but he always told himself that it had been necessary. He was a soldier in the middle of a war to free his country from British rule, and at such times, bad things happen. If he didn't kill, he would be killed, he always told himself, and it was true.

Yet, as he and Father Mike sat in a waiting room, just the two of them in a plain room with four chairs round a small, wooden table, in the middle of which sat a glass ash-tray, almost overflowing with extinguished cigarette ends from previous grieving relatives, he felt sick at the thought of what he was going to see, and worried at what his reaction might be. He stared at the clock hanging on the wall. At one time the décor would have been white, fresh, but the walls wore a sickly yellow shade, the jaundiced skin of death, coated by a million smoked cigarettes. The time dragged, even though they were summoned within fifteen minutes of arriving, the man on the reception desk popping his head round the door to let them know they were ready.

Tommy felt like the sound of his footsteps on the stone floor was deafening, almost loud enough to waken the dead even. Almost. Father Mike remained in the waiting room. Tommy had insisted. It was enough that the priest had accompanied him here in the first place, but this was something he had to do himself. She had called him 'Daddy'.

The man leading the way was small and stocky. He wore a shirt opened at the neck, sleeves rolled up, and a black waistcoat, unbuttoned. He introduced himself, but Tommy immediately forgot the name. Garabaldi. Capaldi. It was something Italian, he was sure.

They walked down one flight of stairs, and then another, and Tommy sensed the temperature dropping with each step, like they were descending into the bowels of hell, but discovering that hell was ice cold rather than red hot. At the bottom of the second flight of stairs, they stopped outside a door, the other man's hand poised on the handle. He glanced round at Tommy, who nodded, and he opened the door, holding it aside to let Tommy in before closing it behind them.

There was a coat-stand in the corner of the room, and Capaldi – Tommy decided that was his name – snatched a jacket off one of the hooks, slipping it on like he was conforming to some sort of macabre dress sense down here. It was a square room, illuminated by a single glowing lightbulb at the end of a cable hanging down from the ceiling in the centre of the room. There were silver cabinets lining three of the walls, giant fridges holding . . . Tommy shuddered at the thought, and shivered as well. He breathed out, and a ball of condensed air crystallised in front of his eyes. Capaldi touched his arm.

'Are you ready?' he said.

Tommy looked at the man, at his blue eyes which held his gaze without blinking, and then he glanced beyond Capaldi's shoulder. On top of a silver table was a shape hidden from view by the dirty white sheet draped over it, but he knew, from the contours, what it was. Who it was. He took a deep breath and looked back at Capaldi, nodding, before slowly following the smaller man over towards the body. Her body. Kathleen. She used to call him 'Daddy.'

They were standing in the church now, the air filled with incense. There were a few coughs as some of it caught in people's throats. Father Mike was slowly shuffling round the coffin, blessing it with incense and then holy water. Everything had been removed from the top of the coffin – Bible, crucifix, white linen sheet. All that was left was a little brown wooden box. It was almost time to carry it out of the church.

Theresa still sat beside him, though her head was bowed

now and her body trembled as she sobbed quietly. The hysterical screams had long since simmered down, to be replaced by a constant stream of tears that left her exhausted. Alice stood in the next row, directly behind her, massaging Theresa's shoulders gently. Tommy was dreading the prospect of coaxing Theresa to her feet so that they could lead the mourners in following the coffin out of the church. He didn't know if Theresa would be able to remain on her feet and, if she didn't, whether he'd be able to catch her if she fell.

He could picture Kathleen's face now, as he looked towards the coffin again, swathed in a cloud of incense. It was like she was a porcelain doll, fast asleep on a steel table, when Capaldi had pulled back the cover. Her lips were red, as if she'd stolen her mother's lipstick and secretly applied some. She's only sleeping, he wanted to say to Capaldi. Wake her up. The cover remained just under her chin, hiding the evidence of where the bullet had entered her body. It was only her face he needed to see, to nod to Capaldi and let him know that this was Kathleen Delaney, the little girl who called him 'Daddy'. He would sign the release form at the reception.

He had barely moved his head when Capaldi started to pull the cover back up. Tommy stopped him. He wanted to see her, just for a few more seconds. Could he stare long enough and pray fervently enough to wake her up? He didn't want the sheet to cover her up again, to hide her from him forever. He didn't know whether he was expected to touch her face or kiss her, or even say her name, but he didn't do or say anything. He couldn't. He just stared and stared until Capaldi whispered 'It's time to go.'

Tommy touched his jacket pocket now. Inside was a

green ribbon. Capaldi had been reluctant to let him take it but he had relented under the pitiful gaze of Tommy's eyes; a dollar bill slipped into his palm also helped. Tommy wanted that ribbon, a reminder of the little girl who called him 'Daddy'. Kathleen. His daughter.

He let out a cry as sudden and unexpected to everyone else as it was to him. He tried to smother it quickly as he felt Theresa's hand slip into his, giving it a quick squeeze, and he stood, holding her hand, as she remained sitting. He stared at Jesus as tears poured down his cheeks.

There had been drinking and singing. Men with fiddles and penny whistles. Jack Gallagher with his mouth organ playing *Danny Boy*, just about in time, and getting a round of applause for his efforts. Jack was old, though no-one knew for sure just how old. He said he'd come over in fifty-one with his father and brother. Two sisters, another brother and their mother hadn't survived the famine. Jack's voice, old and croaky and struggling under the strain of a lifetime of drinking and smoking – 'And whoring!' he always said. 'Don't forget the whoring!' – was a strange cocktail of Mayo and Manhattan. No matter that he would have been just a child when he'd managed to escape the deathly clutches of *An Gorta Mor* – the Great Hunger – a little bit of Ireland remained forever in his character. Tommy noticed the Irish accent became more pronounced on occasions such as these, when there was the prospect of an endless flow of whiskey.

Jack was a regular presence at such events, along with his

mouth organ. No-one knew where he stayed, and Tommy suspected he was forever trawling the city in search of a wedding or a wake, some whiskey and a place to rest his head when he'd taken his fill of the drink.

There were singers, too, women with the voices of angels, and others who croaked their way through songs that the audience struggled to recognise. At first, Tommy had floated between kitchen and front room, playing the dutiful host, checking on cups and glasses, directing people towards the kitchen where an abundance of home cooking was piled on the table and counters – sandwiches and stews, sausages and savouries; enough to feed the five thousand at least. People soon made themselves at home, content to fill their own cups or pile up their plates with food, and he was happy to leave them to it.

He'd stepped into the bedroom. Theresa was sleeping, sedated again by the magical pills the doctor had administered. He was tempted to ask for one himself, if only to guarantee one night's sleep. He sat on the ledge, blowing smoke out through the small gap he'd made when he opened the window. Automatically, he would glance round at Theresa, particularly if she stirred or groaned, or sighed heavily, but she never woke up, and after a while he just kept his gaze on the street below.

There were parked cars lined at the kerbside on either side of the road, while a steady procession of vehicles or varying shapes and sizes rumbled past, spluttering out fumes which lingered in the air. Kids played on the sidewalk, or on the steps that led up to the main door of the tenements. They were chasing each other, laughing and screaming as they did so. Others sat on the stoop like they were sitting in the benches at the Polo Grounds, waiting for the ball game to start, or on the bonnets of cars until an invisible voice boomed out from an open window, telling them to move.

A uniformed policeman strode up the street and Tommy wondered whether he was coming to see him, but he continued walking past the building. A young couple on the other side of the street stopped and glanced over to his apartment. Word of what had happened had obviously spread through the neighbourhood. They didn't point but he knew that they were looking and he stepped back slightly from the window.

There was a knock at the bedroom door, gentle at first, but more insistent after a minute or so. Tommy flicked his cigarette out the window, watching it twist and turn and fall to earth like a bird that had been shot dead. When he opened the door, one of his neighbours, Arthur Maguire, stood before him.

'There's someone here to see you, Tommy,' he said.

'Who?'

'I don't know. Just a guy at the door asking for you.'

Tommy stared down the hallway towards the door, which was closed.

'He's waiting out there,' Arthur said. 'He said he didn't want to come in.'

'And he didn't say what he wanted?'

Arthur shook his head. Tommy closed the bedroom door slowly, keen not to make a noise in case it disturbed Theresa, even though he knew that was unlikely, and walked down the hallway as Arthur slipped back into the living room. As he did so, Tommy heard a snatch of a woman singing *The Mountains of Mourne*. She had a soulful voice, which was a blessing. It was a nice song, and it would have been spoiled by an out-of-tune singer.

When Tommy opened the door, there was no-one there. He glanced back, half-expecting to see Arthur laughing, though why he would play a practical joke on a day like this was beyond him. He stepped over to the stairwell. On the landing below a man leant against the wall, almost in the shadows, though the smoke from his cigarette gave him away. The man moved forward, dropping the cigarette, and walked up the few stairs until he stood in front of Tommy. He took off his cap.

'I'm sorry for your loss,' he said in a clipped New York accent. He was Italian rather than Irish. Tommy could guess an Irish accent immediately, pinpointing the county of origin with a fair degree of accuracy, and while that skill was much harder here, he could still detect backgrounds easily enough. This man wasn't one of them.

'Thanks,' said Tommy.

The man thrust his hand inside his jacket and Tommy instinctively tensed. The man noticed and smiled. He pulled out a brown bag and waved it in the air. Tommy relaxed. The man held the bag out.

'What's that?' Tommy asked.

'It's for you.'

'What is it?'

'It'll help you . . . with all of this,' the man said, nodding towards the apartment. 'Dying can be an expensive business.'

Tommy put his hands in his pockets as the man continued holding the bag out to him.

'Just take it, Mister Delaney. It's for you.'

'Who is it from?'

'Does it matter? It'll come in handy. That's all you need to know.'

'There's more than a few dollars in there,' Tommy said, shaking his head, 'so I know it's not some neighbourhood collection or people at church putting a few cents in a basket for us, so I think it does matter.'

Now it was the man's turn to shake his head.

'I was just told to deliver this here and make sure you got it. Ask no questions and all that.'

Tommy kept his hands in his pockets. The man stepped forward and thrust the bag under Tommy's arm.

'He's really sorry. That's all I know.'

'Who is?' said Tommy, taking hold of the bag.

'The man whose money . . . well, he's sorry. Everyone is. It was a terrible accident. Terrible. No-one wanted that. A little girl. It's not right.'

Tommy grabbed the man by the throat and pushed him across the landing until he thudded into the wall beside the Brogans' door opposite his apartment.

'Who the hell did this? Who killed her?'

The man brought his knee up between Tommy's legs, and as he doubled over, he loosened his grip on the man who broke free, stumbling towards the stairs.

'Jesus! Are you crazy?' he said. 'I'm just the messenger, for Christ sake.'

The man, rubbing his neck, swiftly walked down the stairs as Tommy slowly got to his feet, still holding the brown bag. He didn't look inside it but guessed, just by the bulk of it, that there was at least two hundred dollars in it, probably more. He glanced towards the stairs as the man's anxious footsteps faded until he disappeared out the building and into the street.

Blood Money

The sunlight was dazzling when he stepped out on to the sidewalk, almost colliding with a couple walking arm in arm along the street. He could smell the drink on them. Were they heading home from an all-night party in a speakeasy? There were a few dotted about the nearby streets. You didn't have to look too far to find them. The woman's face was painted, though what had been carefully applied a few hours ago was now showing signs of strain. He didn't think she was a hooker, though he couldn't be sure. She could just as well be a widow looking for a bit of comfort or companionship, and alcohol always helped to provide that.

'Sorry,' Tommy muttered, side-stepping them and stumbling into the road. Luckily there were no cars coming. He stared up and down the street, hoping to catch a glimpse of the man who'd just left. Tommy still held the brown bag in his hand. He could just give it to the drunk couple, and be done with it, but he had more questions for the man. Tommy figured he knew something about Kathleen's death, maybe everything, which meant he would know who had fired that fatal shot. Tommy needed to ask him.

Tommy started running. A car passed him, sounding its horn, telling him to get off the road. He heeded the warning and cut back in between two parked cars and on to the sidewalk. He didn't know why he was heading this way, or what he was looking for. It was like running up a blind alley, and he knew, at some point, he'd have to stop, probably when his lungs were ready to burst and that didn't feel like it would be too long.

He should have fought back, or fought harder when the man broke free, but it had taken him by surprise, and even in the short time since he'd arrived in New York, he'd had little call to resort to violence. The threat of it, or the presence of a gun, was usually enough to do the trick and he'd lost the sharpness he knew had been there when he'd been fighting in Ireland.

He had gone a few blocks when his progress was halted by the traffic racing across Eighth Avenue in both directions. He leant against a street light gratefully, bending over and taking deep gulps of air to try and regain control of his breathing. He glanced round and saw the money man sitting in his car at the junction, waiting for the traffic to clear so that he could continue on his journey. He was staring straight ahead, ready to drive on as soon as he could. Stuffing the bag of money in his pocket, Tommy strode across the road, opened the driver's door and grabbed the man, dragging him out of the car.

He threw the man on to the road, moving forward and kicking him on the head as the man tried to get up. A horn sounded from the car behind, the driver suddenly aware that he was trapped if the traffic started moving, and perhaps alarmed at the impromptu attack, hoping the horn might scare Tommy away. He ignored it. The man was trying to get up on to his knees, still dazed from the blow to his head. Tommy punched him in the face and the man fell back, cracking his skull on the road.

Tommy crouched down and grabbed a handful of the man's hair, lifting his head up and smashing it down on the ground several times. The man groaned, each sound weaker than the last. His face was streaked with blood.

'Who killed her?' Tommy shouted into the bloody face. 'Who killed my daughter?'

More car horns were sounding now, a few voices shouting too, from the build-up of vehicles beginning to stretch back along the street, and also from apartment windows, passers-by on foot as well. Tommy could even hear a whistle sounding in the distance, a siren too, and he wondered if the police were heading his way. He took the brown bag out of his pocket and stuffed it into the man's shirt.

'Tell him I don't want his money,' he shouted. 'Tell him that . . . And tell him I'll find him. I'll find him!'

He let go of the man, who flopped to the ground, and stood up. He started to walk away but turned after a few paces and ran back, kicking the man's body. There was no reaction, but Tommy was sure he heard a crack.

Tommy stumbled back on to the sidewalk, ignoring the people who'd stopped to watch the violent drama unfold, some of them staring at him as he headed back towards home, while others joined a couple of drivers in venturing towards the body which lay prone in the middle of the street. They did so in trepidation, not sure if the man was still alive or not, all of them hoping the siren which was getting louder would arrive on the scene before they had to find out for themselves.

He waited for the knock on the door which he knew would come. When he'd returned home, he called an abrupt end to the wake. There were a few voices of protest but he silenced them with a look he conjured up from his past that was enough to end any further dissent. A bottle of whiskey deposited in Jack Gallagher's jacket pocket persuaded the old man to leave and, besides, at least Jack had done a turn with the mouth organ. Tommy heard it echoing down the stairs, old Jack heralding everyone out like the pied piper of Hell's Kitchen, though where he would lead them, Tommy didn't know or care. A couple of neighbours were concerned about the blood on his hands, but he dismissed their fussing, telling them it would wash off.

'I'm fine,' he said. 'It's not my blood anyway,' he added which was enough to send them away, curious and alarmed, but at least they were out of his home.

He stood at the sink and let the cold water run over his hands until there wasn't a trace of blood left on them. Still, he knew the police would be round soon enough. He hoped it would only be the police. It had happened close enough to the house, to his street, in his neighbourhood, that someone would have recognised him or at least seen where he'd headed.

He sat with a cup of whiskey, nursing it in his hand, as he smoked his way continuously through a packet of cigarettes. Theresa was still sleeping. He was glad of that at least. He didn't know what to say to her, or how to deal with her tears. It was fine in a busy house, with plenty of people milling about, where a concerned neighbour would be happy to sit with Theresa and offer what little comfort they could.

What could he do? Hold her? Promise her everything

would be fine when it was obvious that it wouldn't be? The only thing he could think of was to get the man who killed Kathleen, and then he could at least tell Theresa that. It wouldn't bring Kathleen back. Nothing could, but at least that would be something, if her killer was dead too.

The kitchen table was still littered with food. Trays of sandwiches, plates with half-eaten cakes and the stew and potatoes made by Alice Payne and a couple of other women in the building. The huge pot still sat on the stove. Most of its contents had been consumed by mourners looking for sustenance to line the stomach ahead of a heavy drinking session, but what was left could still be saved for later, tomorrow maybe? There wouldn't be many potatoes left, if any, but a plate of stew with some bread would be enough to fill him up. He'd wait until Theresa woke up, however, and then see if she wanted anything to eat before he decided what to do.

The cigarette ends were mounting up in the ashtray and Tommy emptied the contents in the bin underneath the sink. He was almost out of cigarettes. Normally he would have slipped out to O'Rourke's one block up on 46th Street, which always seemed to be open at any time of day or night, but he was reluctant to leave Theresa on her own. The last thing he wanted was for her to wake up and find the house empty. Even if he didn't know what to do or say, at least he would be there.

There was a knock on the door and Tommy smiled, as if his smoky vigil had been vindicated. Detective Lincoln stood in the hall when he opened the door. He had a uniformed officer with him again, though it wasn't Officer Dolan this time. The other policeman declined the invitation to come into the house, and put his hands behind his back, taking up guard outside the apartment like a doorman at a speakeasy. Tommy showed Lincoln through to the kitchen and the two men sat down.

'He's going to live, in case you're interested,' Lincoln said.

'Who?'

'The guy you attacked on 41st. He's in a mess, though. Broken jaw, ribs too, and a fractured skill. Not a pleasant sight. He's a lucky man . . . and so are you, Mister Delaney.'

'I buried my daughter today, detective,' said Tommy, 'so what do you want from me?'

'I want you to let me do my job, just like I asked you before.'

'Okay.'

'No, not okay. That's just a word, Mister Delaney.'

'Tommy.'

'What?'

'Call me Tommy.'

'I need you to promise not to do anything else, Tommy, and I need you to keep that promise.'

Tommy shrugged.

'I will catch the man who did this. That's my promise to you.'

'Okay, I promise.'

'Why do I feel you're not being straight with me?'

'I don't know . . . because you're a cop and you don't trust anyone?'

'Do you know who that was you put in the hospital?'

'No.'

'Paolo Monti.'

'Never heard of him.'

'What about Gaetano Reina?'

Tommy nodded.

'That's who Monti works for,' said Lincoln. 'You just put one of Reina's men in hospital, Tommy. There are not many who do that and live to tell the tale.'

Gaetano Reina was a big name in the city. Everyone knew that. That didn't tell half the story, though. He was head of the Lucchese family. They ran the Bronx and East Harlem. He had picked a fight with one of the most powerful men in New York, a bit like the Irish fighting the Brits, he thought, suppressing the grin which threatened to break out across his face.

'So you need to back off. These are dangerous people. You should know that and it won't make any difference to them that your daughter's dead.'

Tommy shrugged.

'So let me do my job then.'

'He was Reina's man?'

Lincoln nodded, stubbing out his cigarette in the ashtray.

'So the money was from Reina?'

Lincoln took out a packet of cigarettes from his jacket, offering them to Tommy, who took one without thanks.

'Which means that Reina . . . someone in Reina's gang is the man who killed my daughter.'

'They're not just some two-bit street gang, Tommy.'

'Why else would he offer me all that money? There was at least two hundred dollars in the bag.'

'What did they want you to do for it?'

'Nothing. He just said they were sorry and that it could be used to pay for whatever needed paying for. He said something about death being an expensive business.'

'So what are you going to do with it?'

'What?'

'The money.'

'I don't have it. I left it with Reina's man. I stuffed it into his jacket. I don't want it.'

Lincoln shook his head, lighting up a cigarette and sitting back, blowing the smoke out slowly. He stared through the cloud at Tommy who had to suppress a smile as the detective's tongue automatically caressed the edges of his moustache, and the glow of the cigarette end every time he inhaled seemed to accentuate the ginger traces of his facial hair. Tommy found himself almost beginning to mimic the action, and rubbed his face, which wore the stubble of a few days without a razor, in order to distract himself.

'That's a lot of money for anyone,' Lincoln eventually said.

'I suppose so.'

'I'm not sure I would have done the same as you. I might have kept the money.'

'Well, you are a cop.'

Lincoln smiled, though the expression lasted barely a second. He sat forward on the seat, quickly finishing his cigarette which he stubbed out in the ashtray. He drummed his fingers on the table and Tommy noticed that the detective wasn't wearing his wedding ring. Tommy's own fingers had no jewellery. One day there would be, though maybe he didn't believe that with the same certainly, at least not just now. It would be a while before the subject of a wedding could be broached with Theresa, particularly since when they had spoken about it before, Kathleen was always the flower girl.

'Are you alright, Tommy?'

'What?'

'You looked a bit upset there.'

'I'm fine,' Tommy said with a shrug.

Lincoln stood up, the chair scraping on the floor.

'I'm sure I'll be seeing you soon,' he said.

'No doubt,' said Tommy.

'And remember . . .'

'I know. Leave the bad guys to you.'

Lincoln smiled again and held out his hand which Tommy shook. He followed the detective to the door, holding it open for him and nodding by way of farewell as he stepped out into the hallway. When he could no longer hear the detective's footsteps echoing back up the stairs, he closed the door quietly and stepped softly through to the kitchen. He picked up the packet of Chesterfields which Lincoln had left behind and lit one up. He filled up a mug with cold water and gulped it down. His mouth was parched. He was smoking too many cigarettes, he thought as he drew heavily on the one he was holding now.

He glanced round the kitchen. Something caught his eye and he stepped over to the chair that Lincoln had been sitting on. He picked up the brown bag and this time he looked inside it. There was definitely two hundred dollars inside, probably much more by the looks of it, and he ran his fingers through the bundle of bills. It must have been tempting for Lincoln to have pocketed the money himself, and maybe he'd slipped a few dollars into his pocket, but Tommy was sure that most of it was still in the bag. He suddenly felt much richer, but no less sad.

Picture Perfect

The building was quiet now. It had been this way for a few days now, after all the mourners and moochers had drifted away in search of another wake and another free drink. The wind swirled and swooped up and down 45th Street, howling through tiny gaps in the windows or rattling the metal fire-escapes clinging to the front of the building, though it looked as though they would slide down the brick edifice and crash on to the street below at any moment.

Dirty clouds of dust and debris, car fumes and cigarette smoke mingled together and swirled through the air, the grey mugginess not helped by the dark clouds hovering overhead, ready at any moment to open up and deposit their contents on everyone and everything below. People sensed the impending change in the weather and raced to and from destinations with increased urgency. There was a general air of urgency to daily life anyway. People were always in a hurry, but the need to avoid an unnecessary drenching only made their actions more frantic.

Cars and cabs and trolley cars came and went, only stopping whenever the traffic clogged up at the various junctions along the street, but that was just a temporary delay. They rumbled along the street with a regularity that soon enough made it impossible to keep track of how many vehicles actually passed by. At the busiest intersections, policemen directed the traffic with an impressive degree of control that only rarely threatened to unravel.

Joseph pressed his forehead against the glass, glad of the cold sensation on his skin. He looked out at the street below him, noticing that no-one ever seemed to stop. Even friends or neighbours meeting while going in different directions carried on conversations while walking backwards away from each other, every step leading to an increase in the volume of their voices until they were so far apart that it didn't matter how loud they shouted. He heard snatches of these conversations.

'. . . She said it would be ready on Friday morning . . .'

'. . . Well, I still think they should have kept fighting . . .'

'. . . and a touch of lemon juice always works for me . . .'

'. . . Eighteen. I'm telling you. Eighteen . . .'

'. . . but not when it's too hot . . .'

The Tierney house was quiet. His father was out working. They were building the tunnel that would run under the Hudson River to New Jersey so that people could drive across. Joseph would stare at the water and no matter how hard he tried, he couldn't comprehend how it was possible to build anything under water. Even if they did, what would happen when the cars were under there? His brothers and sisters were out too, at school or work, or wandering the streets doing nothing when they should have been doing one or the other. His mother wasn't in the house either. She had been reluctant to leave him on his own, but she needed to get to Midtown Market. The cupboards were just about bare, she explained, buttoning up her coat and counting the money in her purse one more time before closing it and dropping it into her handbag which she also snapped shut.

'Are you sure you'll be okay, Joseph?' she asked as he sat on the edge of the bed he shared with his three brothers. He nodded. She stared anxiously at him, still in a dilemma over whether or not to go out. He knew she was worried about him. She'd told him to his face, and talked about it to his father or anxious relatives when they had called round to see how he was. He might not be speaking but there was nothing wrong with his hearing. He knew what they were saying. He didn't want to speak. It was his mother who told everyone he couldn't.

'It's the shock of it all,' she'd say with a knowing nod, as if she'd been able to diagnose the problem herself.

It wasn't that he couldn't speak. He knew he could. He'd done so in the bathroom, in a low tone so that no-one else could hear, just to check. He just didn't want to talk. He didn't want to answer questions, or explain what he saw or tell anyone what had happened. He never wanted to speak about it again, and the only way he figured he could do that was by not saying anything at all. Ever. It seemed like everyone had tried to persuade him otherwise. His mother, father, aunts, uncles, brothers, sisters, Father Murphy, the police. Even Kathleen's father had wanted to ask him some questions. He'd come to the house desperate to know what Joseph had seen.

'I just want to ask him a couple of questions,' he explained.

'I don't know if that's a good idea,' Joseph's father said.

'Just a couple of questions. What did he see? What happened?'

'Maybe later,' his father said. 'He's not talking at all just now. He hasn't said a word since it happened.'

Kathleen's father didn't insist, though Joseph, sitting in the bedroom, could hear the desperation in his voice. He was glad his own father was protecting him. He knew the man – Tommy – wasn't Kathleen's real father. He'd only appeared over the last year or two, but the little girl called him 'Daddy'. She was too young to understand and he knew better that to try and explain anything to her. In truth, he hadn't thought about it before… before it happened.

Cars back-firing now made him jump, and then he would race to the window to see if anything had happened, even though his mind was telling him that nothing had. Hadn't he and Kathleen thought they'd heard firecrackers that day? He was anxious when he was awake, and even more so when he was sleeping. It didn't bring him any relief or respite. His nightmares were short but vivid and violent. He'd wake with a scream and everyone else would wake up too. He'd be drenched in sweat – at first his brothers thought he'd wet the bed – and he'd get up and stand at the window, shivering in his nightshirt until exhaustion eventually forced him back into bed where he'd lie in the damp patch of sweat on the mattress.

He hadn't been out of the house since it happened. He was apprehensive about leaving the bedroom, but terrified at the thought of even taking one step over the threshold of the front door. He liked the fact it was quiet in the house and in the building. People had stopped streaming in and out of Kathleen's apartment, so the shouting and screaming and singing which floated up through the floorboards had disappeared. Joseph still heard noises. The building was not able to keep out everything that happened outside, but they weren't as loud and were less likely to scare him.

He'd nodded again when his mother asked him if he'd be okay, and then she left, not absolutely re-assured by the gesture but also knowing that if they all wanted to eat that night, and after then too, then she'd have to make sure the cupboards were stocked up.

It wasn't often that the house was empty. Before, if Joseph found himself enjoying such a luxury, he would have wandered from room to room, savouring the fact he was alone and in charge of the apartment. He would have rummaged through cupboards, sat with his feet up on the table in the front room like his father sometimes did and put the phonograph on, listening to the Four Provinces Orchestra or Ada Jones singing. It was his father's pride and joy. Joseph remembered when his father had brought it home. He'd put the box on the floor in the middle of the room and they'd all stood round it like they were worshipping some new cardboard god. They knew what it was. There was a drawing of the machine on the side of the box, and underneath it, in black capital letters, was printed 'BRUNSWICK MODEL 101', but it didn't lessen the excitement everyone felt.

'Just open it, Denis,' his mother had urged.

She was just as excited as Joseph and his brothers and sisters, but his father wanted to savour the moment, looking at each of them in turn, soaking up the anticipation etched on their faces until he eventually took out his pen knife and ran in smoothly along the top of the box. The phonograph was beautiful. Joseph saw that when his father delicately lifted it out of the box and held it up for everyone to see the way the priest would raise the gold chalice above his head at Mass. Sunlight seemed to burst into the room at that moment, bathing the electrical appliance in its warm embrace, and after a cursory read through the sheet of paper with instructions on it, Joseph's father wound it up.

When Joseph thought about the phonograph, he always heard the crackling which accompanied every song. His father had wound the machine up until it started moving round and round and a man's voice filled the room. It was John McCormack – 'a fine Irishman,' his father declared – and they all stood, staring at the small box, wide-eyed and open-mouthed, almost as if it was God himself who was singing to them.

Every night they would congregate round it, after everything had been washed and dried and put away and tidied after dinner. It was a reward for doing their chores, and they would listen, usually to John McCormack or some other Irish music, before heading to bed, voicing a few protests because they wanted to keep listening. Even when they were lying in bed, the lights out and at least one or two of them already sleeping, Joseph could hear the low murmur from the phonograph through the thin walls separating living room and bedroom, sometimes accompanied by the sound of his parents laughing or his father singing.

He had no inclination to play the phonograph now, even though he had the house to himself and he could listen to whatever he chose, and as loud as he wanted to. He remained in his room, head pressed against the window, staring down at the street below. No-one could see him, or at least, no-one seemed to look up and spot his lonely vigil. He wished he could stay here, in this bedroom, forever. He didn't think he would be safe if, or when, he eventually had to venture out. A feeling of trepidation was already beginning to take root in his mind at the mere thought of actually being outside.

In his dreams he always seemed to be standing on the same street corner. People walked by, jostling him as they headed towards their destination, but he ignored them whenever they barged into him and threatened to knock him into the path of oncoming traffic. His feet remained rooted to the kerb, his eyes focused straight ahead of him, his hand gripping Kathleen's hand. He presumed it was Kathleen, though he never saw the face of the person standing beside him. Even in his dreams he was desperate to find out who it was, and he kept straining his head to see, but there was never a face, just a hand which held his hand just as tightly.

Then came the bang, like a clap of thunder. He jumped, at the kerb, and in his bed, waking up and sensing his grip slipping no matter how frantic his efforts were to hold on. He could feel that all the time now. His palm tingled, like it was touching someone else's flesh, and then he could feel it slipping away, just like Kathleen's hand, almost toppling him over as she fell to the ground. Instead, he let her go, hearing the dull thud of her body on the concrete road.

He hadn't told anyone that he had let her go. Kathleen's mother had warned him to look after her daughter, and he'd promised that he would, but he had let her go and she had fallen down and never got back up.

Joseph stared at his hand, at the palm covered with crazy zig-zag lines like someone had been drawing on his skin with a knife. He closed it and opened it again, doing it a few times to try and get rid of the feeling that he was still holding a hand. Kathleen's hand. But it didn't go away. It never did, no matter how many times he tried to make it disappear, or how many prayers he silently offered up it the hope they would be answered.

He slowly moved away from the window and sat down on the bed, lifting up the mattress and taking out a note-pad. He'd put it there when no-one else had been in the room. He didn't want anyone else to know he had it, not least because he'd stolen it from O'Rourke's store. As soon as he saw the pad, he wanted it. He was mesmerised, picking it up with trembling hands and opening it nervously, almost dazzled by the pure white sheets of blank paper. He quickly put it back down when Mr O'Rourke had looked over in his direction, but he knew he had to have it and it was only a matter of time. It was just a case of waiting until the shop was busy and Mr O'Rourke was distracted before grabbing one, slipping it under his shirt and then heading out as inconspicuously as possible. He already had pencils. They were much easier to acquire than the note-pad, but they were useless until he had some paper.

He opened the pad up and stared at the picture he'd already started. Then he closed his eyes so that he could see the face. He hadn't told anyone what he had seen that morning. He didn't want to talk to anyone, but he had seen the man who had shot Kathleen.

Joseph had heard the sound of gunfire, rapid and angry, and getting closer. Then the rumble of engines, the screech of tyres. The noises drew his attention and he had looked up. It was a thin face, with cheek bones that seemed to be trying to push through the skin; a long, straight pointed nose, hair that was black and shiny, with a moustache to match and eyes that were as blue as the sky over Central Park on a summer's day. But it was the black gap in the man's top row of teeth which stuck in Joseph's mind. He wasn't sure if the man was smiling or glaring as he fired the gun but, either way, the gap was clearly visible. There was a shot and the man's mouth snapped shut just as Kathleen's grip loosened.

He sat down on the bed and pulled a pencil out of his pocket, grasping it with his left hand. He started running it over the white paper, adding a line here, some shade there, colouring in heavily where it was required, so that the image of the man who shot Kathleen continued to take shape. He took his time filling the gap in the man's teeth, but by the time he'd finished, it was unmistakeably the killer, almost as if he was standing in the bedroom facing Joseph at this very moment. The sight sent a shiver down his spine as his palm tingled again and he remembered that he had let her go.

Money Men

He didn't like leaving Theresa in the apartment but what could he do? He had to go out to work. He hoped she understood. She nodded when he asked her, but he wasn't convinced she heard him. She sat at the kitchen table, staring at the mug of coffee he'd made for her, which had long gone cold though she hadn't noticed.

'Jimmy says we shouldn't be too long today,' he said. 'It's just something we need to do over in Brooklyn.'

'Will you be long?'

'No, Jimmy said . . .'

'Okay.'

Her hands, which seemed to tremble all the time, were fumbling with the packet of cigarettes on the table. Tommy resisted the urge to help her but he did have matches ready to provide a light for her. Conversations were disjointed now, making little or no sense, but he rarely pursued them. She sat back and drew on the cigarette.

He moved restlessly around the kitchen, sitting across from her, standing at the sink, arms folded, staring at her body which never moved. Eventually, he walked out of the room and paced up and down the hallway until he had to go back to the kitchen to extinguish his cigarette in the saucer on the table.

'Will you be okay?' he asked.

'Yes.'

'Don't be doing anything about the house. Leave everything until I get back.'

'It's my turn to clean the stairs,' she said.

'It's fine. Connie Brogan did it this week. She said it wasn't right that someone in your condition should be on her hands and knees scrubbing stairs.'

'I'm not ill.'

'I know that.'

She finished her cigarette, dragging every last vestige of life out of it before stubbing it out. Almost automatically, she picked up the mug and took a sip, spitting straight back into the mug and making a face.

'I can make a fresh one,' he said.

'It's fine. I'll get one later.'

Tommy glanced at the clock on the wall.

'I need to be going,' he said. 'Jimmy's picking me up at half past nine.'

He stood over her, and then kissed the top of her head, touching her shoulder delicately.

'I won't be long,' he said.

'Where's my purse?'

'I don't know.'

'I think it's in the bedroom,' she said, standing up and scraping her chair along the floor.

'I'll get it,' he said, rushing out to the bedroom and returning quickly with the purse which had been lying on the bed. He handed it to her and she opened it, rummaging about and then taking out a few coins.

'Light a candle in Holy Cross . . . Light two,' she said,

dropping two ten-cent coins into Tommy's palm. 'For my babies.'

He closed his hand over the coins, thinking of the bag of money wrapped inside one of his shirts and hidden in the bottom drawer of the wardrobe. She was giving him twenty cents when he could easily have taken a couple of dollar bills from the hundreds lying in the other room. He didn't think the amount he donated when lighting the candles would have any bearing on whether God listened or not. He kissed Theresa again, this time on the cheek, though she didn't react or acknowledge the gesture. He left her at the kitchen table, smoking a fresh cigarette, and headed out to meet Jimmy.

He had always enjoyed walking the streets of New York. When he'd first arrived in the city, he would spend hours wandering up streets and along avenues, leading down as far as Battery Park at the tip of Manhattan. He'd stare out at the Statue of Liberty, which stood guard over a waterway that was crammed full of vessels of all shapes and sizes, flying flags, most of which he didn't recognise. Horns sounded, in warning or greeting, and it always amazed him how they all safely navigated around each other without colliding. Battery Park was full of people putting their first solid steps on American soil, having safely negotiated the last stage of their journey – for some it would be the trickiest – through Ellis Island.

He had been lucky. He wasn't sure the papers he carried with him would work, but the dog collar round his neck certainly helped him and Father Mike had been waiting for his arrival, ready to vouch for him if necessary. Sitting in Battery Park could consume hours of the day, though he found he did that less and less now. He was usually working, while familiarity did, to a certain extent, breed contempt. He had seen it all before, he told himself, so why would he need to sit there any more, watching the endless procession of new arrivals filling up the city?

Nor did he wander along Sixth Avenue, gravitating towards Little Italy, where the smells of freshly-cooked food drew him in like a magnet, or drifting further up towards Midtown where, in certain streets, women stood in doorways ready to ask for a light when they were looking for, and offering, a lot more.

His favourite place, however, still remained Chelsea Park in Lower Manhattan. He would find a bench and sit smoking, watching people fly by in a hurry. He'd spot couples walking arm in arm through the park and wonder what she saw in him, or vice versa. He tried to guess the names of babies being pushed along in prams. Sometimes an old man would sit down beside him, gazing longingly at Tommy's cigarette, or offering to share the contents of the bottle concealed inside a threadbare jacket. He was happy enough to share his cigarettes, but always declined the offer of a drink.

He would sit there in the rain or the sun, sometimes staring for what seemed like hours, marvelling at the giant buildings that were racing towards the sky, and he would close his eyes, picturing Donegal with its green landscape broken only by occasional houses, its peaceful tranquillity in sharp contrast to the bedlam erupting on every street of New York. There was nothing pulling him back to Ireland other than fading memories, and that was no reason to leave this new-found land.

One day he had opened his eyes to find Theresa sitting

beside him. She had decided to rest while keeping an eye on Kathleen, who was racing through the park chasing pigeons, and it was like he instantly had another reason to stay in New York. He smiled as Kathleen shouted and laughed, scattering the birds as she ran through them.

'She looks like she's having fun,' he said to Theresa.

'Poor birds, though,' she said in a voice that was soft but unmistakeably New York. She didn't shout or snap when she spoke, unlike many of the natives of the city, and he found her voice instantly captivating.

The birds barely had time to settle in another part of the park and start hunting for the scraps of food discarded by people over the previous few hours before Kathleen would charge at them again. It was all a game to the little girl, but it was unlikely the birds felt that way.

Tommy held out his cigarettes and Theresa took one hesitantly. He liked that she hadn't grabbed at them greedily. As he held a match up for her, cupping his hand to shield the flame from the intermittent flutters of wind, she leant in close to it and he tried to smell her aroma. All he could detect was the tobacco which swirled round their faces as Theresa inhaled her own cigarette.

They had been happy enough to enjoy the cigarettes, their conversations short and precise, broken up by the inhaling and exhaling which created a comforting cloud around them, though it continued to disappear quickly into the air. He had sat with her for a while. He had nowhere in particular that he had to go, while she didn't seem to mind his presence. He had offered her another cigarette but she declined, and that only impressed him even more. She wasn't greedy or desperate. He tried to study her without making it obvious he was looking at her, but sitting side by side, that was difficult.

Occasional strains of her perfume managed to waft their way through the smoke, while he noticed her lips were bright red. He watched them as she spoke. Her eyes focused on her daughter, who seemed to have a never-ending enthusiasm for chasing the birds. She didn't have a ring on her wedding finger. That didn't necessarily mean she wasn't married or that there wasn't a man in her life, but Tommy felt that it was a good sign. He wasn't sure how to engineer the conversation towards the subject, but as his mind worked feverishly on how to bring it up, his demeanour remained relaxed, offering little indication as to what he was thinking about.

He was still thinking about that day when he had first met Theresa even as he and Jimmy drove through Brooklyn. The engine was rumbling in the background as he pressed his head against the window. Jimmy was content to whistle any tune that popped into his head rather than try and spark up any conversations, and Tommy was grateful for that. They'd crossed over the Bridge, climbing slowly up and over towards Brooklyn, and Tommy stared down the East River. Everything looked tiny, the water itself and the vessels that crawled in all directions. Buildings formed a guard of honour along either bank, warehouses and factories, lumber yards and faceless structures housing hundreds of people working feverishly in the traces of light which managed to push their way through grimy windows.

He was glad to be far away from all that, the noise and the smoke and the smells, though he wished he could stay up here on the Bridge all day, enjoying the view and trying to light a cigarette as the chaotic breeze danced through the metal structure which linked Manhattan to Brooklyn.

All too soon they began their descent, leaving the Bridge behind and heading into Brooklyn, the car slowly winding its way through streets bulging with traffic. At times it felt like they weren't moving at all. Jimmy had been vague about what they had to do. They had to collect something from someone or from somewhere. Tommy hadn't really been listening anyway. He didn't care. They'd get the job done and be back home before too long. He hoped Theresa had heard his instruction not to do any work while he was gone. She needed rest more than anything else.

Jimmy turned off Flatbush Avenue and headed to Prospect Place, the car trundling along until he saw a gap at the sidewalk and skilfully manoeuvred the car into the space.

'Are you okay?' he asked, glancing at Tommy.

'Sure.'

'This shouldn't take too long. Just a quick in and out job.'

Tommy started to open his door.

'Here, you'll need this.' Jimmy held out a gun, a .38 Colt revolver.

'Just in case,' he said as Tommy wrapped his hand round the weapon and slipped it into his jacket pocket, hoping it would remain there.

They pushed open the door into the tenement, Tommy following behind as they trudged up four flights of stairs. Jimmy's breathing was getting heavier with every step and he stopped on a couple of landings to rest, bending over with his hands on his knees and taking deep breaths. Beads of sweat were running down his forehead which he would wipe with his sleeve. Eventually they reached the fourth floor and stopped outside a door which had '408' scratched into the black, wooden surface. Jimmy glanced round at Tommy and nodded, Tommy returning the gesture and automatically touching the gun through the material of his jacket.

Jimmy slowly turned the handle and pushed the door. It started to open, which seemed to surprise him and he hesitated for a moment, looking again at Tommy before opening the door. Jimmy led the way, walking slowly and quietly up the hall. He suddenly stopped and leant in close to a door, straining to hear something before giving Tommy the thumbs-up and then pointing towards the room. A gun suddenly appeared in his hand, and he carefully cocked the weapon. Tommy wasn't sure if he should do the same, but his revolver remained out of sight.

Gripping the handle, Jimmy pushed it open and fired his gun. The bullet struck the ceiling, spraying plaster everywhere. A man was lying on the bed, with a girl sitting on top of him. She screamed, and the man pushed her away. She rolled off the side of the bed, falling loudly on the wooden floor.

'Stay where you are, Carlo,' said Jimmy, pointing the gun at the bed as the man tried to scramble across it to join the girl. Her head peeked up nervously over the edge of the mattress and she clutched at the crumpled sheet, pulling it towards her to try and cover herself up. 'You too,' he said to the girl, though it didn't look likely that she would attempt to go anywhere. A few stray fragments of plaster still floated in the air and Tommy stood at the door as Jimmy moved towards the man on the bed, still pointing the gun at him.

'You know why we're here, Carlo.'

Carlo snatched a pillow and tried to cover himself. Jimmy laughed and fired the gun again. The bullet slammed into the wall beside the naked man, leaving a gaping hole in the wooden head-rest. The girl started screaming again.

'Tell her to shut up,' Jimmy said.

Carlo leant forward and slapped the girl on the face, sending her sprawling across the floor. It was enough to silence her.

'I'm here for the money,' Jimmy said, sitting down on the edge of the bed and resting the gun on his lap.

'I know,' Carlo said. 'I know.'

'So where is it then?'

'Jimmy, I'll get it to you. I swear it, I will. I just need a bit more time'

Jimmy glanced round at Tommy and shook his head.

'If I had a dollar for every time someone told me that, I'd be able to buy Staten Island by now.'

'It's the truth, Jimmy.'

'I want the money,' Jimmy said, pointing his revolver at Carlo, 'and I'm not leaving without it.'

'But Jimmy –'

'But nothing, Carlo. You know the score. You're down a thousand dollars, so you need to settle up.'

'I'm going to pay the money, Jimmy. I swear to God I will. I just need to get it for you. I don't keep that sort of dough here.'

Carlo knelt up on the bed, dropping the pillow and clutching his hands as if in prayer.

'Jesus, Carlo, put that away,' said Jimmy. 'I've just had my breakfast.'

Carlo quickly moved one of his hands to cover himself

while the other tugged at the sheet, though the girl on the floor kept hold of it as well and soon they were involved in a frantic tug-of-war with the sheet. Jimmy sighed and then nodded to Tommy who strode over to the girl, lifted her up and as she started squealing and kicking, carried her over towards the door. She let go of the sheet, which Carlo immediately snatched and wrapped round himself, while Tommy dropped the naked girl in the far corner where she pulled her knees up to her chest.

'How much money have you got here?' Jimmy said.

'I don't know. Not much.'

'Where are your pants?'

Tommy saw them lying on the floor under the bed and lifted them out, rummaging in the pockets and pulling out a roll of bills. He threw them to Jimmy who unravelled the money and quickly flicked through it.

'Not quite a thousand, Carlo,' he said, shaking his head. 'What else have you got?'

'That's it, Jimmy. I know where there's more. If you just let me get dressed, I'll go get it for you.'

Jimmy laughed and stood up, putting the money into his pocket.

'You've got another few hundred dollars hidden away somewhere? Is that what you're telling me, Carlo?'

Carlo nodded.

Jimmy stepped forward and cracked the handle of the gun across Carlo's skull, knocking the other man off the bed. He jumped up on the bed and pointed the gun at Carlo, who was now out of sight of Tommy.

'Do you think I'm a thick Mick? Do you think I've just stumbled off the boat from Ireland?'

Jimmy fired a shot and the noise reverberated round the room. There was no reply from the other side of the bed. That was three shots now, thought Tommy. They'd have to get going soon before the police arrived, though he couldn't hear any sirens as yet. The gunshot was still echoing through his head and he suddenly wondered if Kathleen had heard that sound, or maybe screams or sirens as she lay on the ground. Or had it all happened too quickly for her to hear anything? He shook his head, as if trying to get rid of the thought.

'I've got the money.'

Tommy and Jimmy both looked round at the same time towards the naked girl in the corner.

'What did you say?' Tommy said.

'There's money in my handbag. He put it there when we came in.'

Tommy quickly scoured the room, kneeling down and stretching an arm under the bed until he grasped the handle of the bag, pulling it out and pouring its contents on the bed. Amidst the lipstick and hairbrush and coins and mirror which fell on to the mattress, were three rolls of bills.

'Oh, Jesus,' said Jimmy, looking over at the girl. 'Could you not have told me that before I shot him?'

He grabbed the money, stuffing it all into his pockets, though he produced a few notes from the loose pile already there, dropping them on to the bed. He glanced at the girl again, shaking his head furiously, as he walked out the room and Tommy quickly followed.

Out on the sidewalk, Jimmy was muttering as he opened his door. Tommy stepped between the parked cars to get to the passenger side, glancing across the street. A little girl was skipping along the sidewalk, weaving her way through the crowds going about their daily business. He watched her as she moved, lithe and full of fun, and he sighed deeply. He stared harder, the green ribbon in her brown hair glowing like a fiery sky on a clear winter's morning, almost hypnotically drawing him towards it. He stumbled out into the road like a drunk man, staggering across and ignoring the warnings from car horns, irate drivers having to brake suddenly to avoid hitting him.

'Tommy! Tommy!'

He could hear the voice behind him but he ignored it, continuing across the path of traffic, his eyes never leaving the little girl who was still skipping along the sidewalk. As he reached the other side, he tripped on the kerb and stumbled into a woman carrying a shopping basket, who scowled at him, and he temporarily lost sight of the girl. Then he caught a glimpse of the green ribbon again and he was on the move, starting to run now to catch up with her, dodging past people when he could or barging through them when that appeared the only option open to him.

The girl was skipping quickly, or else he wasn't running fast enough, but it didn't feel like he was gaining on her. His eyes remained focused on the green ribbon, even as his mind was trying to tell him that there was an identical one in his pocket. Her movement through the crowd was effortless while his was laboured, his boots like giant blocks of concrete, each step forward draining him of energy.

'Kathleen!' he shouted. He needed to catch her attention and get her to stop. Still she kept skipping. 'Kathleen!'

A couple of people stared at him, while others now stepped out of his way as he bobbed and weaved along the sidewalk, straining his eyes to keep her in his sight and shouting out her name intermittently. He was urging his legs forward, trying to move faster, and he could feel himself slowly beginning to gain some pace as the girl disappeared round the corner.

'Kathleen!' he screamed, suddenly now able to sprint, as if whatever was holding him back had been removed. His momentum almost caused him to fall but he managed to stay on his feet and raced to the corner, careening round it and colliding with a man carrying a crate of bottles, sending both of them sprawling across the sidewalk like skittles in a bowling alley. There was a crash as the glass shattered on the ground and a shout of shock and anger from the man who was touching his forehead which was bleeding.

Tommy glanced down at the man and then looked up and along the street. The little girl was gone. He stumbled forward, his boots crunching through the glass.

'Hey! What the hell!' the man shouted, still sitting dazed on the sidewalk.

Tommy ignored him, though even as he moved forward, he suddenly felt like he was walking blindly into fog. She was gone and so was her green ribbon, and slowly he sank to his knees, tears beginning to stream down his face and he buried his head, smothering the sobs in his lap.

Sound of Silence

Tommy opened the door quietly. It was an instinctive action now. Whereas before he would have burst into the house noisily to announce his presence so that Kathleen would come racing towards him, followed by a smiling Theresa, amused as much by her daughter's reaction as she was pleased to see him, now he crept in like a burglar not wanting to wake the owners of the house.

More often than not, Theresa would be in bed, sleeping or sobbing or just lying there, perfectly still, eyes open, but to all intents and purposes looking as though she was in a coma. He didn't know what to say or what to do, so he did nothing. He gravitated silently in her orbit, but trying to avoid anything which might make his presence felt. He cooked dinner or made cups of tea or coffee, and these Theresa would accept if she wasn't in bed. They would stare at the phonograph and the myriad of tuneful voices coming out of the brown box which broke the agonising silence which filled the apartment.

He stood in the hallway, hearing a murmur from the next room, and he breathed a sigh of relief, feeling almost as if a weight had been lifted from his shoulders. One of the neighbours was in. It was probably Alice, which meant he could stay in the kitchen and out of the way, and not have to think or worry about Theresa, for a while at least. It also meant that she was out of bed, talking even. She might even have made a cup of tea for her visitor, and these mundane rituals of daily life would be good for her, dragging her back to some sort of normality.

He knew it was difficult for her. It was tough for him, too. He wanted to find out who had killed Kathleen and then . . . but it was worse for Theresa. He knew that even if, sometimes, he had to remind himself. It was worse because it was her daughter, her baby, her flesh and blood, and that was something he didn't – couldn't – know about. He would soon enough, of course, and he had to hope that the new baby would help.

As he stepped forward, his foot kicked a sheet of paper lying on the floor. He bent down to pick it up and opened it out. A man's face stared at him. It was a drawing, though in the dim light of the hall, it was hard to get a good look at it. He walked through to the kitchen and sat down, glad to rest his legs. It had just been another normal day at work, loading boxes of bottles into a truck and then unloading the cargo at various locations across the city and beyond. Now, he wanted to relax, enjoy a smoke and a cup of tea, maybe fall asleep for half an hour before dinner.

He looked at the piece of paper again. He definitely didn't recognise who it was, though the face was certainly distinctive; a thin face with cheek bones sticking out so sharply Tommy thought they might jag his fingers if he touched them. The man had a moustache cowering under his long, straight, pointed nose. Everything about the man's face seemed to be jagged, like it had been chiselled out of stone, but it was the mouth which made Tommy smile.

There was a gap in the top row of teeth, a black hole where once there had been a tooth. It made the man look funny, strange, almost demented-looking, and Tommy wondered why the man had never got a replacement. At least a wooden one would look better than the gap, even if its shade didn't quite match the other teeth? Maybe it would? He didn't imagine the man's teeth were as white as the sheet of paper.

He made a cup of tea, debating briefly whether to pop his head into the other room and ask if Theresa and her visitor wanted anything, but he preferred his own, silent company, so he sat down with his cup, lighting another cigarette and stretching his legs out on to the chair opposite him. He should have taken his boots off. He normally did, leaving them at the front door, but now that he was comfortable, he was reluctant to get back up. He didn't think Theresa would notice anyway, and even if she did, it was unlikely she would say anything, or even care.

The piece of paper lay on top of the table, the face watching him as he smoked or drank his tea. Who would have drawn it and slipped it under the door? More importantly, who was the man in the picture? He kept staring back at it, even as he realised he could never out-stare it and that he would always blink first.

'There's someone to see you.'

The voice startled Tommy and he sat up, his legs almost falling off the other chair. Theresa stood leaning against the door, her arms folded. He knew it was her voice – that's what his mind told him – though he had heard it so rarely in recent weeks that it was almost as if a stranger was speaking.

'Are you okay?' he asked automatically.

She shrugged.

He stood up, snatching the paper off the table and stuffing it into his pocket.

'Who is it?' he asked.

'I'll take a smoke,' she said, moving towards him. He handed her the pack of Camels and she took one out, taking his still-lit cigarette and pressing it against the end of hers until it took light. She inhaled deeply and then blowing the smoke out with a slow, almost satisfied sigh; a thirsty woman grateful for a drink of water in a desert. Her free hand automatically ran back and forth over her bump.

He watched enviously, realising he was now scared to touch her. He didn't know how she would react, whether she would press her hand on top of his and guide it across her belly, mustering up what passed for a smile or whether, more likely, she'd flinch or recoil from his touch, almost as if it was painful. He couldn't bear that prospect so he didn't move, instead watching her as she smoked, now leaning on the back of a chair, trying to let the furniture take some of the physical strain of being on her feet.

'It's Mary Hanlon,' she said.

'Who?'

'Mary Hanlon. Pat's wife. She wants to speak to you.'

Tommy froze, alarm spreading across his face as he looked from Theresa and towards the other room, and back again.

'Mary's here?'

'In the next room,' Theresa said, shuffling over to the sink and filling a dirty cup up with water, emptying its contents into the sink and then filling it again, this time drinking the water.

'What does she want?' he asked.

'She says Pat's missing. She thinks he's . . . She's in a terrible way.'

'Is she upset?'

'She looks awful. God knows what happened to her. She says you were working with Pat?'

'When?'

'She wants to ask if you know anything.'

'About what?'

'About her husband. Pat. If you know what happened to him. Do you know, Tommy?'

'Jesus, Theresa, I don't know . . . I don't want to get involved.'

'The poor woman's demented. Just talk to her.'

'What will I say?'

'I don't know. Tell her what you know.'

'But –'

'Or tell her you don't know anything.'

Tommy lit another cigarette. He stared at Theresa, who stood drinking the rest of her water.

'She's a poor soul, Tommy,' she said, but there was no pleading in her voice, no real emotion. If he stormed out the house right now, he doubted she'd be angry. She'd probably walk back through to the other room and calmly tell Mary Hanlon that he'd gone out but that he didn't know anything. She put her cup down and folded her arms.

'Okay,' he said and she nodded, moving forward and past him, leading the way towards the front room. He followed nervously in her wake.

May Hanlon sprung up out of her chair as soon as Theresa walked into the room. Tommy stopped at the door and stared. He couldn't help it. Her hair. That's what startled him. Or rather, her lack of it. Small clumps like lonely bushes on a desolate hillside still sprung out of her skull, but most of her hair was gone. In its place was stubble, like a man's chin after a few days' growth. There were a few dark bruises which still looked as though they'd be sore to touch, and she nervously kept pulling on the tufts of hair. Her left hand was covered by a bandage that had long since lost its pure white colour. Tommy shivered as he remembered what he'd seen at the hut, his eyes not able to look anywhere else but the bandaged hand, no matter how hard he tried.

Mary's eyes were red. He recognised the tell-tale signs of too many tears. Theresa's were the same, though they didn't wear the purple and yellow remnants of bruising. He hoped his own eyes weren't so red that they would betray him. Mary's clothes were torn and tattered like the bandage, and he could smell the mixture of booze, tobacco and stale sweat clinging to her.

'Sit down, Mary,' Theresa said, walking over to the other woman and gently guiding her back on to the seat. Mary rummaged in her pockets and brought out a battered pack of *Luckies*. Her trembling fingers tried to get one out without success, and eventually Theresa had to help, lighting it for her as well before handing it to her. Mary took it, coughing and spluttering as she inhaled. Tommy slowly ventured into the room, remaining on his feet as Mary, her whole body now shaking, looked up at him.

'My Pat,' she began before a sudden burst of tears left her sobbing and shaking. Theresa sat on the side of the chair and wrapped her arm round Mary's shuddering shoulders.

'Take your time, Mary,' Theresa whispered, and the other

woman nodded, slowly trying to compose herself while continuing to demolish the cigarette. Theresa looked up at Tommy, but he could only shrug.

'Do you know?' Mary said slowly, her voice quivering.

'Sorry,' Tommy said.

'I need to know,' she said. 'I need to know!'

Tommy looked at Theresa again, as she still held Mary.

'I don't know what happened,' he said slowly, quietly.

'They did this to me,' Mary said, holding up her bandaged hand. 'Do you want to see what they did?' She started trying to unravel the bandage.

'No!' Tommy said, moving forward to stop her, but then stopping himself.

'Look at her hair, Tommy,' Theresa said, running her hand gently over Mary's head. 'Look what they did to her beautiful hair.'

'I'm sorry,' said Tommy.

'I just want to know what they did to my Pat.'

'I don't know.'

'It was just a few bottles . . . I told him it was stupid,' she said, turning to look at Theresa. 'I told him he was daft and he'd get caught, but he said everything was fine. They'd never notice a few bottles missing.'

She started wailing, rocking back and forth in the chair. It had become a regular sound in this apartment, Tommy thought. The neighbours would just think it was Theresa again. She still held Mary's shoulders, but she let the other woman move, almost in time with her sobs, which were long and loud and painful and well-practised.

'He's gone,' she cried. 'My Pat's gone . . . They killed him, didn't they?'

Suddenly the crying stopped, as did the movements, and Mary stared at Tommy.

'He's dead, isn't he?'

She stared at him and he stared back.

'At least tell me that.'

'Tommy,' Theresa said. 'Please.'

'Yes, he's dead,' Tommy said with a sigh, looking at Theresa rather than Mary, who had buried her head in her lap, almost as if she wanted to stifle any sound, though her body still shook with each tremor of emotion.

'I don't know what happened. I swear to God, I don't, Mary, but he's not coming back.'

Mary knew that. She would have known it from the moment that Gorevin's men had burst into her house and 'persuaded' her to tell them where Pat had hidden their booze. Someone would have punched her, others would have held her down while a pair of scissors destroyed her hair. Then, as she tried to comprehend the scale of her attack, they would have flipped her on to her front, held her arms, buried her head in the pillow, while one of them cut her finger off, wedding ring and all, though there were few screams as she passed out with the shock and the pain. They left her lying on the bed, the white sheet drenched in the blood spurting out of the wound in her hand.

When she'd regained consciousness, weak with the blood loss, though the flow had more or less stemmed itself, she slowly rolled on to her back and held her arm up so that she could see her hand. The scream bursting out of her mouth from the pit of her stomach had neighbours racing into the house within seconds, while people several blocks away halted, shivering as they heard the piercing sound.

'I'm sorry,' he muttered.

Mary looked up and nodded. He was merely telling her what she already knew. She would never get to see her husband again, to mourn for him, to grieve, or to bury him. She could kneel in church, head bowed in prayer, her face hidden by a black veil of mourning, or light a candle in front of a statue of Our Lady, or some other saint who promised miraculous intervention, but they couldn't help her either. There would be no graveside to visit, no headstone to record the merest details of a life or to touch for consolation. He couldn't offer any of that to her, and she knew it.

Theresa picked up the cup at the side of Mary's chair and walked over to the small cabinet underneath the window. She glanced round at him as she took out the silver hip flask and he nodded before she poured some of its contents into the cup. Mary took it gratefully and gulped it down, and it was like a slap to her face. She was alert, looking round her like she was only taking in her surroundings for the first time. Another lit cigarette was placed in her good hand and she sucked on it gratefully like a baby on a teat.

Theresa sat across from her now, suddenly looking exhausted as well. The temporary distraction of someone else's problems was gone now and she had to think again about her own pain. Tommy stood awkwardly in the middle of the room before shuffling back towards the kitchen. There was nothing else to say to Mary. There was nothing else she could ask. As he passed Theresa, she stretched her arm out, and their fingers lightly touched. It made him smile.

New Dawn Fades

It had been raining during the night. Some people had heard it battering off the roofs of parked cars, or cascading off the fire escapes and on to the ground. Occasional bursts would be blown against window panes, like handfuls of gravel thrown by a gang of passing children intent on making mischief or looking for a chase by irate occupants of the building. Traffic hissed through the wet streets; cabs on their never-ending journeys, delivery trucks heading from warehouses to shops or factories, or on into the night, with the driver imagining a warm bed and a warm body to press against. Footsteps could barely be heard, but restless sleepers who leant out of opened windows smoking, while keeping their cigarettes sheltered from the erratic raindrops, could see the dark outlines hurrying along the street, covered as best they could against the elements, and eager to reach their dry destination.

At some point before dawn, the rain stopped. It was as if a tap had been turned off but not completely. There were drips everywhere, most of them unnoticeable, but a few beat incessantly, eventually forcing themselves into the consciousness of those beginning to stir from their slumber. One or two, still half asleep, thought it might be a leaky tap in their bathroom.

There were people already awake, those living on the top floor apartments who found the new day was greeting them with water seeping into their homes, drops running down walls, or pregnant bulges in the ceiling that would soon burst if they hadn't already done so. Buckets were hastily placed underneath, while curses littered the rooms and the man of the house sleepily clambered into clothes before climbing up to the loft or out on to the roof to see if he could spot where the water was coming through. The search would only be assisted when daylight had fully formed.

Ship horns sounded from the docks. Some of the vessels were impatiently waiting to leave the quayside, perhaps only travelling across the Hudson River to New Jersey, or maybe heading out towards the open sea, and on up the coast to Boston. One or two of the larger ships were ready for even longer journeys, sailing back across the ocean to Europe, passing countless other ships of all shapes and sizes heading in the opposite direction, towards the 'new world.' Barges hovered in the middle of the river, waiting for a green light from the dockside before moving forward to unburden the holds of cargo they'd carried all the way to New York. Coal, lumber, stone, foodstuffs of a million and one varieties, clothes destined for Fifth Avenue boutiques, material for shops in the Bronx to be bought by women with a sewing machine, a creative mind and tight household budget, electrical goods to light up rooms or chill food, or bring music into rooms all over New York.

The city was waking up. Bakers were already hard at work, hidden away from view in kitchens behind shop fronts still closed, or buried in cellars, but the smells of their work silently wafted out on to the streets, through tiny gaps in windows, or out of grates in the sidewalk, and everyone who caught the aroma of freshly-baked bread, doughnuts, bagels, biscuits or cakes found their stomachs rumbling, wishing they'd eaten breakfast before leaving the house, or already making plans about where to get a coffee and a plate of eggs when everywhere started to open up for the day.

Garbage trucks groaned and grumbled their way up and down the damp streets, with bins emptied into the back, or discarded bags of rubbish tossed in by men who worked quickly but silently. There were times that they felt they had barely cleared the streets before more rubbish was dumped out on the sidewalk for them to clear away.

Solitary men slipped out of the mouths of the buildings, having left behind sleeping families, heads down, hands in pocket, maybe a paper bag with their lunch stuffed inside their jacket, ignoring anyone they passed as they trudged towards their place of work; factories spewing out all sorts of goods for people and filling the air with dense smoke that never seemed to disappear; building sites erecting the latest skyscraper to fill the Manhattan skyline, a never-ending procession of concrete reaching up towards the sky. Where would it end? Or maybe the men were working on roads throughout the city and beyond; digging them up, filling them in, flattening down, building up; a constant demand to meet the proliferation of cars. Many of these men walked to their work. Some caught trolley cars that went rattling West to East or South to North. Or trains which carried them further afield – over to Brooklyn, up to the Bronx, or to Queens. Men streamed to the ferries which would carry them across to New Jersey. Cars were on the move too, the rumbling of engines growing ever louder with every passing minute.

The men were on the move first but before too long the women would follow. Domestic servants, cleaners, maids, kitchen staff heading to fancy houses on the Upper East Side, or to hotels and boarding houses dotted around the city. Waitresses threw coats over uniforms, the regulation skirts peaking out shyly from the hem of their coats, off to cook and serve breakfast to workers going on or coming off their shift, making sure there was an endless supply of coffee to accompany the food. Women hidden from view behind dull, grey buildings, the stonework long since stained black by car fumes and smoke from industrial chimneys, hunched over machines making clothes and electrical goods, or packing food and drinks into boxes and bottles.

Long shifts. Ten hours with a half-hour break to quickly devour the sandwiches they'd brought with them, washed down with a cup of weak coffee supplied by the factory owners. Then they would all congregate in one room to smoke as many cigarettes as they could in the time available before the bell rang or a horn sounded or the foreman blew a whistle to signal a return to work. In smaller places, it would merely be a shout, but it all meant the same thing. Break-time was over.

As the workers streamed out of the tenements, a whole host of others streamed in; barmen and doormen, gangsters and girlfriends, dancers and strippers and hookers. All of them desperate for bed or still drunk after a night out; the onset of dawn seeing speakeasies open their discreet, or not so discreet doors, to spew out the flotsam and jetsam of New

York on to the streets. Drunks would shout and swear, want to fight their best friend or befriend total strangers. Occasionally there would be a bang – a firecracker, an engine backfiring, a gun fired in anger. No-one who heard ever knew for sure, though everyone knew better than to ask.

Couples staggered home. Men with women on their arms, heading to his home or hers, depending on what their living arrangements were; an empty bed was all they needed, for a few hours at least. More often than not, there would be no names, or forgotten names, false ones even from men whose wedding rings temporarily jangled in their pockets along with the loose change they carried.

A dog barked in one street, a baby cried in another building. Voices were raised in random domestic arguments. A phonograph was turned up too loudly. An old man sat in the communal toilet on a landing, smoking quietly in the dark, the orange glow from the tip of his cigarettes the only illumination. Children fought against the impending daylight which would see them head to school.

Behind closed doors, a drunken husband would grip his belt and swing it across his wife's face. In cheap boarding houses rooms, a gleaming blade was held against a hooker's throat before she was punched, held down, clothes sliced open, and raped while the blade remained pressed against her flesh. Maybe there was only one man, or maybe there were more? She knew not to scream either way.

Other women lay in bed sleeping safely. Mothers. Wives. Girlfriends. Daughters. Women whose husbands had slipped out of bed quietly so as not to wake them, leaving behind an imprint in the mattress, residual warmth still floating under the covers, the odour of sweat and farts which always seemed to hang in the air like an unwelcome guest at a party. An arm would fall across the bed, expecting to connect with a body but instead finding nothing. Some might wake up, if only with momentary panic, before quickly realising the workers were already on the move. Widows grew accustomed to the absence beside them, but it still made them sad when their arm stretched across into that eternal nothingness.

Some of them might have dropped back to sleep with the sweat of early-morning sex still running down their bodies; fumbling and thrusting, half-asleep, fully aroused, maybe trying to keep the noise down so as not to wake sleeping children in the next room or babies in the same room. That sweaty, sticky memory between the legs remained as they wrapped the cover round them and drifted back to sleep. Some would smile, satisfied. Others sighed, having done their duty. Different prayers were whispered. Please let me be pregnant. Please let me bleed.

The wind scurried up and down streets, along avenues, up staircases, lifting up any debris left in the gutters. And in a hundred houses or more, someone breathed their last; an old woman who no longer knew where she was, a father-of-six who had a heart attack while sitting in the kitchen smoking, a baby not yet reached its first birthday. And in a hundred more rooms, new life burst into the city, screaming and kicking and covered in mucus.

Into this world of chaos and cohesion, of love and violence, of a million competing voices in a hundred different languages, something was different. On street lights, railings, shop windows and restaurant fronts fluttered sheets of paper. People in Hell's Kitchen, the area that stretched from 34th to 59th Street, noticed. Not all of them. Those who were in a hurry never lifted their heads to see anything, their eyes focused instead on their feet, but others saw and stopped.

A few stared at the image on the paper, others pulled down copies and studied the drawing more closely. Many of them didn't know who it was, but a few of them did, enough to send a chill through the streets and up and down tenement buildings, in and out of apartments. And, as always, in the way of Hell's Kitchen, word got back to those who would want to know about such things; a drawing which landed in the wrong hands and suddenly there were more questions being asked and answers demanded.

Hidden Treasure

He held out the piece of paper which Jimmy snatched from his hand.

'Do you know who that is?'

Jimmy studied the picture, holding it close to his face and then at a distance before shaking his head.

'That's a face only a mother could love,' he said, handing the paper back to Tommy. 'Who is it?'

'I don't know,' said Tommy, 'but I'd like to find out.'

He folded up the paper and put it back in his pocket, taking out a pack of cigarettes in its place and offering them to Jimmy.

'What did he do?' Jimmy asked as he took a cigarette and lit it.

'I don't know that either.'

'You're not exactly helping much.'

'The picture just landed on my door. Someone drew it and delivered it to me. I want to know why.'

'Why they delivered it?'

'Why they drew it and sent it to me . . . and I figure if I can find out who it is, I might find out why.'

'Let's see it again.'

Jimmy unfolded the sheet of paper that was handed to him and flattened it out on the table. Stray specks of ash floated aimlessly in the air before coming to rest on the pencil drawing, giving the man a spotty complexion.

'What's the deal with the black tooth?' he asked.

Tommy shrugged.

'It's a face you'd never forget in a hurry,' Jimmy said.

'It's the name I'm after.'

Jimmy shook his head.

'I'll ask around,' Tommy said. 'Somebody must know who it is.'

'Just be careful,' said Jimmy as Tommy folded the paper away again. 'You know what people are like when someone starts poking their nose into things they shouldn't.'

'But I just want to know who it is.'

'Well, it's still better to watch your back. People don't like questions around here. You know that.'

The two men sat at the table, content to smoke in silence. A brown suitcase rested on the table in front of them. It was battered and bruised and showing signs of age, but the locks still worked and there were no holes that would let the rain in. Tommy didn't know what was inside. That wasn't quite true. He guessed that it was full of money. How much he didn't know, but it had been heavy enough when Jimmy had asked him to carry it up from the car. Either it was packed with dollar bills or it was full of bricks. He didn't ask Jimmy about the contents. The warning about people not liking questions being asked also applied to him. If Jimmy wanted you to know something, he would tell you in his own good time. If he didn't, he wouldn't.

They were sitting in an apartment in the Upper West Side. The door had been unlocked. Jimmy seemed to know that this would be the case, and once inside, he was happy to sit in the kitchen, smoking and drinking cups of coffee, which he made with monotonous regularity. As soon as one cup was finished, he was back on his feet making another.

Tommy had only been able to get the briefest of glances in the other rooms as they walked along the hallway to the kitchen, though he managed a closer inspection when he went to the bathroom. It was clear no-one lived here on a regular basis. One of the rooms had a double bed in it, and everything seemed tidy and in its place, though the layers of dust which settled over everything were evident to the naked eye. No-one had been in the room for a while. The other bedroom was a refuge for all sorts of junk, an old bed frame, crates of empty bottles, various items of furniture including a cabinet, a chest of drawers and a wardrobe, on top of which sat a lady's hat, pink and wide and dusty.

The living room was cleaner. An ashtray full of cigarette ends sat like an ornament on the glass table in the middle of the room, while two dirty coffee cups stood guard at either side of it. There was a clock on the wall above the fireplace, though it had stopped at twenty past eight. Whether that was morning or night, Tommy didn't know.

Jimmy hadn't said anything other than their destination when Tommy had got in the car, and he didn't press the matter. There were no sign of guns, either in the car or the apartment, so Tommy figured it wasn't dangerous work they were undertaking, and after the disaster of their last trip, he was relieved. He could hear the faint strains of music coming from elsewhere in the building, though it was too faint to recognise who was singing, and passing traffic kept drowning out the noise. He started whistling – *The Ballad of Dan Foley* – but that soon stopped under Jimmy's withering gaze. All that was left was to light another cigarette as Jimmy filled up the kettle, shut his eyes and enjoy the silence.

They both heard the footsteps approaching, loud clunks on the wooden stairs leading up to the third-floor apartment. Jimmy glanced in the general direction of the noise, but continued making his coffee while Tommy sat up straight, more alert, also looking towards the door.

He had instinctively guessed it was Gorevin even before he appeared in the doorway of the kitchen. It was something in the way he walked along the hall, the rhythm of his footsteps which made Tommy think of him. The last time he'd seen Gorevin had been at the hut. He was as smartly dressed now as he was then, though his smile was a more friendly one this time around.

'Gentlemen,' Gorevin said, walking into the kitchen. 'Apologies for my lateness. I was unavoidably delayed.'

Jimmy smiled as Gorevin sat down across from Tommy.

'Coffee?'

'I don't know how you can drink that filth,' Gorevin said.

Jimmy took a sip from his freshly-made cup of coffee and let out a satisfied sigh.

'Just water for me,' said Gorevin.

Jimmy began searching cupboards for a glass as Gorevin took out a silver cigarette case from his inside jacket pocket, flicked it open and offered it to Tommy. He hesitated until Gorevin nodded encouragingly, and Tommy took a cigarette.

Gorevin held out a lighter for him and he leant in close to the flame until his cigarette was lit.

'Nice lighter,' Tommy said, sitting back.

'Thanks,' said Gorevin, holding the silver lighter up. It seemed to glint whenever strands of sunlight caught it, but it was the engraving on the side of it which had caught Tommy's attention – a diamond with an eye in the middle of it, all-seeing.

'I'm sorry for your loss,' Gorevin said, putting the lighter back in his pocket.

'Thanks,' mumbled Tommy, slightly taken by surprise.

'A terrible, terrible thing,' Gorevin said, shaking his head.

'There are no glasses,' Jimmy said.

'A cup will do.'

Jimmy filled the cup up with cold water and sat it down in front of Gorevin, who picked it up daintily and took a sip.

'Perfect,' he said.

Jimmy took a gulp from his own cup. 'Coffee's still better,' he said, holding it up like he was ready to give a toast.

'So how are things at home, Tom?' Gorevin asked.

Tommy was startled. No-one had called him 'Tom' for a long time now. He'd left that name far behind, etched on a gravestone in a cemetery on a remote Scottish island. He was Tommy Delaney in this city, ever since he'd met Theresa. She didn't mind that he'd done so. It made everything more . . . respectable. His accent was still distinctly Irish but his attitude was becoming more like a New Yorker every day. The papers he carried with him to America, nestling in his jacket pocket close to his heart, proclaimed him as Thomas Costello, which had been his uncle's name, but he told everyone he was 'Tommy'. It sounded more American to him, even though that would seem daft if he tried explaining it to anyone. He'd discarded the surname as soon as he could and had no wish to start wearing it again.

Suddenly, Gorevin calling him 'Tom' made his past come rushing back to him like a hurricane; fighting the British on the hills on Donegal, heading to Glasgow to try and kill a British general, falling in love – if that's what he felt . . . Her name was Bernie, and if he hadn't heard himself called 'Tom' for a long time, he'd tried not to think of her name for just as long. She was gone now, and it was better, less painful, to try and forget her. Then there was the island where his escape plan was hatched, the brain-child of an uncle who was also his namesake. It had only been two years but sometimes it seemed like a lifetime ago. Why had Gorevin called him Tom? He looked at the man who smiled through the haze of smoke hovering around the table.

'Are you okay, Tom?'

He kept staring at Gorevin. He remembered the boat that had taken him from the island in the dead of night. He'd cowered in the tiny space under the deck, nervously fingering the priest's collar that pressed tight against his neck as the boat's skipper charted a rocky route back to the mainland. Underneath the black shirt he could feel the holy medals and wanted to touch them for comfort. He knew, elsewhere on the island, a small rowing boat was being pushed out to sea, unoccupied except for some of his clothes that he'd left behind.

He imagined a foot being pushed through the floor of the boat or perhaps it had been more subtle than that, a few discreet holes that would, slowly but surely, allow the water to leak into the boat until it sank, and the clothes would float tellingly in the water until they were discovered and the alarm raised. By then, he would be far away, heading towards a new life and a new land, leaving Tom Costello behind.

'Tommy! Tommy!'

It was Jimmy's voice, dragging him back to the here and now. He looked round, his eyes focusing on Jimmy who looked slightly concerned.

'Sorry, I was dreaming.'

'Are you sure you're okay?'

'Yeah, Jimmy, I'm fine. I've just got a lot on my mind.'

'Don't worry about it, Tommy. We understand,' said Gorevin.

Tommy looked back at Gorevin, who smiled as he extinguished his cigarette in the ashtray. Did he just call him Tommy? It had been Tom just a minute ago and now it was Tommy. Was he hearing things now or losing his mind? He already thought he'd seen Kathleen running down the street and had chased after her, and now this.

'Now to business,' Gorevin said, standing up and unclipping the suitcase locks, slowly lifting up the lid with a grin that seemed to get wider as the contents of the suitcase became more visible.

'What a beautiful sight,' he said as he opened it fully.

Both Jimmy and Tommy stood up and stared at it as Gorevin let his fingers graze over the money which packed every inch of the case. Tommy just stared at it. He'd figured it was money but, even so, seeing so much of it together, crammed into the suitcase, still rendered him momentarily speechless. Jimmy handed over a sheet of paper, which Gorevin glanced at, nodding occasionally.

'It's all there,' Jimmy said. 'Down to the last dollar.'

'I know it is,' Gorevin said. 'I trust you . . . Have you ever seen so much money, Tommy?'

'Nope.'

'Twenty-one thousand, four hundred and twenty-two dollars,' he said slowly, savouring every word like it was a mouthful of food. Jimmy whistled, even though he'd brought the money, and Tommy presumed the paper he'd handed Gorevin detailed the amount. It was hard not to be impressed.

Tommy felt an urge to touch the money too, so he was glad he had the cigarette to occupy his fingers. He didn't think Gorevin would be impressed if he suddenly started pawing the notes.

'You did well, Jimmy,' Gorevin said, taking out a large bundle of notes and flicking through them.

Jimmy nodded. It had been the money they had been out collecting, either when they made deliveries or, in the case of Carlo, when they gathered up unpaid debts. Gorevin obviously trusted Jimmy. That was a lot of money to leave with one man, and while Tommy was sure they would catch Jimmy if he ever tried to run off with the money, it must still have been tempting to take a few dollars here and there in the belief that they wouldn't be missed. Yet, here he was delivering all the cash to Gorevin, and with an accompanying written record as well. Maybe what had happened to Pat Hanlon was still fresh in Jimmy's mind as well, and if that's what they did to someone who stole a few bottles of booze, then it was too horrific to imagine how they'd treat a larcenist.

Gorevin started counting through one of the bundles

before removing a handful of notes which he handed over to Tommy.

'Just a little thank-you,' Gorevin said, nodding towards the money as he sensed Tommy's hesitation.

'Thanks,' he mumbled.

An even larger amount was handed over to Jimmy, who immediately slipped it into his jacket pocket, tipping the edge of his cap by way of acknowledgement.

'And this,' Gorevin said, handing over what Tommy guessed was about one hundred dollars, 'is for the Hanlon woman.'

'Mary Hanlon?' Tommy said automatically, though immediately regretting blurting out her name.

'We did what we had to do,' Gorevin said with a shrug, shutting over the suitcase and locking it, 'but it wasn't her fault. This will make amends. See that she gets it.'

Jimmy nodded, putting that money into a different pocket. Gorevin lit another cigarette and smiled as he saw Tommy cast another admiring glance at his lighter. He held it out and Tommy picked it up, turning it back and forth, nodding appreciatively.

'It was a gift,' said Gorevin as Tommy gently placed it back in the other man's palm.

'It's very impressive.'

'So Carlo's dead,' he said, blowing smoke in Jimmy's direction.

'It was an accident.'

'I don't like accidents.'

'I know,' said Jimmy. 'I'm sorry, Mr Gorevin.'

'Carlo was an imbecile but these things are avoidable difficulties.'

'It won't happen again.'

Gorevin stood up, grabbing the handle of the suitcase and dragging it off the table. It almost fell to the ground.

'Who'd have thought money was so heavy?'

'Here, I'll get it,' Jimmy said, moving towards Gorevin, who had rested it at his feet.

'No, it's fine. You wait here ten minutes after I've gone before leaving.'

'Okay.'

Gorevin lifted the case again.

'Mr Gorevin,' Tommy said.

'Yes?'

'Can I show you something?'

The other man sighed and put the case back down on the floor. Tommy could see Jimmy glaring at him, his eyes indicating it was a bad idea, but he ignored the warning as he pulled out the sheet of paper.

'Do you recognise this man?' he said holding the image out before Gorevin. He looked at it briefly and then he seemed to glance quickly towards Jimmy.

'Who is it?'

'I don't know,' Tommy said. 'Someone drew it and posted it to me. I just wondered whether you maybe recognised who it is.'

'Let me see it,' Gorevin said, snatching the picture out of Tommy's hand and studying it more, closely. After a few moments he shook his head. 'Sorry, Tom,' he said. 'I have no idea. I've never seen this man before.'

'Thanks anyway,' Tommy said as he took the sheet of paper back and folded it away.

'Gentlemen,' Gorevin said with a nod as he picked up

the suitcase and walked out of the apartment, his footsteps slowly fading until nothing could be heard. Tommy knew that Jimmy's furious eyes were still focused on him but he didn't look round. He kept staring at the door through which Gorevin had disappeared. He had called him 'Tom' again. Why had he done that?

Warning Shots

'He's getting too big for his boots,' said Jimmy as they drove slowly back to Manhattan. 'He's long forgotten that the arse used to hang out his trousers the same as the rest of us.'

Tommy glanced at Jimmy, who continued muttering and shaking his head. Jimmy didn't usually talk like that. He'd never heard the older man speak disparagingly about anyone they had dealings with, and certainly not any of their superiors.

'Is everything okay?' Tommy asked.

'It's just that eejit,' Jimmy sighed. 'He thinks he's a big-time Johnny just because he wears a fancy suit and talks proper and uses big words. Any fool could do that.'

Tommy smiled.

'I knew his father.'

'Who? Gorevin?'

'He was a good man. Patrick Gorevin. County Cork. He was a hard-working man, on the roads, the railways. Wherever there was work to be done. Give him a shovel and he'd bloody well dig through anything. And he was handy with his fists too. He did a bit of boxing in his time. Travelling shows. That sort of thing. 'The Cork Cannon', they called him.'

'The Cork Cannon?' Tommy laughed.

'As God is my witness, that man could fight. One good punch from him and you'd be out for the count. Not that I ever experienced it myself, but I saw him fight. God, it was something to see. He'd take on all-comers. A dollar a time. Last man standing. Sometimes he'd be fighting from dawn 'til dusk. Slipping and sliding on the bloody floors . . . but he was a good man. Hard but honest. Not like that son of his with his fancy ways, forgetting who he is and where he comes from. His father, God rest his soul, would have had something to say about it, that's for sure.'

Tommy didn't want to admit to Jimmy that he didn't much like Gorevin either. He was uneasy in his presence; not scared, since he was scared of no man, but Gorevin unnerved him. Behind the façade of the well-dressed, well-spoken gentleman lay a cruel and brutal character. Hadn't he seen a glimpse of it in the hut with Pat Hanlon, and he certainly didn't want to get on the wrong side of him.

Hearing Jimmy voice such negative sentiments about Gorevin was also unnerving. Was he just letting off steam, although Tommy wasn't sure about what? Gorevin had been pleasant enough, and they both had a bulge in their jacket pockets to illustrate he'd been generous too. Maybe it was a test and Jimmy was trying to induce him into muttering some equally disloyal sentiments which would be eagerly reported back to Gorevin, after which it would only be a matter of time before Tommy was summoned to his own hut rendezvous. He didn't think Jimmy was that devious, but he decided it was best to ignore any temptation to join in with the chorus of disapproval.

He was grateful for the money, of course. It was always welcome, particularly with the baby on the way. There was an envelope of money lying under his mattress, secreted away from prying eyes. Detective Lincoln had left it, and Tommy hadn't had a chance as yet to return it to him. He didn't want to touch one single dollar of the blood money, and he also wanted to make sure Theresa never found out about it. He knew it would be tempting to remove the envelope from its resting place and start spending the money, but he felt it was wrong to even think about that, given the circumstances.

Tommy's unease, however, was more than just a feeling aroused by Gorevin's presence, or the menace which always hung in the air when he was in a room. It was the way he spoke to him, the fact that he had called him 'Tom' on more than one occasion. No-one called him that here. He'd never used that version of his name so he was suspicious when it suddenly made an appearance like a ghost from a previous life. He didn't say anything to Gorevin, and if the other man was deliberately trying to tell him something, he didn't elaborate beyond the name. Tommy wracked his brain as the car rumbled along the streets, Jimmy taking right and left turns as if at random in a bid to avoid the most congested roads.

Father Mike was the only person in New York who knew the story of his arrival. He'd been part of it, recruited by Tommy's uncle, and unless he had told someone in a moment of uncharacteristic indiscretion, there was no way Gorevin could know of his past. Tommy believed the priest treated the information with the same sanctity normally reserved for the confessional box. Maybe Gorevin didn't know anything? It could have been a slip of the tongue and Tommy was reading too much into it.

'Do you want to give the Hanlon woman the money or will I just do it?' Jimmy asked.

'You can do it,' he said, immediately picturing the distraught and dishevelled woman who'd sat with Theresa in his front room, clawing anxiously at the tufts of hair that still remained on her skull after she'd been 'punished'. He didn't want to see her again, to have to look into those red-rimmed, despairing eyes that pleaded for an answer, and have nothing to tell her, no hope to offer, not even false hope. The money wouldn't ease her pain or dispel her misery. It would still be gratefully received, of course. Mary Hanlon wasn't stupid enough to look a gift horse in the mouth, but she still wanted to know what had happened to her husband, and where his body was. It was probably better she didn't find out.

'I'm surprised, right enough,' said Jimmy.

'What about?'

'Gorevin giving her the money. He doesn't usually do anything like that.'

'Maybe he felt sorry for her.'

'Who, Gorevin? You've got to be kidding, Tommy boy. That man is a cold son of a bitch. I'm not sure he's even got a heart.'

Tommy smiled at Jimmy's Dublin brogue attempting to say something so clearly American. It was impossible not to pick up the vocabulary of New York, or find the roughest edges of their accent being smoothed down, and he knew he was guilty of it too, though it wasn't as if he was doing anything wrong. There were definitely words which didn't sound right in an Irish accent and 'son of a bitch' was most definitely one of them.

'She's a poor soul,' Tommy said.

'Who?'

'Mary Hanlon. Pat's missus. The money will come in handy.'

'I suppose it will. Still, I don't imagine Gorevin will want to make a habit of it or even let people find out about it. They'll start to think he's some sort of charity. Either that or he's gone soft.'

'There's no chance of that.'

'None at all. He really is a mean son of a bitch.'

Tommy said the word in unison with Jimmy and the two men laughed, relieved to be away from Gorevin, glad to have a few dollars in their pockets – more than a few – and desperate to get back to the safety of their own homes. Tommy, as he always did, got Jimmy to drop him off a few blocks from home.

'I'll be in touch in a few days,' Jimmy said. 'We might have something on down in Soho.'

Tommy didn't ask what it was. He figured that Jimmy would tell him if, and when, he needed to know. As he opened the door and began to step out, he stopped and looked back at Jimmy.

'Did you see Gorevin's face when I showed him the picture?'

'What picture?'

'My picture! The drawing I showed you.'

He took out the piece of paper and unfolded it, studying it for what seemed like the millionth time.

'What did he do?' Jimmy asked.

'He blinked.'

'What?' Jimmy started laughing and coughing at the same time.

'He blinked. Furiously. As if he had something stuck in his eye.'

'Are you sure?'

'Positive.'

'I didn't see him do anything.'

'He definitely did. It was as if the picture reminded him of something, or someone, that he didn't want to remember.'

'You got that from the blinking?'

'If you'd seen him then you'd know what I mean.'

'Well, I didn't.'

'I know.'

Jimmy shrugged and Tommy took that as his signal to go. He stood on the sidewalk for a few minutes after Jimmy's car had been swallowed up in the mass of cars pouring along the streets, the piece of paper still in his hand, fluttering slightly in the gentle breeze. He thought about Gorevin again, calling him 'Tom', blinking at the sight of the pictures, and he felt uneasy again about the man.

Tommy carried the picture everywhere he went. The image was still distinctive despite the folds in the paper that cut across the man's face. Sometimes his cheeks looked as though they were scarred. A couple of times, warm raindrops fell on to the white sheet before he had time to shelter it, smudging the pencil drawing slightly.

He found himself scanning crowds or examining faces, hoping to spot the man himself though realising that was unlikely to happen. He had committed the image to memory, and if he closed his eyes, the man's face immediately appeared in his mind. He wondered what he would do if he came face-to-face with the man.

It had been another tiring day at work as he trudged home. At least it had been a sunny day. It was still warm even now, in the late afternoon, the sky clear blue and cloudless, the sun hovering imperiously above the city. When it did eventually begin to sink away for the night, shadows cast by the buildings lining either side of the streets would race to meet each other in the middle of the road, and it would become cooler, though a cool summer's evening in New York was generally warmer than the warmest day in Donegal. Sometimes, in the height of summer, people would escape to the roof of their building to sleep under the stars, glad to be out of the stifling heat of their homes.

Tommy saw a car edge its way out from an alleyway that ran up the side of two tenement buildings. It stopped at the junction, its way barred by the traffic driving along the road. There were plenty of gaps in the flow of vehicles for it to pull out, but instead, the passenger got out the car and stood leaning against the side of the vehicle. Tommy glanced up and noticed it was a policeman.

The cop took his hat off and mopped his brow with a white handkerchief, which disappeared back into his pocket before he put his hat on. As Tommy reached the car, he swithered over whether to cut in front of the car or walk round the back of it since it was barring his way.

'You look like a man in a hurry,' the cop said as Tommy started to walk round the back of the car.

'Me?'

'Where are you heading?' the cop said, pushing himself off the car and stretching.

'Home.'

'And where's that.'

'45th Street . . . West and 10th.'

The cop nodded, and took off his cap again, this time wiping his brow with his sleeve. Tommy didn't think it was that hot.

'So where have you been?'

'Just out,' said Tommy.

'Just out for a walk or just out asking questions?'

Tommy frowned. The cop moved towards him.

'No-one likes a man who pokes his nose into things that don't concern him.'

'I'll bear that in mind.'

'You would be as well to do that, Mister Delaney,' the cop said, now standing toe to toe with Tommy, so close the tip of his cap was almost touching Tommy's forehead.

'You know who I am?'

The policeman smiled. 'Of course we do,' he said, glancing to his right. The other cop who had been driving had now got out of the vehicle and was making his way round the car to them.

Tommy looked from one man to the other, very much on edge now. It was like being questioned by the Brits when he was back home in Ireland. They already knew who he was, and they were just waiting for any opportunity or excuse to use physical force. The trick was to keep calm, and not provoke them. He looked back to the cop directly in front of him. He smiled and almost in the same moment Tommy felt the air being sucked out of him and he sank to his knees, holding his stomach where he'd been hit. He caught a glimpse of the black truncheon the cop was holding and guessed that's what had been used. He braced himself for another blow, this time to the head, but it never came. Instead the cop crouched down so that, once again, he and Tommy were face to face. Tommy sensed the officer's partner standing behind him.

'Take a friendly warning,' the cop said. He was so close that specks of spit landed on Tommy's face but he didn't bother wiping them away. He was taking deep gulps of air to regain his breathing.

'Enough with the questions. People are getting a bit tired by it and you'll get no answers anyway.'

'I just want to know who killed my daughter,' Tommy mumbled.

'What's that?'

'I want to find my daughter's killer.'

'Leave that to us,' the cop said.

'Well, if you'd do your job I wouldn't have to be out there asking questions.'

Another blow was delivered to his body, this time from behind, and he fell forward, struggling to find any breath at all. There was a hint of panic beginning to grip him even though he kept telling himself that everything would be fine and he'd soon be able to breathe again. He heard the policeman behind him laugh.

'We're just trying to help you, Tommy,' the first cop said. 'No good will come of poking your nose into things that don't concern you.'

Tommy started to pull himself up on to his knees and the cop helped him, taking his right arm and holding his steady. Tommy coughed and spluttered and spat out on to the sidewalk. The cop, with his free hand, rummaged in

Tommy's pocket and pulled out the picture. Then he stood up and Tommy could hear the paper being torn before the tiny pieces floated around him like snowflakes. They landed on the sidewalk at his knees and he picked up a couple of pieces, which carried random traces of what had been a distinct image of a face just moments before. He dropped them again. There was no point keeping them now.

'Just let it be, Tommy. It's for the best.'

The cop patted him on the back as he returned to the car. Tommy heard the doors click open and then slam shut before the car drove away. He remained kneeling on the sidewalk, the paper snowflakes scattered around him.

Clouding the Issue

The bar was dark when he stepped inside, the door closing behind him and blocking any real light from entering. Everything was artificial here, and the dull glow of lights hanging from the ceiling offered more by way of concealment than illumination. The doorman was at his shoulder and Tommy could feel breath on his neck. There was an edge in here, a wariness of unexpected guests and unpredictable movements. He'd already been patted down to make sure he was unarmed. He knew better than to turn up with anything that might have been construed as a weapon, and while the search was rigorous, it proved fruitless.

A haze of smoke hovered just below the low ceiling, much of it having lingered there from the previous night, although the few customers now dotted about the room were adding to the cloud. None of them seemed to pay any attention to Tommy, though it was hard to tell in the gloom whether they were watching him or staring into their glass. He didn't want to catch anyone's eye. Sometimes that was enough to spark a fight, with cross words leading to crossed swords. He'd worked often enough in places like this to know the etiquette. Besides, he was here for a reason and had no time for any distractions.

In the far corner a man sat at a piano playing a slow, sad

song that Tommy didn't recognise but which was in keeping with the mood of the bar. He could see the top of the man's head, his thinning grey hair visible over the top of the battered piano, which still managed to retain a tuneful sound even if it had seen better days. Tommy knew that, later on, when the place was bulging with people, loud and lively with a drink in their hands, the tempo of the music would be quicker and struggling to be heard above the hum of chatter and laugher rippling through the room.

He wanted a cigarette himself but he would wait until he was asked or at least until he had sat down. Any move towards his pockets, despite the fact he'd already been searched, was not advisable. He also hoped there might be a drink on offer. It didn't feel right to be in this place without a whiskey in his hand.

He saw the figure sitting at a table in the shadows. A cigarette lay smouldering in an ashtray which was positioned beside a bottle of rum and a glass which was filled with the brown liquid. A couple of ice cubes bobbed in the glass like buoys in the water. Tommy stopped in front of the table and waited. The man picked up his cigarette and took a draw, blowing the smoke out towards Tommy before balancing it on the ashtray again and taking a large gulp of his rum, draining the glass. He poured more into the glass and Tommy could hear the clink of the cubes on the glass, even above the sound of the piano.

The gesture was barely noticeable, just a nod towards the seat opposite, but Tommy knew to sit down. The doorman who had accompanied him withdrew, only as far as the bar, where he stood leaning against it, his eyes never leaving the table where they sat.

'You want a drink?'

'Whiskey.'

A wave of the hand brought a barman scurrying over to the table.

'A whiskey for my friend here.'

'Sure thing, Mister Dwyer.'

'And another one for me,' he said, holding up the bottle of rum.

Tommy watched as he picked up the cigarette again, hoping he'd be given one as well, though the offer wasn't forthcoming. He tried to study the man facing him without making it too obvious. He didn't want to stare, not at someone as powerful as Bill Dwyer. He was a man that everyone knew. He ran the main bootlegging operations out of Manhattan, smuggling rum up and down the coast. It was rumoured that his set-up even stretched all the way to Europe. Tommy pictured all the ships cluttering up the bay and wondered how many of them were laden with secret cargo destined for the warehouses Dwyer had at his disposal before it was distributed throughout Manhattan and beyond by people like Jimmy and himself.

It was Jimmy who had set up the meeting. He'd asked for help, and Jimmy had agreed without asking why. They'd done work for Big Bill plenty of times before, though this was the first time he had met him. Tommy immediately thought of Gorevin and the hut where they'd left Pat Hanlon. He wondered whether the man sitting opposite him knew about that, but it didn't matter either way. Tommy suspected he would approve of how the theft had been dealt with. It sent a message to everyone else. There was a heavy price to pay for stealing from Big Bill Dwyer. Had

Gorevin vouched for Tommy or would Jimmy's word have sufficed? Either way, he was grateful for the opportunity.

Bill finished his cigarette and sat back with a smile as the barman returned with the drinks. Tommy sipped his whiskey, allowing the golden liquid to run smoothly down his throat. Bill filled his glass up again. Tommy had already seen him down two drinks, but he looked none the worse for it.

'So Jimmy tells me you want my help?'

'That's right, Mister Dwyer.'

'Call me Bill,' he said, holding out the pack of cigarettes to Tommy, who took one gratefully.

'Thanks . . . Bill.'

'It's a terrible business, Tommy. This is the life we choose, and these are the risks we run, but not our children . . . not our children.'

Tommy took a drink of whiskey.

'It's not what we want for our kids. We work and do what we have to do so that they won't have to. Am I right?'

Tommy nodded.

'So what do you want from me, Tommy?'

'I need your help. I need to find who killed my daughter.'

Bill nodded, his face suddenly sombre.

'I'm sorry for your loss,' he said, blessing himself.

'Thanks.'

'I'm a father myself, Tommy. It's terrible . . . terrible. How is your good lady?'

'As well as can be expected,' Tommy said.

He didn't know what that meant but it was as much as he could tell Dwyer, or as much as the other man was interested in hearing. He wouldn't care that there was silence in the apartment where before there had been laughter, or that they lay, back to back, in bed at night, two rigid bodies terrified of any contact. He would stare at the wall facing him, wondering if Theresa was doing the same thing. Sleep would eventually come, but it was fitful and restless, and sometimes he was more scared of the nightmares that might visit him than he was of the pain which was his constant companion when he was awake.

'I can make some enquiries,' Bill said. 'I'll ask around. See what I can find out. Someone will know something.'

'It's one of Reina's gang.'

'Gaetano Reina? From the Bronx?'

'Yes,' Tommy said.

'How do you know?'

Bill lit another cigarette, shaking his head as he did so and frowning. Tommy thought of the man with the black tooth and he wished he still had the drawing to show Bill. He might have identified the man right away. Tommy was still convinced that there was a flicker of recognition in Gorevin's eyes when he had seen the picture, even if Jimmy had laughed at him when he'd mentioned it.

'He sent the police to warn me off.'

'Reina did?'

He told Bill what had happened, describing how the cops had ripped up the picture, and as he recounted the incident, he felt a slight twinge in his stomach like the pain from the baton had still lingered.

'So I can't take Reina on myself.'

'And you want me to take him on for you?'

'No, with me.'

'But I have no quarrel with Reina.'

Bill took another drink, and once again his glass was empty. This time, however, he didn't immediately fill it up again.

'I still don't know what you want me to do, Tommy.'

'I can't do it myself.'

'Well, I told you, I have no quarrel with Reina.'

'Even if they thought you were in my corner, it might help.'

Bill shook his head.

'That's a dangerous game for me to play. I don't want to get involved in a fight that has nothing to do with me, and has nothing to do with my business.'

'But they killed my daughter.'

'I know, Tommy, and if there was anything I could do to help, I would.'

Tommy drained his own glass. He shouldn't have been surprised but he felt desperate and it didn't do any harm to ask. The idea that Big Bill Dwyer would go out of his way on his behalf was a crazy one, but at least he could say that he had tried. He wasn't any further forward but it hadn't been a setback either. It was still him, on his own, looking to find the man who had shot his daughter. Suddenly, he wanted to go home, the dark and oppressive atmosphere of the speakeasy suddenly one that he felt uncomfortable with. He started to stand up.

'Sit down, Tommy. Sit down.'

Tommy sat back down again.

'How is the old neighbourhood?' Dwyer asked.

'Same as ever, Bill.'

'I'm not sure if that's a good thing or not,' he laughed.

Bill Dwyer was a product of Hell's Kitchen. Maybe he

was the most famous person to have come out of the neighbourhood, or maybe that should be infamous! He'd been a name that had hovered in the background when Tommy had first arrived in New York, but over the past couple of years it was one that he heard more and more. It was no surprise that Bill was drinking rum. He had that operation tied up in the city, along with some of the politicians and policemen as well, if the stories Tommy heard were true. Reina also had influence with the New York cops, and it was that which had made Tommy realise he needed help.

He wasn't sure what he'd been expecting from Bill. Maybe nothing. Maybe everything. In an ideal world, Bill would have agreed to help, found out who was responsible and either delivered the killer to Tommy or made sure the man was punished. Tommy almost laughed at his own naïveté. Bill Dwyer was an important man, and far too busy to be getting involved in what was a minor dispute which, as he'd already pointed out, was nothing to do with him. It was just Tommy's bad luck that the man who had killed his daughter was linked to one of the top gang bosses in New York. He knew that, regardless of the police warning, he had to figure out how to exact justice on his own.

He thought of Theresa, sitting at home and staring into space, or lying in bed, her hand absent-mindedly caressing her bump while her thoughts would still be of Kathleen, trying to keep the image of the little girl fresh in her mind while worried that one day it would fade away. Tommy guessed that's how she felt, because he felt the same way too. He wanted to tell her that the man who had killed their daughter had been dealt with, but whether he ever would or not was still uncertain.

'I will ask about for you, Tommy. You need to look after your own, don't you?'

Tommy nodded.

'But once I've found out what you want to know, then you're on your own. You need to pick and choose your battles in this world, Tommy, and I'm afraid this isn't my battle.'

'I know that, and I appreciate your help.'

'Gaetano Reina is a business rival, but this is not a matter to fall out over. You understand that, Tommy?'

'I do, Bill.'

'So are you sure this had something to do with Reina?'

Tommy explained about Paolo Monti and the money, picturing it hidden away in the apartment. He wondered what Theresa would say if she stumbled upon it. It was more money than she'd ever seen before in her life, and it might confirm to her that what he was involved in wasn't digging roads or putting up buildings. She had never really questioned him before. It was better that way. It saved him lying to her or, worse, telling her the truth. What she didn't know wouldn't hurt her, as long as he never got as greedy or stupid as Pat Hanlon.

'You were taking a chance attacking one of Reina's men,' said Bill.

'I didn't know that was the connection. It was Detective Lincoln who told me.'

'Who did you say?'

'Detective Lincoln. He's in charge of the case. He told me who Monti worked for and warned me to let him do his job.'

'So what happened with the money?'

Tommy hesitated. Bill was watching him now through the haze of smoke and Tommy wished he could have another drink. He glanced at his glass, only for a moment, but Bill immediately signalled towards the bar and within seconds the barman was at the table, filling up Tommy's glass. He took a large gulp as the barman refilled Bill's glass before retreating back to the bar.

'I've still got it,' Tommy eventually said, running his tongue along his lips and tasting the remnants of the whiskey lingering on them. 'Lincoln left it for me.'

'The detective gave you the money?'

'Well, he left it behind after he left. He told me about Monti and his connection to Reina, and wanted me to promise not to do anything else but leave him to catch the killer. Then, when he'd gone, I noticed the bag of money.'

'Reina's money?'

'Yes.'

'How much was there, if you don't mind me asking?'

'About three hundred?'

'What price a life, Tommy?'

'I haven't touched it, Bill. I can't. It's not right. I'll give it back to Lincoln next time I see him.'

Bill nodded, draining his glass again and sighing. Tommy was impressed at the way he drank without seeming to show any effects of it. Tommy could already feel his head beginning to spin a little, and that was after less than two glasses of whiskey.

'It is important we always stick together, Tommy. These people are not like us. They don't understand us. They're different, do you know what I mean?'

Tommy nodded, even though he didn't understand what Bill was talking about.

'I'll help you Tommy. You're a Hell's Kitchen boy, and a good Irishman as well, and that's important in my book.'

'Thanks, Bill.'

'What sort of world are we living in if one Irishman can't help another?'

'I know.'

'It's a bad business back home, is it not? Fighting each other now when we should be fighting the British. It doesn't make sense to me.'

'Me neither, Bill.'

Tommy thought briefly of Michael Collins and hoped that his friend was okay. He wanted to touch the medals he wore, but realised that it would look strange to Bill if he suddenly started pawing at his clothes. He didn't think that Bill Dwyer or any other gang leader would be particularly interested in what was happening back in Ireland. For most of them, it was a place they'd never seen. It had been parents who passed on their memories, or it had been drunken relatives singing maudlin songs at parties which gave them a vague sense of Irish identity or at least a tenuous connection to the old country.

'Anyway, let me have a think about what I can do for you, Tommy. It's always best to have a plan, but the devil is in the detail.'

Tommy still didn't really understand what Bill was talking about. He'd already said he would make enquiries, ask a few questions and then deliver whatever information he acquired to Tommy, who would then be on his own.

That was as much as he could have expected, and probably more than he was entitled to hope for.

'Just sit tight and wait. Tommy I'll let Jimmy know what's happening.'

Bill gave a small nod, and suddenly the doorman was back at the table. It was time for Tommy to leave. He stood up and Bill held out his hand, which Tommy shook.

'Thanks again, Bill.'

'Don't mention it, Tommy. I'm happy to help,' Bill said, already beginning to fill his glass with more rum, though the ice cubes had more or less melted away.

It felt strange being back outside, and Tommy had to adjust his eyes to the daylight which greeted him when he left the bar. He stood on the sidewalk, taking time to light a cigarette and glancing back towards the door he'd just appeared from. The man who'd escorted him had disappeared back inside, but Tommy was sure that he hadn't gone far and was probably lurking just on the other side of the door, ready to block the way of anyone wanting to venture inside for a drink until they passed whatever inspection he carried out. He wondered whether Bill Dwyer had already forgotten about him, and would either be dealing with the next request to find its way to his table or continuing to work through another bottle of rum.

He still wasn't really sure what had happened. One minute Bill was muttering about asking a few questions, the next minute he was talking about plans and telling Tommy to sit tight until he got word to him through Jimmy. Everyone expected him to do nothing. Lincoln had advised as much, and now Bill was saying the same thing. They hadn't lost a daughter, however, so the thought of sitting and doing nothing was not an option for Tommy.

He was reluctant to head home. It didn't feel like an inviting place these days, and even though Theresa had no idea where he'd been or what he had been asking, he still felt she'd be able to read in his face the cocktail of helplessness and guilt he felt . . . but maybe that would change soon.

Paying the Price

Joseph saw the Chevrolet parked at the side of the road about fifty yards ahead of him. It was impossible to miss, not least because everyone seemed to be looking at it, throwing admiring glances in its direction or pointing it out to companions and extolling the virtues of the luxury car. Its purple frame shone majestically in the sunshine, and surrounded by the monotony of black Ford Model Ts, it was no wonder that it gathered attention and admiration in equal measure. He somehow sensed it was waiting for him, though he kept walking towards it like it was drawing him in, hypnotically.

As he reached the vehicle, the passenger door opened and a man emerged out on to the sidewalk. His bulky frame blocked the way ahead and he stood, arms folded, waiting. He took a step back as Joseph reached him, nodding towards the car. He hesitated, glancing around him in the hope that someone might be nearby that he could call on for help, but the man quickly nudged him into the vehicle, immediately following behind and closing the door. As the car started moving, he found himself squashed in the middle of the back seat between two big men, and he could hardly move his arms as they pressed in on him. One of the men pulled a black hood from his pocket and slipped it over Joseph's head.

He was completely in darkness now and he could feel his chest tighten as a sense of mounting panic quickly swept over him. His eyes were frantically trying to adjust to their new surroundings but it was a futile effort. Everything was black. It wasn't like when he was lying in bed at night, his eyes tightly shut and trying to force himself to sleep while his brothers slept either side of him. Then, he knew he could open his eyes, and even in the gloom of the room, shapes would be visible, outlines of familiar objects in the room. Sometimes, if the curtain hadn't been pulled over properly, the moon cast a lazy illumination on the room, perhaps focusing on the face of one of his brothers who slept, oblivious to the lunar attention. He wished he was back there now, squashed in the bed and unable to turn either right or left without disturbing someone. It felt a bit like that now, stuck as he was between the two men. He tried to control his breathing, but it felt like he was being smothered and there was nothing he could do to stop it.

'Calm down, sonny. The hood is just for the journey,' one of the men grumbled into his ear, leaving a hand on his shoulder.

Tears were streaming down his cheeks and he was glad at least that the men couldn't see how upset he was, though he was sure they probably heard the muffled sobs above the rumbling of the car engine. Had anyone seen him being bundled into the car? It had happened so quickly and quietly that the car was gone before anyone was likely to have noticed. Perhaps they might have wondered what had happened to him. One minute he was there, the next he was gone, but then they'd start to question themselves. Had there really been a boy there at all? At that point, he'd be forgotten as they put it down to a trick of the light, a shadow bouncing off the wall of the building.

The car continued on its journey, which seemed bumpier and more disjointed in the dark. There was no point trying to figure out where they were. The car made various turns, right and left, but he couldn't even begin to guess their location. So he closed his eyes, which seemed pointless in the dark, but it did bring him a slight comfort, like the darkness was a choice rather than being forced upon him. He knew, however, that he was merely playing tricks on his own mind, and that panic was liable to set in again if he opened his eyes and found himself in a darker place than if he kept them closed.

Eventually, the car stopped. He couldn't say how long they'd been driving since the darkness had dulled his sense of time, but at a guess, he would say it was about twenty minutes. A door opened and one of the men got out. Immediately there was more room on the seat and Joseph stretched, though he was quickly guided out of the car, banging his head on the door frame.

'Sorry,' muttered a man's voice.

He stood still in the darkness for a few moments, glad of the steadying hand on his arm, and then they were on the move again, crunching along a path before entering a building. Joseph felt helpless, and though he hadn't lost the power of his legs, it did feel like he was incapable of walking at all without assistance. When they eventually stopped moving, having walked up a set of stairs and along what he presumed was a corridor, he was guided on to a seat and he dropped on to it gratefully.

The hood was pulled off and he opened his eyes and let

them adjust to the light this time. Slowly, a man came into focus, his shadowy form taking shape and substance. His frame was large, bulky, like he was wearing about ten layers of clothing though it was only a shirt which covered his torso. His arms were folded and an almost demented grin spread across his face. His head wore the stubble of a few days' growth but Joseph could tell it was normally shaved until it was smooth and shiny. Joseph tried not to stare though he couldn't help but notice that the top part of the man's left ear was missing. He didn't want to imagine how that might have happened.

It was the same man who had 'invited' him into the Chevrolet, though he hadn't noticed his ear before. He glanced round the room registering his surroundings. On the wall facing him, hanging above the cabinet, was a framed picture of a country scene, a horse and cart driving along an empty lane, endless green fields to the right, and bushes and trees to the left. A man and woman were in the cart. He was holding the reins while she linked her arm in his and pressed close to him. Perhaps they were heading out for a picnic. Maybe they were going home after being at church. He wondered if they had children waiting for them at home, or maybe, like Theresa, the woman was pregnant and a baby was on the way.

'Where am I?' he whispered.

The man shook his head.

'Why am I here?'

'No questions, kid.'

The man stood at the door, blocking any chance Joseph might have had of making a run for it, but the thought barely entered his head. He knew he'd never be able to outrun the man anyway, and he didn't want to imagine what would happen if he tried and was caught. He wondered whether anyone would miss him or, indeed, if they would even notice that he was gone. His parents were relieved that he had managed to venture out the house again, though he never revealed what he was doing, and the fact he still spoke very little in the house, and never about what had happened with Kathleen if either of them tried to broach the subject, didn't seem to unduly concern them. If it did, they never mentioned it in his presence.

Maybe when the sun went down and a quick head count in the house revealed his absence, then the alarm might be raised, but he didn't think anyone had noticed him being taken, and even if they did, they wouldn't know where he'd been taken. He didn't know himself. A sudden surge of fear raced through his body and he tried to stifle a sob, though not completely successfully, and the man glared at him. Joseph stared at his feet, too scared to look anywhere else in case he started crying for real. He feared that, if he started sobbing, he wouldn't be able to stop, and he guessed the man's only solution for stopping him would be to hit him. There was a knock on the door, and both Joseph and the man glanced towards it. Another man's head appeared briefly.

'It's time,' he said, disappearing before Joseph was able to get a good look at him beyond his black hair which clung to his skull, no doubt saturated with hair wax.

The man gestured for Joseph to lead the way and he followed. They walked out of the room and down a long hallway. Then it was down two flights of stairs to the cellar. The man held the door open for Joseph, who walked in.

Sitting at a table in the middle of the room was a familiar face. It was the man from his picture. There was a chair facing the man and Joseph was guided towards it. When he sat down, the man smiled and he spotted the black gap in his teeth immediately, which sent a shiver down his spine.

'What is your name?'

Joseph stared at the man, who was now lighting a cigarette. He could feel his heart pounding at being so close to the person who had killed Kathleen, and he knew, if he closed his eyes, he could conjure up those few moments from Saint Patrick's Day again, when they stood at the kerb and he had let her go. He guessed it wouldn't be a good idea to close his eyes, however, and as he watched the man slowly smoking, there was a tiny element of pride taking root in his head. He had made a good job of drawing the man, which had all been done from the memory of a few fleeting moments.

'Do you not have a name?'

Joseph kept staring. One of the other men clipped the back of his head.

'Answer Angelo when he asks you a question. What's your name, kid?'

'Joseph,' he whispered.

'What did you say?'

'Joseph.'

'Joseph,' said Angelo, nodding like he knew all along and he just wanted confirmation of it. 'Do you know why you're here, Joseph?'

Joseph shook his head. Angelo laughed.

'Empty your pockets, Joseph.'

Joseph hesitated, not quite sure what Angelo meant,

but another clip on the back of the head prompted him to take out the contents of his jacket pocket. He put the folded sheets of paper on the table and looked between them and Angelo. Every one of them contained the image of the man sitting opposite him. Angelo picked the bundle up and took one sheet, unfolding it and putting it on the table. He did the same until there were eight drawings looking up at them. Joseph chewed on his bottom lip nervously as Angelo laughed again, this time shaking his head as he did so.

'What am I going to do with you, Joseph?'

Joseph shrugged.

'Posting these pictures of me all over the place . . .' Angelo shook his head. 'You're a whole heap of trouble for someone so young.'

Joseph hadn't imagined he would get caught. As he wandered the streets with a bundle of drawings in his pocket and in his hand, he looked for places to leave them. It never crossed his mind that anyone would stop him, and he definitely didn't think it would be the man in the picture. Angelo. He hadn't really thought too much about it at all. He hoped that people might recognise who it was, but he realised now that, even if they did, they wouldn't know why the picture had suddenly started appearing everywhere, and what Angelo had done. Even Kathleen's father wouldn't have known when he found the drawing. Yet, Joseph didn't know what else to do. He couldn't speak about it – he wouldn't speak about it – so the only thing he knew to do was pick up his pencil and draw.

'I have to admire your nerve, Joseph, but I can't be having this. Not here in the Bronx. What will people think if I let this go unpunished?'

Joseph shrugged again.

'You don't have much to say for yourself, do you?'

Angelo dropped his cigarette end on the floor and stood on it. He said something in a language Joseph didn't understand – Joseph presumed it was Italian - and the two men appeared at the table. One of them remained behind Joseph while the other stood to the side of the table, a stick dangling at his side.

'Do you like baseball, Joseph?'

Joseph shrugged.

'Typical Irish,' Angelo said to the two men, who both laughed. 'You're an American kid now, Joseph and baseball is an American sport. It's a wonderful game. You really should follow it.'

In truth, Joseph's dad had taken him and his brothers and sisters to the Polo Grounds a couple of times to see the New York Yankees, but he didn't really understand what was going on. He cheered when the others did, always hoping no-one would ask him why he was cheering. He now noticed the man's stick was, in fact, a baseball bat. Angelo put the paper drawing down on the pile and brought out a pen from his jacket pocket. He held it out for Joseph.

'Draw me a picture, kid.'

Joseph looked at the picture and then glanced towards Angelo, who nodded in encouragement. Slowly, Joseph stretched out a hand and grasped the silver pen, and then taking one of the sheets of paper, turned it over so Angelo's image was face down on the table. He started to draw. The pen had barely touched the paper before it was snatched out of his grasp by the man behind him who now held Joseph's left arm straight on the table, pressing the boy's hand on the hard surface and gripping his shoulder. The other man swung the baseball bat swiftly, connecting with Joseph's forearm.

He heard the crack, like ball on bat. There was a delay of a few moments before shock was replaced by pain and Joseph screamed. Now the man gripped Joseph's elbow and his accomplice brought the bat down on Joseph's hand. Strike One . . . it smashed his fingers. Strike Two . . . it broke his knuckles. Strike Three . . . it shattered his wrist. When the man released his grip, Joseph collapsed, falling noisily to the floor.

The baseball man brought a bin over to Angelo, who pushed all the paper in it. A lighter was held to it until the flames started dancing up from the pile of burning images.

'No more drawing for you, kid,' Angelo muttered, lighting another cigarette and staring at Joseph's motionless body.

A Sort of Homecoming

Joseph didn't recognise the room when he opened his eyes. He was lying on his back and at first he stared at the ceiling, then out the corner of his eye he saw a small pink rabbit on the window ledge which seemed to be watching him, and he stared at it for a few minutes. The rabbit stared back, never blinking, but it always seemed to be on the verge of saying something. Joseph sighed. He knew it was just a toy. That's what his mind was telling him, though when he looked back at it, he could almost swear that the rabbit winked at him.

Slowly, like the emerging dawn sunshine that crept up from way beyond New Jersey, shooting its rays over all the land it surveyed before bouncing off the water of the Hudson River and stretching across the whole of Manhattan, he became aware of a pain that was spreading out from his fingertips to his shoulder. He tried lifting his left arm but screamed out. His right arm was fine. He lifted it up and down with ease, waved it in the air, held his hand close to his face to examine it, but when he tried again to do the same thing with his left arm, he screamed even louder than before. He caught a glimpse of the white bandages covering his hand and stretching all the way up to his elbow. He was sure he knew what had happened, but his mind couldn't quite focus, so he couldn't say for definite.

'Are you okay?'

He heard the woman's voice and looked round towards the door. It was Kathleen's mum. She stood, framed in the doorway like a picture, her arms folded.

'I heard you scream,' she said, moving slowly towards the bed.

Joseph glanced at the rabbit again. It still hadn't looked away. He gazed up at the ceiling, knowing that, through the wood and plaster was his own home, his own parents, his brothers and sisters. He glanced back at Kathleen's mum again. Theresa. That was her name. He knew that, but smiled gratefully at the rabbit as if it had just whispered it to him.

'Is it sore?' Theresa asked.

Joseph nodded as he tried to peer down towards his arm, though he didn't dare move it this time.

'It's best if you don't move it,' she said. She sat on the edge of the bed and he could see that her eyes were brimming with tears. One or two had already started to stream down her cheeks and he wished he could stretch across and wipe them away, but he didn't want to move because he knew it would only hurt him.

'How are you feeling?' she asked.

He wanted to cry, but for some reason he found himself trying to fight back the tears. Crying was for girls. That's what his father had always told him and his brothers, and that message had taken up residence in his brain, even though every part of him wanted to scream and sob. Theresa gently touched his right arm, her fingertips caressing his skin. She kept her hand on his arm, like she was trying to reassure him.

What about his parents? Wouldn't they be worried that he wasn't in his own house? He'd woken up in a strange bed in a strange house, so he had no idea how long he had lain here. His family would be getting worried.

'Mum,' he whispered.

'Your mum knows you're here,' Theresa said, giving his arm a gentle squeeze.

Joseph was almost startled by the sound of his voice, hearing it out loud, even as a whisper. He hadn't really spoken since Kathleen's death, and certainly not to another person.

'Mum,' he said again, this time louder, which sounded ever stranger, like he was listening to someone else's voice. Did he really sound like that?

'It's fine, Joseph. She's upstairs. I can get her if you want?'

He looked over at the rabbit but it didn't offer any suggestions as to what he should say to that.

'She just thought you'd get a better rest down here,' Theresa said. 'It's quieter here, not as many people . . .'

She let the words hang in the air with a heavy sigh and Joseph looked at her. He didn't know whether to try and offer a smile by way of comfort, but he sensed it would just look like he was in pain, so he did nothing.

'You've had a terrible fright,' Theresa said. 'You need to rest and get some sleep. That's what the doctor said.'

'Thirsty,' he mumbled.

'Do you want a drink?'

He nodded.

'I'll get you some water.'

Theresa disappeared out of the bedroom and Joseph stared at the ceiling again. His own mother was up there, feeding children or scolding them. Maybe she was sitting thinking about him, worried for him? Her rosary beads would be wound through her fingers as her lips moved in silent prayer.

'Our Lady, Queen of the Angels . . . please take care of my boy.'

A stray tear escaped from the side of his eye and rolled down his face and into his ear. He was glad of the quiet, and the isolation. It didn't matter how much his mother warned his brothers and sisters, they'd still be rough and loud and curious to inspect him, firing questions at him, none of which he could answer. He didn't want to deal with that, but he still missed his mother.

'Here you go,' Theresa said, re-appearing with a glass of cold water. She helped Joseph to hold his head up, tilting the glass back so that he could drink the water. After a few sips, he lay back on the bed.

'Thanks,' he said, licking his lips.

'I'll just leave it here at the side of the bed if you want another drink,' she said, placing the glass on a small wooden cabinet. He wasn't sure he would be able to reach it, certainly not without moving and possibly causing more pain to shoot up and down his left arm, but he didn't say anything. He could always ask for help later.

'Do you want me to get your mum?'

This time it seemed like the rabbit shook its head and so Joseph did too.

'She said she'll pop down when your dad comes home from work. What a fright they got. We all did.'

Another tear spilled from his eye, followed quickly by another, and he blinked to try and stem the tide.

'It's okay,' Theresa said. 'It's okay to cry.'

He shook his head slightly but realised there was no way to stop the tears. He let them fall now, adjusting his head so they fell on the bed rather than continuing to drop into his ears, which was cold and uncomfortable. Theresa stood up to go and then, just as she was about to move away from the bed, leant back over and planted a gentle kiss on his forehead. He closed his eyes but the tears still poured out.

'Don't go,' he whispered as she was halfway to the door.

'What?'

'Don't go.' He said it louder this time, opening his eyes but it was like staring at a blurry figure in the street on a rainy day. Theresa walked back and sat down on the bed again.

'I'm not going anywhere,' she said, giving his arm another squeeze.

'Thanks,' he whispered, wiping some of the tears on his face with his right hand. He didn't dare risk moving his left arm because he knew the pain would still be unbearable.

It was darker when he woke up again. He didn't know how long he'd been sleeping but he guessed it had been a few hours. The sunlight was slowly fading and shadows stretched across the bedroom walls. It was easier for his eyes to adjust this time, though the first thing they focused on, once again, was the ceiling. He could hear footsteps above him, heavy ones that he guessed belonged to his father, slowly clumping from one room to another. There were other ones, quick and continuous; his brothers and sisters racing through the house, chasing each other while staying out of the kitchen where his mother would probably be preparing dinner, and avoiding their father, who was always in an unpredictable mood when he came home from work.

He felt suddenly hungry and imagined he could smell the aroma of meat pie and potatoes wafting through the floorboards and filling the bedroom, making his stomach rumble. The glass of water remained at the side of the bed. He still didn't think it was a good idea to try and attempt to reach it. His left arm felt heavy now, like a dead weight was pinning it to the bed and he knew better than to try and lift it this time.

There were other noises too, drifting in from the street outside. An endless rumble of traffic, cars and trucks and trolley cars. Occasionally, he was sure he could hear the sharp bell pulled by a passenger to let the driver know they wanted off. The rattle of metal came and went at intermittent moments. He didn't know if it was from trains rattling along the Ninth Avenue Elevated line, heading through Midtown going north towards the Bronx or down to Lower Manhattan, or was it nearer, perhaps a gust of wind shaking the fire escapes clinging precariously to the front of their building. Voices shouted and screamed and laughed. Neighbours stopped for a few minutes of snatched conversation before continuing on their different journeys. Children played on the sidewalk. His friends. Their activities illuminated by street lights until a voice from an open window shouted them up for dinner or bed-time. It was only then that the noise began to simmer down.

Joseph had no energy to move. He knew his legs still worked. He wriggled his toes every now and then just to prove to himself that they did, but the thought of putting them on the ground so that they would support the weight of his body, and then attempting to move them, putting one foot in front of the other, seemed beyond his current physical capabilities. He waved his right arm in the air, but his left arm remained limp on the bed at his side.

He couldn't hear any noise in the apartment. Theresa wasn't sitting on the edge of the bed. He guessed she had moved when he fell asleep. Would she be in the kitchen, cooking dinner for her husband, or maybe she was sleeping in an armchair in the front room. He hoped that she was making dinner and that some of it would be for him. The rabbit remained on the window sill. It still stared at him, though it too was now in shadow and it seemed like the pink colour had drained from it. He stuck out his tongue at it, but got no response. The door opened and Theresa walked in. She was carrying a tray, and the plate and cutlery rattled as they collided with each other.

'I've brought you some soup,' she said. 'Ham and potato. I thought you might be hungry.'

Joseph could smell the soup as Theresa got closer to the bed and his stomach automatically rumbled in anticipation. She picked the glass up, putting it on the tray so there was enough space to put the tray down on the cabinet. It took a few painful minutes before she managed to prop up the pillows and then lift Joseph so he could sit up and lean against them. He let out a cry when she tried to take a grip under his left armpit, and she immediately stopped, apologising to him. He knew he had to endure the pain, however, if he wanted to eat the soup, certainly without having to be spoon-fed, so when Theresa suggested trying again, he nodded in agreement. He flinched several times as she dragged him up the bed and rested him against the pillow, but he bit his tongue to stop crying out loud.

She placed the tray on his lap and he started eating it hungrily, not bothering that several drops fell on his shirt. It was awkward having to use his right hand. Theresa took up her place at the side of the bed again, lighting a cigarette, though she was at pains to blow the smoke away from Joseph.

'Did you get a good sleep?' she asked.

He nodded, not breaking the rhythm of his eating, his spoon relentlessly moving from plate to mouth and back again.

'I'll let your mum know you're awake now. When she popped down earlier, you were sleeping.'

The spoon was clattering the plate, which was almost empty now.

'My goodness, someone's hungry. Do you want more?'

He looked up and nodded. It felt like his stomach was rumbling again and the plate of soup had barely filled it. Theresa lifted the plate with a smile while Joseph held on to the spoon. Soon, she had returned, and the plate was miraculously filled almost to the brim with more soup.

'There's plenty more if you're still hungry,' said Theresa. 'Or I can make something else if you want? What about some bread pudding? Do you want some of that?'

'Soup's fine,' he said, shaking his head.

Theresa resumed smoking, and for the next few minutes the only sounds filling the room were Joseph slurping his soup and Theresa drawing on her cigarette.

'Your arm's still really sore.'

It was less of a question than a statement of fact, but Joseph nodded anyway.

'What happened? . . . No, you don't need to tell me. It's none of my business.'

She got up and went to the window. She picked up the rabbit before opening the window and flicking her cigarette out. It floated slowly to the ground. She closed the window but kept hold of the rabbit which rested on her lap when she sat down.

'I'm sorry,' Joseph said, putting his spoon down in the empty plate.

'Do you want more?'

'No thanks.'

Theresa lifted the tray and placed it back on top of the bedside cabinet.

'I'm sorry,' he said again.

'What for?'

'Kathleen,' he whispered.

The name hung in the air for a few moments, like the residual noise from a ship's horn that still seemed to echo even after it had been sounded. Theresa took a deep breath and looked at Joseph.

'It was my fault,' he said.

'Don't say that,' she said quickly. 'You're a good boy, Joseph.' She squeezed his hand. 'You're a good boy.'

'You asked me to look after her.'

'It's not your fault, Joseph. There was nothing you could have done. It wasn't your fault. You shouldn't blame yourself.'

'I'm sorry.' He said it again, barely a whisper this time.

Theresa was crying now, quietly, and she leant over and gently hugged him, trying to make sure she didn't press on his left side at all.

'You're a good boy,' she kept repeating.

Joseph closed his eyes, picturing the morning when he'd been asked to look after the little girl. His left arm continued to throb, while he didn't dare try to move his hand. He could move his right hand, and his palm tingled suddenly, the sensation of a tiny hand within his own palm so realistic he had to open his eyes and check to make sure that wasn't the case. The rabbit on Theresa's lap looked up at him, and this time he was sure it did wink at him.

'I saw him,' he said.

'What?'

It was Theresa who spoke, even though Joseph had been speaking to the rabbit.

'I saw him,' he repeated. Now he was crying, and even though his shaking shoulders sent tremors of pain shooting up and down his arm, he didn't stop.

'Who did you see?' Theresa asked, trying to wipe some of Joseph's tears away.

'The man,' he said. 'The pictures.'

'What pictures?'

Joseph remembered grasping the silver pen which was held out to him, a hand gripping his shoulder, his arm stretched out on the table; a baseball bat being swung once, twice, three times . . .

He screamed again and again and again, his whole body now convulsing and his left arm feeling as though it was going to explode. He continued screaming, even after Theresa had wrapped her arms round him, not caring now that she might hurt him and aggravate his injury, but instead wanting to smother his pain with her own, hurting body.

Blazing Mad

There was a cool early-morning breeze in the air, but Tommy knew that it would soon disappear, banished for the day by the rising sun that was already beginning to stretch from its slumber and cover the city and beyond in its warm embrace. For now, though, he wore a cap, as much to conceal his face as to keep his head warm, and he made sure it was pushed low so that his features remained in the shadow cast by the peak.

From his vantage point about one hundred yards along the street, he could see the truck. It was parked outside the warehouse, a lonely presence in an otherwise empty street. The building itself was dark and dismal, as if it had just emerged from days underground and needed to wash off the grime and grit that clung to its skin. It was a common condition in this part of the city, street after street of tenements and warehouses and store-rooms and workshops, all within a stone's throw of the river. Sometimes, in the dead of night, it was possible to hear the water lapping the docks if the river was particularly restless. Now, though, Tommy couldn't have heard anything, even if he was to strain his ears to listen.

There were two men inside the truck. He'd seen them emerge from the building and jump up into the vehicle, the driver taking his place straight away while his passenger walked round to the back to check the cover which concealed the contents of the truck, before joining his companion in the cabin.

Every few minutes puffs of smoke floated out from the truck as if it was slowly smouldering, though Tommy knew it was just the two men smoking. They had obviously opened the windows. He was tempted to light up himself, but the clouds which would emerge from the doorway where he was hiding would reveal his presence to anyone taking even a cursory glance along the street. So he continued his vigil with his mouth parched, his throat throbbing and his lungs almost crying out for a fresh intake of nicotine.

The minutes slowly ticked by, though he showed no signs of impatience. He had watched the truck often enough in the past few days to know what was going on. The men were waiting for someone, content to enjoy a smoke as they did so, and whether that wait lasted a minute or an hour was immaterial to them. The truck would remain parked until all the formalities of their early-morning schedule had been completed.

Tommy knew there would be renewed activity when a Ford Model T appeared round the corner, into Hubert Street and drove up to the building. It pulled in behind the truck, though leaving a safe distance between the vehicles. The passenger emerged, his face hidden by the black fedora perched on his head, and he strode into the building, disappearing inside the grimy structure, quickly followed by the driver of the truck.

Tommy waited for a couple of minutes before taking a deep breath and emerged from the shadows. He walked briskly along the street on the opposite side from the two vehicles, head bowed, and hands in pockets. He looked, to all intents and purposes, like a man heading towards work. He didn't have much time. The car passenger was only ever inside the building for fifteen minutes at most, and often it was less than that.

He clenched his fists as he approached the vehicles, quickly going through his mind exactly what he planned to do. He crossed the street, not bothering to check whether there was any traffic coming, relying on his hearing to let him know the road was clear. By now his pace had quickened and he was soon at the truck. He gripped the handle of the driver's door and opened it, springing up into the cabin in the same movement. His fist slammed into the man's face, crushing the startled expression which had greeted his sudden entrance. The man sprawled across the cabin, thudding to the floor. Tommy scrambled across the seat, punching the man three more times in quick succe-ssion before leaning over him and pushing open the door. The man was launched head-first out of the cabin, crashing heavily on the sidewalk where he remained motionless as Tommy shut the door.

He started up the truck, glancing briefly in the wing mirror to see the car driver, hands clutching his own steering wheel, his mouth gaping wide and his brain still trying to register what he'd just witnessed in the space of a few moments, and then trying to figure out what to do next.

Tommy pushed the truck into reverse, released the hand-brake, pressed the pedal to the floor and the truck sprung back, slamming into the car. The crunch of metal on metal reverberated along the deserted street as Tommy drove the truck forward about ten yards, stopped and then repeated the manoeuvre, colliding once more with the car, whose front was slowly disintegrating. As he moved forward again, he could see the driver frantically trying to open his door to escape, terrified that if the truck hit the car again, it would be him who'd be crushed.

Tommy wasn't stopping this time, however. He kept driving as figures emerged from the building, alerted by the noises that must have sounded like the dull thud of explosions from inside. The truck driver was the first to appear, his head frantically spinning from the crushed car to his own vehicle which was disappearing along the street. He started searching his pockets, clumsily pulling out a pistol, but as he started to aim it at the truck, the man in the fedora hat who'd rushed out the building just after him, laid a firm hand on his arm and the man lowered his gun.

Tommy drove round the corner and into Greenwich Street without slowing down, and the truck almost lost balance. He gripped the steering wheel, fighting to retain control of the vehicle as the sound of breaking glass could be heard from the back of the truck. The last thing he needed now was to crash the truck before he'd managed to escape. He was sure that no-one from the building would be able to pursue him, and as soon as the truck had steadied itself, he allowed himself the briefest of satisfied smiles. So far, so good, he thought. He remained on edge, however, glancing every few minutes in the mirror to check in case he was being followed.

There were other vehicles behind him, but none were paying attention to the truck. He'd taken them all by surprise and they appeared to have no means of pursuing him. He lit a cigarette as he drove, heading back up towards Hell's Kitchen. Traffic was getting busier now and he had to stop at every junction. At one intersection, a traffic cop was standing in the middle of the road directing and controlling the flow of traffic which seemed to be going in all directions. He didn't envy the man, whose movements seemed choreographed like he was dancing to a piece of music no-one else could hear. A few horns sounded in frustration, which seemed to lead to an extra delay for the cars coming from that direction, but for the most part, drivers seemed content to wait their turn, and the cop continued expertly manipulating the traffic to avoid everything grinding to a halt.

Tommy glanced out his window. A little girl was on the sidewalk staring at him. He felt his chest tighten and he had to gasp for a breath. He looked at her again and let out a sigh of relief. It wasn't Kathleen. The girl was holding a lollipop that she would occasionally lick. She looked a little older than Kathleen, he thought as he stared at her. A horn sounded behind him just as the girl stuck her tongue out at him. He smiled. The horn sounded again. He glanced in the mirror and then looked ahead. The cop was waving him on, and he quickly started moving the truck across the intersection. The little girl's attention had already been distracted by an older woman walking along the sidewalk with a dog on a lead, and she ran towards the animal, shielding her lollipop from its hungry attentions.

When he pulled into the street he saw that Jimmy was already waiting for him, holding, as always, the customary cup of coffee. It made Tommy smile. He saw the other man drain the cup and then drop it into a trash can as he stepped forward. He waved at the truck, even though Tommy knew it was him. It was the address they'd arranged to meet. It was Jimmy who had explained what they were going to do.

'Bill doesn't want any of this getting back to him,' Jimmy emphasised right away. 'So if anything goes wrong, you're on your own.'

The plan was to take a truck belonging to Reina and steal the booze. It was as simple as that. Tommy stared at Jimmy after he'd explained it to him, waiting for the second part of the plan.

'Is that it?' he'd eventually said when Jimmy hadn't added any more information.

'What do you mean, is that it?'

'We steal a truck of booze. Big deal. How is that going to help me find Kathleen's killer?'

'We can't just go in all guns blazing,' Jimmy said. 'Bill doesn't want a full-blown war with Reina, so there's got to be a plan. The devil's in the detail, Tommy.'

'So Bill told me.'

'Well, trust him then.'

'But what's the point of stealing the truck?'

'To provoke a response. Reina will want to know who's responsible and we wait and see how he goes about that and who he sends to find out.'

'And what if he doesn't?'

'Come on, Tommy. Think about it. Someone steals one of his trucks, from outside his own warehouse. That's an insult to a man like Gaetano Reina. He'll want answers.'

'I hope you're right. It seems a big risk for very little return.'

'And because it's happening right in Manhattan, he's liable to come asking Bill for information.'

'What if he thinks it was Bill?'

'He won't. We've to make it look like a robbery, plain and simple. So no guns. We don't want to give any impression that it's been well-organised.'

Everything had gone to plan so far. Now they had to unload the cargo into one of Bill's garages. Tommy and Jimmy worked quickly and quietly. The strenuous physical activity left no energy for conversation, and they both knew that the quicker they emptied the truck, the better. Word would quickly get back to Reina about what had happened, and then he'd start looking for answers. By then, however, the plan was to have the booze safely hidden away, and the truck disposed of.

Within half an hour, the truck was empty. Jimmy walked out of the garage with a single crate, putting it in the back of the vehicle.

'It'll help you get rid of the truck,' he said and Tommy nodded.

He jumped back into the cabin while Jimmy locked up the garage. Jimmy tipped his cap as Tommy started up the truck, moving in the opposite direction as he headed towards the final destination they'd decided on. He realised that he'd taken most of the risks, but since it was meant to be helping him, he didn't mind. He still wasn't convinced that it was much of a plan beyond stealing some booze, which would benefit Bill, but for now there was nothing else to do but go along with the instructions Jimmy had passed on and hope that, at some point, it would lead him to the killer.

Eventually, after half an hour of crawling up through Manhattan, he steered the truck over Willis Avenue Bridge and into the Bronx. He was heading for Denman Street.

He slowed the truck down, glancing out either window now, his senses alert for any possible danger, but no-one would be expecting him. He pulled into the kerb about halfway along the road and stopped. Jumping down on to the sidewalk, he quickly headed for the back and unhooked the tarpaulin cover, pulling it up so that he could clamber up into the truck.

He opened the crate and took out a bottle of rum. He was tempted to open it and take a gulp, but the less time he spent there the better, and he needed to be alert and on guard. He struck the neck of the bottle on the side of the wooden crate, having to repeat it a couple of times before the glass smashed, spilling some of the dark liquid on to the floor, a few drops splashing on to his boots. He poured the remainder of the rum over the opened crate. Then he took out the matches from his pocket and struck one, dropping it into the crate, where it immediately caught fire.

As the flames began to take hold, burning wood and straw, and being constantly fed by the alcohol, he jumped back down from the truck, stretching to pull the tarpaulin back down so that it concealed the fire inside. There were a few tiny trails of smoke escaping from gaps underneath the tarpaulin, but nothing that was likely to immediately alert or alarm passers-by.

Tommy stepped back on to the kerb and lit a cigarette. Pushing his hands into his pockets, he began walking up the street away from the truck and back in the direction he'd come from. His cap was still pushed low on his head, hiding his features and he pressed his chin in towards his chest. He couldn't afford to be recognised.

'Hey! Mister.'

He heard the shout but kept walking. It was a woman's voice but she might not be shouting him. People were always hanging out buildings shouting on husbands or wives or children or neighbours.

'Hey! You with the cap on.'

Maybe she was trying to catch his attention. His instincts told him not to stop.

'Your truck's smoking.'

He quickened his pace. He guessed that she was shouting from a window, so she was unlikely to chase him but somebody else might if they heard her, and maybe try to stop him. He spat his cigarette out on the sidewalk ahead of him, standing on it as he started to run, slowly at first. A sprinting man always aroused suspicion, day or night.

The woman shouted again, but her voice didn't carry far enough up the street to be distinguishable. He looked up to see whether there was any oncoming traffic. It was clear, though just as he stepped on to the road there was an explosion and he stumbled forward, just about managing to get his hands out of his pockets quick enough to cushion his fall. He landed on his knees, the palms of his hands taking the brunt of the fall as they scraped along the ground and he glanced back down the street.

The truck was now a blazing skeleton, flames dancing high in the air and singeing the branches of nearby trees. There were a few more sporadic explosions, though none with the same ferocity as the initial one. Tommy quickly got back on to his feet, wiping his hands together to clean them. The flesh of his palms stung but he ignored the pain. A couple of cars which had turned into the street stopped and one of the drivers stuck his head out the window.

'What the hell happened there?' he said, glancing briefly at Tommy before his eyes were drawn inexorably back to the blazing truck.

'I don't know,' Tommy mumbled, beginning to shuffle round the back of the car as there was a further explosion. The man shook his head and whistled.

'It's like the fourth of July,' he said.

He was no longer paying attention to Tommy, who had reached the corner of the block. He peered back, momentarily mesmerised at the flames, which shimmered and shook in the breeze rippling up and down the street. A few people were out now, drawn towards the truck, but still having enough sense to remain just out of reach of the fire. Each tiny explosion would send them back a few cautious paces, but they remained enthralled by the spectacle. Tommy turned away after a few more minutes. He knew the cops would be on the scene soon enough, the fire brigade too, while there would be other people asking questions, taking notes, checking out strangers. Word would reach them of the missing truck and they'd figure it out quickly. He'd made his point and sent a message and he was satisfied with that. He walked swiftly away, still with his head down but taking care to avoid people rushing in the opposite direction. He'd be on the train soon and heading safely back to Hell's Kitchen. Then, as Jimmy told him, he was to wait until Dywer sent word for him.

Fourth of July

Tommy could see fields and hills stretching forever, and he knew it was Donegal. He would always recognise his home. It had felt, as he grew up, like he'd covered every inch of this land. It was his garden and offered endless hours of fun. His mother was always there, just out of sight, but keeping a watchful eye over him.

He spotted a cottage sitting on its own, isolated at the foot of a small hill. Smoke was billowing out of the hole in the peat roof, sending indecipherable signals far and wide. It wasn't his own cottage, but he was getting closer. It was a warm sunny day, so it seemed strange to him that there would be a fire burning. The door of the cottage swung open and he stepped inside, a wave of heat almost knocking him over. Beads of sweat ran down his face, one or two landing on his lips, and he could taste their saltiness. It was so warm he was finding it difficult to breathe, and he gasped for fresh air, frantically looking for the door as an escape route. It was so close, almost within touching distance, but whenever he stretched out an arm, the door was just beyond his reach.

He turned towards the peat fire which was burning bright

against the far wall of the cottage. Orange flames were dancing excitedly in the hearth and waves of heat lapped the room. An occasional snap from the fire disturbed the silence and every time he heard it, Tommy was startled and stared into the flames, trying to search out the culprit.

There was a small figure sitting in front of the fire on a wooden stool, so close it looked as though, at any time, the flames were going to jump out and engulf them. A black veil was draped over her head like she was at Mass, and her shoulders rocked back and forth like she was praying or being pushed by an invisible hand. He stood watching for a few minutes, not wanting to move or say anything. He sensed it was best not to disturb her. She must be almost melting, he thought, but if she was, she made no effort to move away from the mouth of the fire.

Slowly, she turned round, and as she did so, she pulled the veil off her head. He saw the brown hair and gasped.

'What are you doing here?' she asked softly.

He shook his head, not able to find his voice.

'Why are you here?'

'This is my home,' he whispered.

She laughed and stood up. The wooden stool toppled over and for a few moments it looked as though it would roll into the fire, but it seemed to stop itself and rolled back and forth for a minute or so before it came to rest.

'Why are you here?' he asked, his voice trembling.

'This is my home,' she said.

He watched her, mesmerised, as she walked confidently over to the bed in the far corner. She sat on the edge of the bed and began stroking the hair of the figure lying in the bed. She began singing as well – *Dáimh Gaeilge Briste*. That had been the one his mother always sang. Kate's Song, they always called it. How did she know that? Her voice was like how he imagined an angel would sound.

'Close your eyes,' she said, 'and don't look back . . . 'Cause what you see would break your heart.'

'Kathleen?' he whispered as the little girl continued singing.

The figure in the bed stirred. It was his mother, looking exactly the same as she had when he'd last seen her. But she had died. The news had followed him to Glasgow and found him. She was gone. He knew that, so why was she lying here now, in this bed, as Kathleen sang to her? He cried out, though it was just an incoherent noise.

'Ssh!' the little girl scolded. 'You'll wake granny up.'

Tommy woke up with a start, like someone had slapped his face or thrown a bucket of ice-cold water over it. He looked around, expecting to see the little girl, or the peat fire still burning brightly. He stared towards the dark corner, but instead of his mother's death bed, there was the outline of an armchair. He was lying on the couch in his own apartment. He lay back and wiped the sweat off his forehead with his shirt sleeve. His heart was slowing down too, and he took long, deep breaths until he felt calm, although he remained unnerved

He ran a hand through his hair, which was damp with sweat. His cigarettes were lying on the ledge underneath the window and he shuffled across the room, hoping that a cigarette might steady his nerve after his dream. He often sat at the window during the night, opening it a fraction and blowing smoke out of it. Anyone walking past who might glance up would have taken a second glance, just for reassurance that the house wasn't on fire. That wasn't an uncommon sight. So many apartments packed together, row after row of them with very little breathing space between each one, people living side by side and on top of each other. Sometimes it might be a chip pan that suddenly took light and engulfed a kitchen within seconds; it might be a cigarette dropped by a snoozing drunk. Sometimes the fire was started deliberately, for reasons that could never be ascertained when raking about in the smouldering ashes later on. When people realised it was merely someone smoking, they continued on their journey, relieved there was no need to raise the alarm or venture into the tenement building to try and rescue any occupants who might be trapped.

He could smoke his way through a whole packet if he didn't feel tired or want to go to bed and lie beside Theresa. He was scared to touch her or even just disturb her when he slipped under the covers.

He liked sitting in the darkness, the room only illuminated a fraction whenever he drew on his cigarette, the orange glow from the tip lighting up like a lighthouse beam in the distant sea. There was something soothing about the night time gloom. It seemed to dampen down his worries while promising that tomorrow's sunshine would bring with it a better day. He liked it best when he thought of nothing, when he could close his eyes, drawing the nicotine into his lungs and letting it slowly escape from his body, sighing as he did so. He tried to clear his mind of everything – Kathleen's body lying on the mortuary slab, Theresa's quiet sobs or silent pain, Pat Hanlon's dying screams, Mary Hanlon's desperate pleading, even the face in the picture.

He never quite succeeded, of course, but those tiny snatches of time, perhaps no more than a few seconds, were the most precious of all. He could even pretend he was back in Donegal rather than in New York. That always made him smile, especially when a delivery truck rumbled along the road outside and brought him straight back to Hell's Kitchen.

Was it really hell though? He glanced towards the bedroom where he knew Theresa was lying awake, eyes wide open and staring ahead of her at the blank wall. He wished he could go to her and help her, talk to her, touch her, comfort her, hold her. If he could find out who had killed Kathleen, that might help a little bit. At least that would give him something to talk to her about. He hoped that stealing the truck would bring him a little closer to that aim. At least, that's what Bill Dwyer had told him would happened. He remained unconvinced.

He thought again of the cops who'd stopped him and 'warned' him. He shouldn't have been surprised. Asking questions had undoubtedly aroused interest, even annoyance and sending the cops to speak to him had obviously been a sign of that, as well as an indication of Reina's power and influence. That's why he had to ask for some help himself. The fact the cops also roughed him up a bit had angered him. He wasn't used to being told what to do, and certainly not in such terms. He tended to do the opposite in those situations, and he'd gone over the various arguments in his head these past few days.

Whether Theresa expected him to exact revenge for her daughter's death or not, he didn't know. It wasn't a subject that was ever broached. So even if he did nothing, it was unlikely that she would be disappointed, or if she was, she wouldn't let him know. It was the easier option. He knew that. He could have slipped back into the life he once had, of working with Jimmy on whatever job he'd been tasked with, and trying to make a life for himself here with Theresa and the baby hoping that, in the fullness of time, she would re-engage with life and, while the pain of losing Kathleen would always be there, it might become just about tolerable some day.

That was the easy option. Doing nothing always was, but that wasn't normally what he did. Doing nothing would have stopped him picking up a weapon and joining the fight to get the British out of Ireland; doing nothing would have kept him away from Michael Collins and the War of Independence, or the special mission Collins had given him, which had taken him to Glasgow. He wondered how his friend and former comrade was doing now. He'd split opinion in Ireland by signing the treaty with Britain. More than that, he had divided the country, and not just given the Brits the six counties – Tommy was sure that Collins would fight to get them back at a later date – but the divide was a fierce one, with Irishmen taking up arms against each other. Who would have thought it would come to that? He knew what side he would have been on now if he'd still be in Ireland – standing shoulder to shoulder alongside Michael Collins – the Big Fella.

Doing nothing wasn't part of his nature and even if he'd been warned about his actions – and he had done nothing more than ask questions and show people a picture – he still had to do what he felt was right . . . and finding Kathleen's killer was the right thing to do. What he would do once he'd achieved that – if he achieved it – remained to be seen. He'd have to figure something out that kept him in the clear and his family safe.

He lit another cigarette and shook his head, trying to get rid of the images of the cops from his mind, as if, by simply shaking his head, it would dislodge the images from his brain and he'd be able to think of other things.

Whenever he glanced out of the window he could see the bunting that hung between the lamp-posts on either sidewalk. Red, white and blue, they stretched up and down the street. People had been out with ladders earlier in the day to complete the task. It was something replicated throughout the city. The Star Spangled Banner was draped out the windows of random apartments, while just about every business, be it a clothes shop, milliner's, restaurant, convenience store or butcher's, had the flag flying above the door of their business or adorning the window. Special July fourth offers were written in shaky handwriting on the glass, all in preparation to entice patriotic customers inside once daylight broke. Independence Day hats for less than ten dollars. A leg of Founding Fathers' lamb for a dollar-fifty. Add a couple of chops to make it two dollars. Freedom cookies. A bag of six for fifty cents. Wash them down with a cup of American coffee before heading out to enjoy the day's festivities.

Tommy wished that the sunrise would never come, because the decorations would only remind him of the last parade, and what had happened that day. He and Theresa would be staying in on the fourth of July. They hadn't spoken about it, but he knew that she wouldn't set foot outside the apartment at all during the day. How could they, and run the risk of inadvertently getting caught up in the celebrations, trying desperately to avoid being dragged along in the undertow of independence fervour that would no doubt be fuelled by a few surreptitious gulps of liquor. No-one would know why they'd be resisting efforts to involve them in the festivities. How could they?

It would be safer to stay out the way and out of sight, hoping that the strains of marching bands from the parades wouldn't reach as far as their building. Just to be on the safe side, the apartment windows would be closed. They would both stay away from the window throughout the day, lest their eye catch sight of the bunting. They would both just have to smoke in the kitchen.

The boy would be here too. It seemed like he was always here. Theresa was looking after him. He hadn't offered even a word of explanation for the terrible state of his arm. Tommy could only speculate about what had happened, but he could see that someone, possibly the police or one of Reina's men, had taken an iron bar, or something similar, and battered the boy's limb into submission. Tommy would occasionally watch him, and even just breathing in and out seemed to send a spasm of pain rippling through his body.

Theresa had insisted on taking care of him. She had insisted to Tommy and, in turn, Tommy had to go upstairs and explain the situation to the boy's parents. They were frantic, understandably, particularly the mother, and it was actually Theresa who had offered the soothing words of comfort, explaining that, in their quieter apartment, he would have a better chance of recovery. No-one knew what had happened. All that could be said for certain was that

Theresa had found him lying, unconscious, on the sidewalk outside their building, and from that moment onwards, her only focus was to nurse him back to full health.

Whether that would ever happen was unlikely, judging by the state of his arm, but it was better to remain optimistic, even if it was only for Joseph's sake, as he would surely read the situation. Tommy didn't imagine the boy was stupid. He would only have to look at his arm to realise the extent of the damage. He was also the only one who knew what had happened and, so far, he had shown no inclination to share that information with anyone else.

Tommy guessed that Joseph would want to avoid any of the fourth of July celebrations as much as him and Theresa. His memories of Saint Patrick's Day would be just as painful, and even more vivid, and he was certain the boy wouldn't want to re-create any of them. Everything was bound to be busier and noisier. Back in March, that had been an Irish occasion, although many people seemed to be claiming Irish heritage on the day. This time, however, it was a day for everyone to enjoy, regardless of where they originally came from. They were all Americans here and this was their special day to mark as citizens of their new country.

Children would clutch small flags in chubby hands, which they waved intermittently whenever they remembered they were carrying them. They would pester parents for food, which was in abundance and on offer at every street corner. Hot dogs. Ice-cream. Cakes. Long strips of candy in appropriate red, white and blue colours. The din of the crowd battling to be heard above the marching bands, whose procession was boosted in number by soldiers and sailors, men who had fought alongside the Brits during the Great War, marching proudly down avenues that, at times, looked as though they were being attacked by a freak summer snow storm with the shredded paper that was poured out of office windows into the air, floating chaotically until, eventually, it fell softly to the ground.

What could this day offer Tommy other than painful memories? He knew the same thought would have crossed Theresa's mind too. He imagined taking Kathleen out to enjoy the day, the little girl just as excited as he guessed she had been for Saint Patrick's Day. He shook his head, not wanting to start picturing moments that had never happened and never would.

He'd finished another cigarette and stepped over to the couch, leaving the window open to try and let a little cool air into the room, though in the stifling head of the July night, that was virtually impossible. He thought of going through to the kitchen to make some coffee, but as he sat down on the edge of the couch, yawning as he did so, he realised he was tired. Part of him was reluctant to fall asleep because his dreams scared him, but his brain was pleading with him to give it a rest. He yawned again and lay down slowly on the couch. It was warm enough that he didn't need a cover, though he would have used it if one had been there.

His eyes were heavy and it was a struggle to try and keep them open. He could feel them rolling about in their sockets and he yawned a third time, this one heavier and more prolonged than the previous two. If he was going to dream about Kathleen, there was nothing he could really do to prevent it. He was finding it difficult to keep his eyes open, and even harder to think of a reason for doing do.

The tune of *Kate's Song* was swirling round and round in his head and he began humming until he slipped quietly back into a sleep, though it was never anything other than a fitful and restless couple of hours on the couch until he woke up again, the rest of the house still sleeping.

Needle in a Haystack

He preferred her apartment to his own. It was quieter for one thing. Most of the time, it was just the two of them. She always had a cigarette hanging out her mouth, and a trail of smoke following in her wake, but he loved the smell that clung to his clothing long after he'd left and slowly trudged upstairs to his own family. At first he would knock on the door quietly, dancing nervously on his feet as he waited for her to answer. She was careful when she hugged him before standing aside so he could come in. He still couldn't lift his arm, or really move it at all, and it hung limp at his side, a reminder of the consequences of what he'd done. Lying in bed with his brothers didn't help either, no matter what position he occupied in the bed. If he rolled on to his side, he woke up screaming. If one of them rolled into him, he woke up screaming. His parents didn't seem to mind that he'd taken to sleeping downstairs in Theresa's apartment.

When he did fall asleep, it was either on the couch, when Theresa would drape a cover over him and gently kiss his forehead before turning off the light and leaving him in the soothing darkness that was only ever illuminated by pale blue streaks of moonlight pushing through the flimsy curtain, or she would let him sleep in her bed. On those nights, when she knew her husband wasn't coming home, she let him use the big bed, while she would lie in Kathleen's bed. He could never do that, not when it would only remind him of what happened.

As he lay in the big bed staring at the ceiling, he could hear Theresa crying, the steady rhythmic sobs pulsing through the thin wall dividing the rooms. He wanted to shut off the sound, blocking his ears from the pain that pierced them, but even if he tried, he could only use his right hand so the sound never left him. Sometimes it made him cry too and he would roll over on to his side and bury his head in the pillow. He cried softly, almost silently, not wanting to let Theresa hear him.

He wondered whether he should go in and see if she was alright, but something held him back. He still felt it was his fault. She had told him to look after her daughter and he hadn't been able to, so maybe if she saw him when she was upset, it would just remind her of that. It was painful listening to her, but he didn't know what else to do.

There were times when no-one answered his knock on the door, so he would turn the handle and push the door open – it was never locked – and walk into the apartment. Theresa might be dozing on an armchair or sleeping in Kathleen's bed. He even walked in on her singing at the kitchen sink one day. She looked round guiltily, as if there was no justification for her singing after all the sadness and heartache she had suffered. He liked when she sang. She had a lovely voice and he wished he could hear it more often.

Most times when he walked in to the apartment uninvited, it was empty. He'd wander slowly from room to room, shouting 'Hello?' and 'Theresa?' without ever getting a reply. She had insisted that he call her by her first name, which had sounded strange at first when he'd said it, but he soon got used to it. He would pour himself a cup of water and then sit in the living room, waiting until she arrived home. It didn't seem to bother or startle her when she came in and found him sitting there as if it was his own house.

'Hello,' she'd say, either sitting down on the chair opposite to loosen the laces of her shoes before slipping her tired feet out of them, or trudging through to the kitchen with the bags of shopping she carried. On those days he would head in to the kitchen behind her, helping to put everything away, happy to stand silently and wait for instructions as to where all the items should go. When it was all packed away in the correct cupboards and drawers, Theresa would make a pot of tea and they would sit at the table, both of them slurping their tea, content with that noise without the need to engage in any conversation.

Today he had walked into the apartment and found her already at the kitchen table, a pile of cigarette ends mounting up on the saucer in front of her. She was enveloped in a haze that hovered like a spectre round her body.

She didn't look up, so he filled the kettle with fresh water and put it on the stove, taking the book of matches that was on the table and lighting the gas under the kettle. He rinsed out two cups until they looked more or less clean, and put them on the table. It was a slow and awkward process, but one that he was beginning to cope with as his right arm became accustomed to its increased activity. Even the clatter of the cups as he put them down failed to get a reaction from Theresa.

When he had filled the cups up with tea, clouds of

steam spiralled up from the hot surface and he sat down and pressed his right hand round his own cup, allowing the heat to warm through to his flesh. He looked at the pile of cigarette ends and then at the smouldering one in Theresa's hand, and he was tempted to take one out of the packet and smoke it himself. The taste of the nicotine was already coating his tongue every time he breathed in the clouds of smoke swirling around the kitchen. He'd tried cigarettes before but they had made him sick when he'd inhaled too much nicotine in one go. He contented himself with savouring Theresa's smoke, though if she wasn't here, he might have tried one again. He didn't want his coughing and spluttering to disturb her, however.

Eventually, she stubbed out her cigarette which had just about burnt down to nothing and sat back with a heavy sigh. Automatically, she picked up the cup and took a gulp of tea. It had cooled down enough for her to drink, and she had soon drained the cup of its contents.

'How's your arm?'

Joseph wasn't sure if he'd heard her right, or even if she had spoken at all. Her eyes still stared off into space and her hands clutched blindly in front of her until they located the pack of cigarettes. She instinctively retrieved one and lit it without glancing once at what she was doing.

'Is it still sore?'

He looked down at his arm, bruised and swollen, and his hand, crushed and useless.

'Yes,' he said.

'That's a shame.'

He didn't know what to say. She must have heard him, even though she barely acknowledged him. He didn't even know if she liked him always being in the apartment, though she had never once said anything. Tommy was out most of the time. They weren't husband and wife. Joseph knew that from overhearing his own parents speaking when the Irishman had moved in, but when he and Theresa were both in the apartment they seemed to move awkwardly around each other like they were strangers. He was used to seeing his own mother and father talking and laughing and shouting and fighting and kissing and making up; the creak of the bed or the occasional gasps or moans which could be heard through the walls was always a sign that they had made up. He saw nothing between Theresa and Tommy. They hardly ever spoke to each other. He did try, sometimes, even if it was just to ask her how she was feeling but, more often than not, she never replied. Maybe that was why Tommy stayed away so often now?

'You're a good boy,' Theresa mumbled, her mouth barely able to form the words. It was like she was drunk and slurring her speech. Her eyes were beginning to roll and occasionally he could only see the whites of her eyes, which made him shiver.

He stood up and took her by the elbow, gently at first but then with a greater firmness when she ignored that prompting. She stood up slowly, letting the cigarette slip out of her grasp. It dropped to the floor and Joseph immediately stamped on it. He knew he would have to guide her, since he could only really use one arm, but she let him steer her with little nudges and squeezes until they were in Kathleen's bedroom.

She waited at the edge of the bed while he pulled the cover back and then she slowly climbed on to the mattress and lay down, her head sinking into the pillow which still held the impression from when she had previously lain there. Her eyes shut immediately and it seemed like she was already sleeping. A tiny smile broke out on the edges of her mouth as if her body was grateful for the rest.

Joseph watched as her shoulders rose and fell with an almost hypnotic regularity. He remembered when his mother had put him to bed when he wasn't well. Those were rare occasions when he was allowed the bed to himself, for an hour or two at least. She would pull the cover up until it was at his chin and only his head peeked out. Then she would lean in close to him and gently plant a kiss on his forehead.

'Go to sleep, my precious boy,' she'd whisper, and even though his eyes were shut tight, he heard her voice and it always made him smile.

Joseph stood up and then leant over the bed until he was close to Theresa's face. His lips barely grazed her cheek and he only mouthed 'Goodnight,' but it still felt like the right thing to do. It wasn't even evening either, but he couldn't think what else to say. He watched her for a few more minutes, and it seemed like for the first time since Kathleen's death, that she actually looked peaceful and content. He knew that was only an illusion, however, and even if there was a temporary respite in her dreams, it was only that, and when she woke up, after those initial few seconds when her brain was adjusting to being awake, the gut-wrenching, agonising, never-ending pain would engulf her again, and it would take an enormous effort just to pull the cover back and think about getting out of bed. He knew that was how she would feel because that's the way he felt too.

He slipped quietly out of the apartment, closing the door behind him and stood in the hallway. He glanced towards the stairs which led up to his own home but quickly turned and started walking the other way until he was outside. He kept walking, not wanting to bump into any of his family, and he didn't stop until he was a couple of blocks away. He didn't want to meet them or face any of their questions. He knew that he could come and go as he pleased anyway. It wasn't like his parents had thrown him out, but Theresa had offered to look after him, and it was one less mouth to feed and one more space in bed at night.

They had wanted to know what happened, of course, though they knew they wouldn't get any information from Joseph, who had resumed his vow of silence. He only spoke when he was alone with Theresa. Whatever Tommy had told them seemed to suffice as an explanation, though as he glanced down again at his arm, he wondered why they hadn't made more of a fuss about it. He didn't know because he never spoke and was spending as little time as he could in the house, preferring the sad solitude of downstairs.

He was heading for the Ninth Avenue Elevated train, and cut up 42nd Street to where the station was. He stopped outside Rabovitz's Deli, halted as much by the smells drifting out of the open door as by the sight of all the freshly-baked goods piled in the window. He pressed his nose against the glass, breathing on it until the window steamed up and he couldn't see any more. Then, he rubbed his sleeve on the pane to clear it.

'What are you doing there?' a voice shouted from the doorway. 'Leave my window alone.'

He looked up at an old man shuffling towards him, shaking his head and scowling.

'I clean those windows and you mess them up. Get away. Go!'

Joseph stepped back slightly as the baker got closer. He had a cloth in his hand and he began wiping the glass where Joseph's sleeve had done just the same thing moments before. The wet material glided over the surface, taking away any remnants of Joseph's breath. The old man shook his head again.

'You are a nuisance,' he said.

'Sorry,' Joseph mumbled.

The old man frowned, though Joseph sensed he wasn't really angry. His face looked tired, rather than irritated, and he took off his spectacles, wiping his eyes before putting them back on again. He stared at Joseph, looking him up and down.

'What happened to you,' he said, gesturing towards the bandaged limb which hung at his side.

Joseph shrugged.

'Who did this to you?'

Again, Joseph shrugged, and the baker threw his hands in the air, muttering something in a language Joseph didn't understand. He began heading back into the shop before stopping and glancing back.

'Are you hungry?'

Joseph nodded enthusiastically.

'Wait here,' he instructed before disappearing inside his shop. Joseph stood on the same spot, his eyes remaining focused on the doorway and refusing to be distracted by any passers-by, heading up and down the sidewalk outside the baker's. After a couple of minutes, the old man re-appeared. He was holding a brown paper bag.

'Here,' he said, holding it out to Joseph who hesitated for a moment, before the bag was thrust towards him. 'This will fill your stomach.'

The bag was still warm. Joseph could feel the heat radiating out through the paper. He was desperate to find out what was inside but wasn't sure whether it would be rude to look while the baker was still standing in front of him.

'Thank you,' he managed to say, though without looking up at the baker.

'They are very good. I made them myself.'

Joseph nodded.

'Now, on your way,' the baker said, and Joseph started to move away from the front of the shop. 'And don't be messing up my window any more,' he said with a laugh.

Joseph didn't look back, though he suspected the old man would already be heading inside his shop to take his place behind the counter. He clutched the bag close to his chest, feeling the heat cling to his clothes. He took a deep breath. The smell was incredible, enough to make his mouth water, and he was tempted to stop and delve into what he was sure would be the delicious contents, but he resisted. He'd decided that he would wait until he was on the train. The thought of how the baking would taste when it rested in his mouth after he'd taken his first bite was enough to make him increase his pace.

Soon enough, he had reached 42nd Street Station, paid

the two-nickel fare, and took his seat on the train which, thankfully, had arrived just as he stepped on to the platform. As soon as he sat down, he opened the brown bag and almost stuck his nose into it, just to savour the smell again. There were bagels – three of them. He took the first one out and sank his teeth into it, taking a large bite which just about filled his mouth. He chewed on the pastry, though some of the chunks he swallowed were enough to make him cough.

'Watch you don't choke to death on that, sonny,' a woman's voice said just behind him and he glanced round. 'That smells good enough to eat.'

Joseph nodded, turning round so that he had his back to her. She was big enough to completely fill her seat, though she still managed to get a shopping bag squashed in beside her. Her skin was black as night, while her eyes were like the moon. He remembered his father's warning, issued many times to him and his brothers and sisters.

'Don't you be speaking to those coloured folk,' he'd said, while his mother would nod in agreement. 'They're not like us, so just stick to your own kind.'

Joseph didn't really know what his father meant, and neither did any of his siblings and, anyway, they never came into contact with any 'coloured folk' anyway. Joseph finished the first of the bagels and his right hand immediately searched out another one. He heard the woman take a deep breath and then almost groan as she sighed.

'Sure smells good on this train,' she said with a laugh that filled the carriage.

Joseph looked round. There was a man further down the carriage reading a newspaper, while a grey-haired woman slumped against the window sleeping across from him. Apart from that, the carriage was empty. Joseph glanced up at the black woman and then back at his pastry. Slowly, he stretched out his arm, holding the bag out for her.

'Don't mind if I do,' she said, her chubby hand plunging into the bag and grabbing the last bagel, almost seeming to squeeze the life out of it. Crumbs fell on to the chair which she didn't seem to notice as she began stuffing the pastry into her mouth.

'Where are you heading, honey?' she mumbled, though her mouth was so full that Joseph could hardly make out any of the words. 'You going home?' she said.

He shook his head. He turned away from her and stared towards the front of the train. He didn't want to speak with her and he hoped that his silence would soon discourage her questions. It seemed to work with everyone else. He could hear her munching her way through the pastry, and soon enough it was finished. He was glad there weren't any more in the bag otherwise he was sure she would ask for another one.

'That was de-licious,' she said, and he could hear her licking her lips in satisfaction. She was right, too. The pastries were lovely and he ran his own tongue across his lips, hoping to catch any stray crumbs that might have been left behind.

He was going as far as Sedgwick Avenue Station, and thankfully the woman didn't want to pursue a conversation with him. She did shout goodbye as he made his way to the door, waiting until the train had slowly rumbled its way into the station and come to a halt at the platform before he opened it and stepped down without looking back at her. A few people were waiting to board the train although they held back until he was past them before darting for the door. He wanted to get away from the crowd, not least because someone might bang into his arm.

Once he'd walked down the stairs and out on to the street, he stopped. He hadn't thought about what he was going to do beyond reaching this point. He knew this was the neighbourhood where they had taken him, though it would still be unlikely that he'd actually spot the man he had drawn, or indeed, the big man who was obviously the boss. He started walking along the street, kicking any stray stones that were in his path.

He had wanted to get out of the apartment, to feel like he was doing something to help try and find Kathleen's killer. He'd drawn the pictures, and that had got him into a whole heap of trouble, and though he'd never actually explained who the drawing was of, he hoped that someone would get the message. That's what he thought Tommy would realise, though he hadn't seen him for a while now, so there was no way of knowing.

Skipping across the road, he walked for a couple of blocks before realising that he could be here all day and not find anything. He began walking along Summit Avenue, aiming to get to the end of the block and then double back along West 162nd and head towards the train station, when he saw the car parked on the other side of the road, in Cross Street. It was a Chevrolet. He stopped and stared at it, closing his eyes to get a better picture. In his mind he heard the screeching of tyres and the car racing round the corner of West 34th, almost spinning on to its roof before the driver managed to regain control as it continued its pursuit of the car in front. His vantage point was on the edge of the kerb, with a little girl standing beside him, holding his hand. There was the sound of firecrackers . . . no, it was gunshots.

He opened his eyes again and knew that he was staring at the car that had been there the day Kathleen was shot. That was the vehicle the killer was in. It was also the car which had taken him. Automatically, he felt on edge, glancing in either direction before taking a few nervous steps backwards until he was leaning against a railing outside a tenement building. His eyes never left the car, even as he slowly headed back up the street, making a mental note of the address, and where the car was parked. If that was the car, then Angelo might not be too far away, he realised, though the thought sent a shiver down his spine and he suddenly longed for the comfort of Theresa's apartment, and to hear her soothing voice as he drifted off to sleep. He would have broken into a run but the impact would have been too sore on his arm, but his pace did quicken, almost in time with his heartbeat, until he came into sight of the station, and he knew that he was on his way home.

Killing Time

There was a knock on the door and they both turned round at the same time. It was a welcome distraction, breaking up the awkward silence that seemed to have taken up residence. It was just the two of them, sitting in a lonely apartment like two strangers thrown together. Sometimes, Tommy found himself wondering why he was still here. A sense of duty? A feeling of guilt?

They said little to each other. She never asked him how his work had been. He asked how she was feeling, but her replies were short and stilted. He preferred the smoky silence which now enveloped them.

'Who do you think it is?' Theresa asked without looking at him.

'I don't know.'

She remained standing by the sink as Tommy got up and walked across the kitchen, a trail of smoke lingering in his wake from the cigarette in his hand. He could hear the tap running as he walked into the hallway. Theresa was either filling the kettle or getting a glass of water.

Father Mike stood at the door when Tommy opened it. His face was grim, the way it had been on Saint Patrick's Day when he'd broken the news about Kathleen.

'Who's died?' Tommy asked and Father Mike shook his head.

'Not here, Tommy. Let's take a walk.'

'I'm just heading out,' Tommy shouted back into the house, closing the door without waiting for a reply, though he doubted he'd get one anyway.

Father Mike swiftly led the way down the stairs and out into the street. He glanced over his shoulder briefly, just to check Tommy was still behind him, before taking off. Tommy almost had to break into a jog to keep up with the priest, who was striding purposefully along the sidewalk, quickly passing one block and then another.

'Where are we going?' Tommy asked, but he got no response. 'Father Mike!'

The priest was just about running himself now and Tommy was almost out of breath.

'Michael!'

This time he shouted and the priest stopped suddenly.

'Sorry,' he said.

'Where the hell are we going?' Tommy said, puffing and panting as he stopped alongside the priest.

'I just need to keep moving,' Father Mike said. 'I had to get out.'

'What's wrong?'

'We're almost at Bryant Park. Let's get a seat there and I'll tell you.'

Tommy knew it wouldn't be good news. He wracked his brain, trying to guess what it might be, but he could think of nothing. The truth was, he couldn't imagine things could get any worse for him, so he walked the last block in silence alongside the priest, who had now slowed down to a more civilised pace, with a sense of curiosity rather than real foreboding.

Bryant Park was four blocks from his house. It was a small, compact oasis of greenery amidst the concrete jungle of the city, though the elevated railway line cast a shadow over swathes of the park. It made him laugh when he thought about railway tracks in the air, and he was sure no-one back home would ever believe him if he tried to describe it. There were several wooden benches dotted around the perfect square of the park, and Father Mike stopped at the first one they came to, and sat down. Tommy followed suit, immediately perching himself on the edge of the bench and staring round at the priest. Father Mike took a deep breath and stared back. Tommy's curiosity was certainly aroused now. The priest dealt with death every day. It was part and parcel of the job, so it would have to take something really bad to unsettle him.

Tommy studied the priest who was probably his closest friend in New York, perhaps his only friend. Father Mike's hair was cropped short and Tommy was suddenly aware of how grey it was. He'd never noticed it before. He guessed the priest was in his sixties. He was a tall man, well over six feet, and he generally strode into a room, back erect, towering over everyone else, and he would dominate, aided by the natural authority and respect that came with the uniform.

He had answered the call to help that had come via a letter from Tommy's uncle. The letter had travelled to the United States almost at the same time as Tommy. Thankfully, it had arrived before him, so there was at least one friendly face waiting for him in the city. He had known

Tommy's uncle for a long time, a friendship forged during studies for the priesthood in Rome, and maintained through correspondence over many years, with the occasional meeting when church business allowed for it.

He had been the first person Tommy's uncle had turned to when he needed help for his nephew. They'd hatched a plan of escape that was, at best, haphazard, or worse, was bound to fail. That it didn't owed much to good fortune, perhaps some divine intervention, and Father Mike's assistance. Tommy had asked his uncle for help. It still seemed ironic to him, given that he'd originally headed to the Scottish island of Benbecula to kill the old man. Instead, he confessed that he needed to get away from everything, mainly his life as an IRA assassin, and he couldn't see how that was possible, not when the war with the British was still going on. If the Brits didn't kill him, and they'd tried their hardest during his mission to Glasgow, then his comrades might do so once he'd turned his back on them.

A new life in a new land seemed like the perfect solution. It was the only solution and that's where Father Mike came in. He was there to meet Tommy when he arrived in the city. He gave him and food and shelter, and even when Tommy began to make his way in this new world, choosing paths he knew the priest wouldn't be happy about, he remained someone Tommy could always turn to when he needed help. That had already proved to be the case after Kathleen died, and it would no doubt continue to be the case in the future. For now, though, it looked as though it was Father Mike who was more in need of help than Tommy.

'The Big Fella's dead,' Father Mike eventually said

quickly, almost breathlessly, though he slumped back in the bench after he managed to get the words out, as if the effort of doing so had drained him.

'What?'

The priest stared at Tommy, almost resentful of having to repeat himself.

'He's dead. The Big Fella.'

'Michael Collins?'

Tommy frowned at the priest, who nodded slowly, blessing himself as he did so.

'Michael Collins is dead?' Tommy asked. Father Mike nodded again.

'I don't understand,' said Tommy. 'It's the Big Fella . . . The Brits would never get him. He's too smart for them.'

Father Mike buried his head in his hands and sighed deeply.

'What is it? Mike!'

The priest looked up.

'I don't know for sure what happened, Tommy. Just that he died. Shot dead in an ambush. We did it.'

'Who?' Tommy whispered.

'The IRA. Somewhere in County Cork. They ambushed his car. The Big Fella got shot . . . Killed by a fellow Irishman. What sort of world are we living in, Tommy?'

Tommy sat back on the bench and closed his eyes. Immediately, Michael Collins was there before him, barking orders to volunteers, sharing a joke and a smoke with others, playfully wrestling with his comrades, Tommy included. He tried to remember the last time he'd seen his leader. His friend. It was in a safe house in Dublin, as he waited to head over to Glasgow on a mission that Collins had given him. He'd turned up to wish him good luck. There had never been any doubt that he would accept the mission. It was an order, after all, and there was nothing to do except obey it. It was also the Big Fella, and Tommy would have done anything for him.

Sometimes he still felt guilty for abandoning the war and escaping to New York to make a new life for himself. When he did that he knew there was little chance, if any, of seeing Michael Collins again. Yet, that was his choice and the prospect of one day returning to Ireland, though slim, still remained an option that was open to him. He never, at any point, imagined it would be an Ireland without Michael Collins. He knew the Big Fella wasn't immortal, but he didn't believe that anyone could kill him. What was worse was the fact that it had been a fellow Irishman who had pulled the trigger and done England's bidding. Tommy blessed himself. He didn't know why. It was an automatic gesture, but it seemed like the right thing to do.

'Are you okay?' Father Mike asked.

'I don't know.'

'Here,' the priest said, offering him a cigarette.

'I can't believe it,' Tommy said.

'I'm going to say a Mass for him.'

'When?'

'This Friday night.'

'How do you think that'll go down?'

'I don't care,' the priest shrugged.

'There are plenty of people who'll be happy at the news.'

'Happy?' the priest said. 'At a man's death? And a fellow Irishman too.'

'You know what I mean. He was a hero to some and a

traitor to others. Sure, the country's at war with itself over that bloody Treaty.'

'Every man deserves a prayer in God's house, Tommy, no matter what their sins might be or what anyone else might say.'

'But there will still be some who won't be happy about it.'

'To hell with them. If they've got a problem, they can speak to me and I'll soon put them right.'

Tommy thought of the Treaty that Michael Collins had signed. It had heralded the civil war, but more than that, it had led to his death. Tommy would have sided with the Big Fella if he had still been in Ireland, regardless of his own misgivings about it. He had fought because he wanted an end to British rule and freedom for the island of Ireland, all thirty-two counties, and for him, too much blood had been split to compromise with the enemy. But he knew that he would have remained loyal and that would always remain the case.

He remembered the drunk man outside the baker's on Saint Patrick's Day, drinking a toast in the hope of Michael Collins' death, and he wondered if that man was slumped somewhere in a drunken stupor at this moment, having celebrated the news from Ireland that he had wished for.

'Well, I'll be there for sure,' Tommy said.

'Even if people don't want to go on the Friday night, there will still be prayers said on Sunday, so they won't be able to avoid it.'

'Are you looking for a fight then?'

'Maybe.'

Tommy dropped the cigarette end at his feet and stood on it. His fingers craved another cigarette, but he realised that his own packet was still sitting on the kitchen table, keeping Theresa company as she sat in the silence of the apartment that would feel less awkward because he was no longer there. Bryant Park was quiet. An old couple sat on one of the benches across from them. The man was reading a newspaper – it looked like the *New York Evening Journal* – and he would open up the pages, trying to make sure the wind which occasionally swooped down and through the park didn't attack and destroy his paper. His wife sat beside him, content to stare ahead of her. Tommy wasn't sure if she even noticed the occasional passer-by who walked through the park. The couple – he presumed they were husband and wife – didn't once speak to each other. He guessed they had been married for many years, so maybe the well of conversation they'd once thought would never run dry, had eventually been completely drained. The two of them looked happy enough, and he wondered how that could be when the silence between him and Theresa felt so painful?

A man in a suit was walking towards them from the far side of the park. Tommy studied him as Father Mike handed him another cigarette, which he accepted gratefully. He kept his eyes on the man as he got nearer. It looked like he was talking to himself. His lips were moving as if in conversation with an invisible companion, while he kept touching the rim of his trilby. As he passed by their bench, his lips continuing to move, Tommy couldn't hear the man's voice and he wondered whether it was a silent prayer, a decade of the rosary perhaps, as he continued on his way.

'So how are things at home?'

Tommy glanced round, his attention, which had been focused on the praying man, suddenly distracted. He turned to look at Father Mike, who stared straight ahead of him, smoking. Had the priest actually spoken or had he just imagined it? Eventually, Father Mike turned to face him, raising his eyebrows. Tommy shrugged. He didn't know what to say.

'She's having to cope with a lot of sadness,' the priest said. 'To bury your own child . . . I can't imagine how that must feel.'

'I know. It's hard.'

Tommy realised that it wasn't just Theresa he couldn't speak to about it. He didn't know what to say to Father Mike either. If the priest was looking for a reply, he didn't say, but if he was, he'd be waiting a long time. He had been a father, more or less, with a little girl who called him 'daddy'. She was gone now and it was a sadness that weighed heavily on him too. But he was a man. There were no tears allowed, no sign of weakness to be shown, no wallowing in self-pity. He was focused on other things anyway, though he didn't mention any of that to Father Mike.

'Stay strong for her, Tommy,' the priest said. 'The last thing she needs now is to lose you as well.'

Tommy wasn't sure that was true, but he never said anything, instead nodding at the priest as if he agreed with what he was being told.

Blast from the Past

Tommy knew where they were going without even having to ask Jimmy. Well, at least he guessed who they were going to see, even if he wasn't sure of the location. Normally, whenever Jimmy picked him up, he'd mention what the job was and where it would be, if he hadn't already done so beforehand, but when Tommy stepped into the car, Jimmy started driving without saying anything. He asked questions without getting any reply, and Tommy soon realised that no information would be forthcoming. He wasn't sure whether it was just his imagination, but he sensed that Jimmy was on edge. They were going to see Big Bill Dwyer.

He rolled down the window so there was a gap he could blow smoke out of. If Jimmy was nervous – and Tommy might be wrong about that – then he was relieved. Ever since they'd stolen Reina's truck, taking the booze before setting it on fire, he'd been impatient to find out what was going to happen next. He was getting fed up with Jimmy brushing off his questions, always muttering that 'the devil's in the detail'. He just wanted to know what those details were. As far as he could tell, nothing had changed after the truck heist, or if it had, no-one had told him.

Reina might have made enquiries. He might have sent Kathleen's killer to look for whoever had stolen his truck, for all that Tommy knew. Jimmy was his only link to Bill Dwyer, and Jimmy wasn't saying anything. He probably didn't know anything either, but he was less anxious about it. That's why Tommy was surprised now to see the other man display such obvious signs of unease. Maybe he should be more nervous too, but he was glad of another opportunity to speak to Dwyer. Whether he would still feel the same way after hearing what the gang boss had to say to him remained to be seen.

He hadn't said anything to Jimmy but it struck him that stealing the truck was only designed to deliver Bill a free consignment of liquor, with Tommy taking all the risks of stealing the vehicle and then destroying it. At any time, he could have been caught, and the consequences of that would have been fatal. 'The devil's in the detail,' they kept telling him. He would find out soon enough if that was true.

The journey didn't take long. Tommy wondered why they hadn't just walked. It was only about ten blocks from where Jimmy had picked him up, and the sun hovering in the blue sky tracked them until they arrived at their destination. Jimmy stopped his car outside a café and glanced at it before getting out the car. Tommy followed him and they walked inside, a small bell ringing above them as they pushed the door open. Mrs Lafferty's Café was quiet as they stood at the counter. Two men sat facing each other, their heads almost touching as they spoke quietly to each other while also glancing at the sheet of paper on the table in front of them. A mother sipped a cup of tea while checking the pram beside her. Tommy wondered if she was making sure the baby was still breathing, or praying that it was still asleep so that she could enjoy a few moments respite. In the far corner, a priest was stuffing a large slice of chocolate cake into his mouth. He didn't look up when the bell rang.

'Table for two?' the man standing behind the cash register asked.

'We're here for a meeting,' Jimmy said, glancing towards the door at the other end of the counter.

'Who will I say is calling?' the man said as he made his way towards the door.

'It's Jimmy Healy.'

'And?' he asked, looking at Tommy.

'Tommy Delaney,' said Jimmy.

The man disappeared beyond the door and Jimmy kept his eyes focused on it, even as Tommy surveyed the café again. A strong aroma of coffee was battling for supremacy with strawberry cheesecake, and for the briefest of seconds, that smell made Tommy think of someone special he had known in Glasgow. He wondered whether it was, in fact, the smell or whether it was just that, after the news of Michael Collins' death, events from that time, and from his past, were now at the forefront of his mind. The priest had finished his cake and was mopping up the stray crumbs with his tongue, holding the plate up to his mouth and devouring them. The mother was smoking and she savoured every draw, which was long and slow and heavy. Tommy was tempted to light up as well, but he didn't want to do so in case, as soon as he had, they'd be called through to see Bill, and he'd have to leave the barely-smoked cigarette behind, letting it smoulder on the floor if he didn't have enough time to stand on it.

It couldn't have been more than a couple of minutes before the man re-appeared, holding the door open.

'Come on through, gentlemen,' he said, and Jimmy led the way with Tommy close behind them. Only the priest seemed to pay any attention to them, though even he was slightly distracted as he lit a cigarette, sitting back and blowing out smoke rings like he was performing tricks for captivated kids. His belly was large and round, much more so than Theresa's currently was, and he would occasionally caress it too, though Tommy knew that at no point would the bump kick him because it had been disturbed.

When they stepped through the door, the man led the way along a narrow corridor before opening another door at the far end. He stood aside as Tommy and Jimmy walked in, and then he closed the door and disappeared back out to take his place at the front counter, serving people hot tea and coffee, or alcohol hidden under the counter to those who knew how to give him the correct nod or wink, and cash, of course.

It was a large room they were in, at least the size of the front room in his apartment, Tommy thought. Facing them, Bill Dwyer sat behind a large desk. Just like when Tommy had met him in the bar, a bottle of rum was on the desk beside a glass that was half-full and a smouldering cigarette which was perched on an ashtray. He smiled at the two men, gesturing for them to sit down. A two-seater couch was pressed against the wall to Bill's left, and both Jimmy and Tommy dropped on to it, immediately sinking into the soft cushions. Both of them tried to push themselves forward, though it took a bit of effort until they were perched on the edge of the couch. Facing them was

Gorevin who sat comfortably on an armchair. He was smoking too, and an ashtray was perched on the arm of his chair. He stared at them without making any gesture or expression. Another man whom Tommy didn't recognise, stood at the back of the room, hands clasped behind his back. He was also watching them

Bill opened up a drawer in his desk and took out two glasses, putting them on the desk.

'What can I get you, gentlemen?' he asked.

Tommy hesitated, glancing at Jimmy, who cleared his throat.

'Scotch, Bill, thanks very much,' he said.

'Same for me,' muttered Tommy with a nod.

'Scotch it is then,' Bill said, going into another drawer and producing a bottle of scotch. He poured them both a generous measure and then gestured for them to take the glasses. Jimmy was first off the couch and he picked up both glasses, handing one to Tommy as he sat back down, this time being more careful not to sink into the furniture. Simultaneously, they both took a sip. Jimmy let out a sigh of satisfaction, while Tommy had to stifle a cough as the liquid raced down his throat, leaving a burning sensation in its wake. He held on to the glass, but was reluctant to take another sip. Bill, as he had done before, drained his glass of rum and filled it up again.

'You did well with Reina's truck,' he said, picking up the cigarette and drawing on it. 'It did the job nicely.'

'Did you get any response?'

Tommy could sense Jimmy glaring at him, though he didn't want to look round and catch the disapproving look from his companion. He knew Jimmy would believe he'd broken some unwritten etiquette about speaking to Bill – basically, that you waited until you were spoken to and invited to respond before opening your mouth. Tommy didn't have the time for such intricacies of behaviour. He needed to know what had happened about the truck, otherwise what had been the point. Bill, evidently, wasn't too bothered by the question.

'Tommy here is not a happy man,' said Bill, laughing. 'Reina wants to find out who did this. There's money been offered, a reward for information. A grand, I believe.'

Jimmy whistled, but Tommy kept looking at Bill. There were three words he was desperate to say but they were the hardest ones of all. 'Is that it?' That's what he wanted to ask. Reina had put up a few dollars to try and find out who had stolen the truck. 'Is that it?' A thousand dollars for someone like Reina was nothing, and if nothing else happened, then he would eventually forget about what happened and write it off as a hazard of the job. 'Is that it?' He could have been caught, shot, tortured or killed. They told him the devil was in the detail, but there didn't seem to be much detail, although there definitely was a devil, and maybe more than one.

'Our friend here is not a patient man,' Bill said, smiling, and Tommy could sense all eyes on him.

'It's not that, Bill, it's just . . .'

'It's just that you wanted someone's head delivered on a plate to you.'

Tommy shrugged.

'It's not that simple, Tommy. I told you, I don't want a war with Gaetano Reina or the Lucchese family.'

'I know, Bill.'

'So you need to trust me. Do you trust me, Tommy?'

Tommy looked up as Bill stubbed out his cigarette. His eyes never left Tommy.

'Yes, Bill,' he said. 'I trust you.'

'Good man. Stealing the truck was only the first move . . . Do you play chess, Tommy?'

'No.'

'It is a wonderful game. You should learn.'

Tommy nodded.

'Well, we've got a few moves to make in this game before we achieve checkmate.'

Tommy nodded again, though he wasn't sure what Bill was talking about. He had never played the game before. He had sometimes seen men appearing in the park when he used to sit there, producing a chess board and putting it on the bench between them, quickly becoming engrossed in their game as they moved the small wooden pieces across the board. He didn't understand what they were doing, so quickly lost interest after a few minutes.

'And the next move will put us closer to a winning position, certainly as far as you're concerned, Tommy.'

Bill glanced at Gorevin, who hadn't moved until this point, but he now stood up and walked to the back of the room, taking a bag off the man standing there. He returned to the desk and put the bag on top of it. Bill stood up, gesturing for Tommy and Jimmy to stand up as well.

'What do you think is my most valuable possession?' Bill asked.

Tommy looked at him, and then at the other two men standing in front of the desk, hoping for some help or at least a hint of what the answer might be.

'I don't know, Bill.'

'Information, Tom. That is priceless.'

Tommy stared at Bill now, who smiled back at him. Had he heard right? Had Bill just called him 'Tom'? He glanced at Gorevin, who gave him a short smile. He had been the last man to call him that, and now he was beginning to think that wasn't a coincidence either.

'So you've come to me, asking for help in finding the man who killed your daughter. I understand that, Tom, and I respect it. Who among us here wouldn't do the exact same thing if, God forbid, we were ever in that situation? And you need my help because you can't do it alone. I want to help you, Tom, because what happened is wrong, and we also have to look out for each other. But I need you to help me.'

Tommy stared at Bill, sensing that the best thing to do was to say nothing. When he needed to speak, then he would do so, but he didn't know what Bill wanted him to do, and the fact he was calling him 'Tom' only put him on edge. He'd replayed Gorevin's words in his head over and over again. Sometimes he believed that he'd deliberately called him 'Tom' and he was making him aware that he knew about his past, while other times, he decided it was just a coincidence. There was no coincidence about Bill doing it, however. He knew that, but it was still better to wait for the gang boss to show his hand.

Gorevin stepped forward and opened the bag, taking out a Smith and Weston rifle and placing it on the desk before taking the bag and placing it beside his seat. Tommy looked at the rifle, and then at Bill.

'Information is power, Tom Costello.'

Tommy nodded, while Gorevin let out a short, sharp laugh

'How did you find out?' Tommy asked.

'It's my job to know these things, Tom. And I have Francis here to thank for that,' he said, nodding at Gorevin,

'Who's Tom Costello?' Jimmy asked.

'Sorry, Jimmy. Let me introduce you. This is Tom Costello.'

Jimmy looked at Tommy with a puzzled look and Tommy shrugged.

'Tom here fought with Michael Collins,' Bill said.

'You fought the Brits?' Jimmy asked.

Tommy nodded.

'In nineteen-sixteen?'

He nodded again.

Jimmy whistled. The rest of the story was too long and complicated to share with Jimmy. Maybe some other time. He had no wish to share it with the rest of the room just now either. He wasn't sure how much Bill really knew but it was enough to know who he was and what he did.

'You think you know someone,' Jimmy said. 'You're a dark horse, Tommy boy.'

'And now we have Tom Costello, one of the best shots the IRA ever had, here before us, in this city and in this room. It is a pleasure and a privilege, sir,' Bill said with a brief, mocking bow.

Gorevin smiled again.

Bill picked the rifle up, grinning as he did so. He held it out for Tommy.

'Here, take it. You know you want to hold it.'

Tommy hesitated. It had been a long time since he had

held a weapon like that. Before, when he used a rifle, it always felt like an extension of his arm. Now, he was nervous, and not just because he'd hoped never again to hold a weapon like this. He didn't know what Bill wanted and he feared that it would mean he'd be doing a lot more than just holding the gun. Bill held the rifle out.

Tommy hesitated, but as soon as he grasped it, he knew that this was his weapon. He remembered lying in cold, damp fields, his eye staring through the sight, his fingertips poised on the trigger, anticipating the recoil that would slam the butt of the rifle into his shoulder. He had killed men with a weapon such as this many times before, too many to recall. He went through the motions of checking the loading action of the gun before pointing it at the window and staring through the sight, finger on the trigger again.

'Old habits die hard, Tom.'

Tommy lowered the rifle and turned to stare at Bill. It seemed strange that the news of Michael Collins' death had barely filtered across the Atlantic Ocean, a memory of the life he left behind, and suddenly his past was rising up to confront him. It was as if they'd always known who, and what he was, but it was only with Collins out of the way that they were able to confront him about it.

'So who told you?'

Bill shook his head. 'I can't tell you that, Tom. Confidentiality is almost as important as the information itself. It's enough that I know. Francis is my eyes and ears in Hell's Kitchen.'

Tommy looked at Gorevin again, who held his gaze without blinking. He could only imagine that he'd persuaded Father Mike to reveal Tommy's secret. He felt disappointed.

He thought the priest would have maintained a confessional confidentiality with the information, but he'd obviously been induced or intimidated. Either way, his secret was no longer that. He put the rifle back down on the table.

'Did that feel good, Tom?' Bill asked, taking a drink of rum.

Tommy shrugged.

'You always told me you hated guns,' Jimmy said. 'You could hardly bear to touch them whenever I gave you them.'

'I do hate touching them.'

'That's not what I'm hearing.'

'That was in the past, Jimmy. I'm not that person any more.'

'Well, I hope that's not quite true, Tom,' said Bill. 'Sit down, have another drink.'

They all sat down again, including Gorevin, who slowly lit a cigarette. A few stray fragments of ash floated on to his black suit and he lightly brushed them away before crossing his legs. Tommy and Jimmy remained perched on the edge of the couch, their eyes focused on Bill, though Tommy sensed Gorevin's eyes boring into him. Bill filled up the glasses with scotch and then stood up, picking them up and walking round the desk. He handed the drinks to the two men and then leant against the desk, folding his arms. Jimmy took a drink but Tommy just held the glass.

'I need a man like you, Tom, with a good eye and a steady hand,' said Bill. 'This is a job which requires a certain degree of expertise.'

'What do you want me to do?' Tommy asked, slowly, reluctantly, glancing at the rifle on the desk as he did so.

'I want you to shoot someone.'

'What?'

'With this,' Bill said, picking the rifle up and waving it in the air. 'I need Tom Costello's help.'

'I'm not the person you want, Bill. That's in my past. Tom Costello is dead to me.'

'Resurrect him,' said Bill.

Tommy shook his head. He was being honest. As far as he was concerned, Tom Costello was lying six feet under in a small, weather-beaten graveyard on a remote Scottish island. It wasn't possible to resurrect him.

'I'm sorry, Bill . . .'

Bill threw the rifle towards Tommy, who instinctively caught it, dropping the glass in the process, the scotch spilling over the carpet. Gorevin started laughing.

'You want my help, Tom, and I'm happy to oblige. Now I need your help.'

Tommy looked at Bill. He could hear Gorevin sniggering but he didn't dare look round, otherwise he felt he would either punch the man, or worse. He'd use the rifle. He could feel his shoulders sag and he felt sick in the pit of his stomach. He sensed there was only one answer that would suffice in this room, and it wasn't the one he wanted to give. He had asked Bill for help and, as the gang boss said, he had agreed to do just that. Tommy was now annoyed at himself for not really considering that there would be a price to pay for that help. He was now going to have to pay it, and it seemed like it was a heavy price. He couldn't bring himself to say yes, but he shrugged his shoulders, like he knew there was no point voicing any more objections.

'This is the next move in our game, Tom. You need to trust me on this. Do you trust me, Tom?'

'I just want to find who killed my daughter, Bill.'

'I know, Tom, and we will find him. This will help us in that.'

'What do I have to do?'

'Good man, Tom. You know it makes sense.'

Bill walked back round the desk and sat down, pushing his chair back and putting his feet up on the desk.

'Francis has all the details, Tom. He will fill you in on what has to happen, and when.'

Gorevin nodded towards Tommy.

'My business interests rely on smooth operation and organisation,' said Bill, 'and when that doesn't happen, everything is disrupted. That's when I need to iron out those blips. This is one of those moments, Tom, and I need you to iron out the problem.'

'What do I have to do?' Tommy asked again.

'I want Tom Costello to kill someone for me, a troublesome man who is bad for my business.'

Secrets

Joseph wanted to tell Theresa about what he'd found. More importantly, about who he'd found. The knowledge he was carrying around with him felt like a heavy weight on his shoulders, and he wanted to unload it. He liked talking to Theresa. It felt like she listened to him, that she actually took in what he was saying. She was the only one he really talked to now. Sometimes his mother would try and engage him in conversation on the odd occasion when there weren't other children in the apartment, but it was awkward and clumsy, and both of them were almost relieved when it ended.

She was worried about his arm. She kept staring at it, even while they were talking, and it just made him even more self-conscious. It was still sore, but that was only when he forgot about it and tried to do something that required both his hands. The pain which shot up his arm was an instant reminder that he was different now, and he wasn't sure that would ever change. Sometimes, when he was sitting on his own, he tried to wriggle his fingers, just a tiny bit, to see if there was any life in them. He was scared as he did so, and at times it looked as though nothing moved. He felt it, however, even if no-one was able to see it.

He imagined what it would feel like to hold a pencil again and guide it across a white sheet of paper, marvelling as it transformed the blank canvas into something tangible that came from his head. He missed being able to draw. He didn't think he was very good at anything else, but once he had a pencil in his hand, he was able to create things on the page. He prayed that, one day, he'd be able to do it again, and he had to keep that hope in his head otherwise . . . he didn't want to think about otherwise.

Theresa was in the kitchen, baking some bread. Sometimes he liked to sit at the table and watch her as she moved around the room. It seemed to him that she was gliding, even though she actually moved awkwardly, her big bump slowing her down. Other times, like today, he would sit in the front room, close his eyes and let the aroma of the bread as it baked drift through from the kitchen. When it reached his nose, he felt his stomach rumble and there was a temptation to instantly spring up and race through to the kitchen, hoping that the bread would be ready to be eaten. If it was, he'd stuff a piece into his mouth regardless of the fact it burned his tongue. If not, he'd hover around Theresa, ignoring her gentle chastisement until a plate was put down in front of him.

He glanced at the door, concentrating on the gap at the bottom to see if he could spot the smell of the bread floating through and into the room. He knew that wasn't possible, but he still dropped to his knees and shuffled across to the door. He crouched down and breathed in. Theresa's baking was nearly ready. His mouth began to water as he imagined how it would taste when he took a bite. He breathed in again. The door opened, colliding with his head and he let out a cry.

'What's wrong? Joseph?'

'Sorry.'

He moved away from the door, still on his knees, and rubbed his head with his good hand.

'What are you doing down there?' Theresa said, now able to fully open the door.

Joseph didn't immediately reply. He kept rubbing his head and avoided making eye contact with Theresa.

'I was just . . .'

'Just get up before I end up knocking your head off.'

She helped him to his feet and clipped the back of his head.

'Sorry,' he mumbled, and Theresa smiled.

'The bread's ready,' she said. 'And it's burning hot, just the way you like it.'

They walked through to the kitchen and he spotted the chunk of bread on a plate on the table. The heat was still rising off it, and he was barely on the chair before he was stuffing it into his mouth.

'Slow down, mister,' Theresa said. 'Here, you'll need this.'

She put a glass of water down in front of him and he immediately realised that he was in danger of choking. After he'd taken a drink, managing to squeeze the cold liquid into his already congested mouth, he felt better and he chewed on the bread in a much slower and less excitable manner. Theresa sat across from him, folding her arms and smiling. He didn't have to tell her how good her baking was. She could tell by the way he quickly devoured the bread that he was enjoying it.

'That was always Kathleen's favourite,' Theresa said and he looked up.

He was surprised to hear the name, and the fact it wasn't followed by tears. It still made him feel sad when he heard it, but he tried his best to smile for Theresa.

'She would always stuff her face too,' she said, shaking her head. 'And then she'd start choking, so I'd have to give her a drink and then hit her back until she spat out the bread. She never learned.'

Joseph had finished eating and he drained the glass of the water.

'Do you want some more bread?'

He shook his head. Theresa picked up the plate and glass and took them over to the sink. He watched her as she held them under the water before placing them at the side of the sink. It was strange to hear her talk about Kathleen, though it was nice too, when he thought about it. He was always too scared to even whisper her name in the house, but maybe it wouldn't be so bad if he did.

'I found the man,' he said.

It was so quiet that Theresa didn't hear him and for a few minutes he wondered whether he should repeat it. What could Theresa do with the information anyway? It was only liable to upset her, and he was reluctant to do that when she actually looked almost happy today. Yet he'd carried the information with him like a heavy burden and he needed someone to help share the load.

'I found the man,' he said, louder this time.

'What's that, darling?'

'The man who killed Kathleen . . . I know where he lives.'

Theresa stopped what she was doing and stared at him.

'Are you sure?'

He nodded.

'Oh my God. How . . . ?'

He explained about his trip on the Elevated train, and spotting the car outside the house in the Bronx.

'Are you sure?' she asked.

He nodded again. She walked over slowly and sat down, touching his right hand gently, which rested on the table.

'It was definitely him?'

'Yes.'

'The man who . . . ?'

'Yes.'

'Oh my God.'

They sat in silence for what seemed like an eternity. Sometimes Theresa stared at him and looked to be on the verge of saying something. Other times, she gazed off into the distance and he wondered what she was thinking about.

'You'll have to tell Tommy,' she eventually said.

'Why?'

'He'll know what to do.'

'Do I have to tell him?'

'Yes, you do. He has to know.'

Joseph frowned, even though he knew that she was right. Tommy was the only one who would know what, if anything, was to be done with the information. He was just reluctant to speak to anyone else but Theresa. Maybe she could be the one to tell Tommy?

It was a false hope. He knew that, even as he wished it. When Tommy came home, she ushered him into the kitchen. He could hear the murmured voices as he sat nervously on the edge of the seat. He tried to imagine what she was telling him and his mind was still racing with a host of possibilities when Tommy appeared at the door.

'Theresa said you've got something to tell me.'

Joseph looked up nervously at the figure looking through the haze of smoke billowing from his mouth. Theresa brushed by Tommy and stood in the middle of the room, offering an encouraging smile.

'I saw him,' Joseph said softly. Nervously.

'Speak up, son. I can't hear you.'

'I saw the man,' he said again. 'I know where he lives.'

'Who did you see?' Tommy asked, his eyes glancing between Joseph and Theresa.

'The man who killed Kathleen,' he said, the sentence trailing off to a trembling whisper. 'I know where his house is.'

The Killing Field

Tommy lay perfectly still in the thicket. He'd barely moved from this position for the last hour and he could feel himself stiffen up. He really wanted to get up and stretch, but he couldn't afford to desert his post, not even for a few moments. He knew it was a case of waiting. He had always been good at that. Patience was a virtue and one of his strengths, certainly when he'd been out on an ambush in Donegal, waiting . . . waiting . . . waiting for an army patrol to pass by. Sometimes it was a futile exercise, and the operation would eventually be called off and they'd all trudge home, cold and wet and miserable. Other times, their patience was rewarded. So far, today, nothing had happened.

He touched his holy medals, remembering Danny, his cousin who had worn one of them before he'd been killed by the Brits during an ambush. Tommy had always glanced at his cousin, who would wink at him, before they began shooting. It gave him a sense of reassurance, and he instinctively glanced to his right now. There was nothing there except some heavy shrubbery but he still winked anyway, smiling as he did so.

Jimmy was back at the truck, his patience no doubt similarly tested, though at least he could get out and stretch his legs whenever he wanted. What a luxury that was.

He hoped the other man wasn't smoking, or if he was, that he did so inside the vehicle and that the window was closed. They had to avoid anything that might attract attention, and a trail of smoke escaping out of the forest would give their position away. The sight was trained on the front door of the farm house. It was like he was back in Ireland. The feelings were the same, adrenaline flowing through his body in anticipation of what was to come, while his mind remained composed and focused on the task in hand.

Jimmy's task was also a straightforward one, if also much easier. As soon as he heard the shot, he was to start up the engine and be ready to drive the vehicle away as quickly as possible once Tommy was safely inside as well. They were in a secluded spot, and Jimmy was sure they'd remain undetected. It had been deliberately selected because it offered concealment and a clear view of the farm house, which meant a clear shot too. Tommy had no doubts that he would be successful. It might have been a while since he'd fired a rifle but he was confident enough in his own ability to know that he wouldn't fail.

It had been Gorevin who had explained what was expected of him. Bill had sat back, content to watch Tommy's reaction, which seemed to amuse him. Gorevin found it funny too, though a smug grin was all that he allowed himself to display.

'You want me to kill Lincoln?' Tommy had said.

'Yes,' said Gorevin.

'Detective Lincoln?'

'Yes.'

'Detective John Lincoln?'

'Who else do you think I'm talking about? Of course I mean Detective John Lincoln. We want you to kill him.'

Now it was Tommy's turn to laugh.

'Please explain the joke, Mister Costello?' said Gorevin.

'You're asking me to kill a policeman, a detective even. That's just crazy.'

Gorevin stood, arms folded and leaning against Bill's desk. Tommy could tell that he wasn't used to being questioned, and he wondered what the reaction would have been if his boss hadn't been there. It was crazy, what they were asking him to do, and Tommy had no choice but to question it. He didn't like the idea of killing anyone, certainly when there was no cause or movement to kill for, and to shoot a New York detective was . . . well, it was crazy.

'If you kill a cop, the whole police department will come after you,' he said.

'Not a crooked cop,' said Gorevin.

'A cop's still a cop.'

'Detective Lincoln works for Gaetano Reina. How do you think he knew about Paolo Monti and got the money back to you?'

'He knows who killed your daughter,' said Bill, standing up and walking round to the front of the desk. 'He tells you he's trying to find the killer, but he already knows because they're both part of Reina's organisation.'

'But if I kill him, how does that help get the killer?'

'Lincoln has overstepped his authority,' said Bill. 'He's trying to hinder my operations down here in order to help Gaetano. I can't have that.'

'But he's still a cop, Bill. You can't just shoot a cop and expect to get away with it.'

'He's a crooked cop, Tommy. Remember that.'

'A crooked cop with an apartment full of booze and money that his colleagues will find after he's dead,' said Gorevin. 'They'll put two and two together and realise he was up to no good. As you sow, so shall ye reap.'

Tommy shook his head. 'I don't know, Bill. It just seems . . .'

'Trust me, Tommy,' said Bill. 'I know what I'm doing. The police won't be happy, at least not publicly, but it will be one less bad egg in their basket.'

'And I still don't understand how this helps me.'

'It helps you because it helps me. Reina will get the message, loud and clear, and he will feel he has to respond. When you knock your opponent off their guard, they make mistakes, and that's when you pounce . . . Checkmate!'

Tommy shifted slightly on his elbow in the bushes and stared through the rifle sight which was trained on the front of the farm house. Whoever stood at that door would have no chance of escape. Mind you, they would be unaware of the weapon trained on them, and they'd already be dead before the sound of gunfire reached their ears.

Lincoln was on his way here to collect a pay-off from a contact. It was Gorevin who had found out about it, informing Tommy of the time and the place. Lincoln would be alone, Gorevin had told him with a certainty that offered no option to voice any further doubts, but it was better that he was on his own. The last thing Tommy wanted was to kill anyone else, or get caught up in a gun battle. Now, he just had to watch and wait.

He thought again of Dwyer and his game of chess. Tommy had started to suspect that he was being strung along. First it was stealing the liquor truck and destroying it. Now he was expected to kill a cop. Dwyer kept promising him that it would bring him closer to his daughter's killer, but maybe Dwyer just wanted Tommy to do some of his dirty work.

Information is power. That's what Dwyer had told him, revealing his knowledge of Tommy's past. Now Tommy had information himself, about Lincoln and, more importantly, about where Kathleen's killer lived, though he didn't reveal that to Dwyer. The truth was, he didn't really need Dwyer any more. He could just head over to the address that Joseph had told him and take matters into his own hands. He'd been tempted to do just that, but the more he thought about it, the more he realised that it was a risky move, and one that would make an enemy of Dwyer, as well as Reina.

He thought of Michael Collins. His former leader was never far from his mind theses days, ever since Father Mike had broken the news. It was still difficult to believe he was gone. Tommy knew that, just as before when people he knew died, they would slowly begin to fade from his memory. It had happened with his mother. It had happened with someone he had loved and lost in Glasgow. It hadn't really happened with Kathleen yet. She still haunted him, whether he was awake or asleep, and that was a different worry as to whether that would ever stop.

He would forget about the Big Fella again, just as he had, more or less, these past three years in New York. The difference, of course, was that before, Collins was alive, and there was always the prospect, however remote, that one day they would meet again. The fact that Tommy had fled here after faking his own death in order to escape from the fighting made that unlikely, but still, when Michael Collins was alive, there was a chance. Now he was dead, and that chance was gone.

What would the Big Fella make of him now, lying in undergrowth and waiting to kill a cop? He would want to know why. The Big Fella hadn't been averse to ordering the execution of police officers, but that's because they were the enemy, working for the Brits. Where was the cause that justified killing Lincoln, he would have asked Tommy, probably shaking his head in disbelief or lecturing him on the folly of his actions? Maybe the Big Fella would be more impressed if he knew what Tommy's plan was. He wasn't sure if it would work, but the last thing he wanted to do today was press the trigger.

He heard a rustle in the bushes to the left of him and he froze. There was no way he could spin the rifle round in the confined space and having positioned the weapon and sighted it, he didn't want to knock it off. He had no other weapon, and as he thought about what to do next, he held his breath, not wanting to make a sound that might alert whoever, or whatever, was in the bushes. As he eventually breathed out, he heard another noise. This time he slowly glanced round to his left. A rabbit sat watching him from a few yards away. Its nose moved incessantly, while occasionally, its head moved like it was glancing left and right to check everything was okay. He stared at it, realising that it didn't blink at all. He had to look away momentarily when he found himself blinking.

Tommy relaxed. It would have been worse if it had been a larger animal, perhaps a fox or a deer, but the rabbit seemed content to watch him. He was sure it would soon get bored because nothing was happening. He'd hardly moved in all the time he'd been lying here, and if the rabbit was looking for some excitement, it had stopped at the wrong place.

It moved its head, looking round towards the farm house and Tommy looked round too. Nothing to see there, he said out loud, immediately smiling as he realised he'd just spoken to a rabbit. He was still smiling as the car came into view, driving slowly along the dirt road that led to the house. Tommy glanced at the rabbit which had resumed looking at him. He shook his head and then crouched down, pressing his eye to the rifle sight while his finger gently touched the trigger.

The car was sending dust clouds up into the air in its wake, making it difficult to identify the make of the car from Tommy's vantage point, but he presumed that it was Detective Lincoln who was driving. Who else would be coming out to this isolated place? It must be something that Lincoln was used to doing, otherwise it would have aroused his suspicions.

He could feel the rifle pressing against his shoulder and anticipated the recoil that would follow if he pressed the trigger. He glanced again at the rabbit, winking at it with a smile before resuming his vigil. He missed his cousin, even though he was another person that he rarely thought about.

At this precise moment, however, he wished Danny was lying here beside him, ready to play his part in the mission.

The car drew to a halt a few yards away from the farm house and, slowly, the dust clouds began to dissipate until the vehicle emerged fully in his sights. It was Lincoln's car, a black Buick which now wore a layer of dust that would have to be washed off later. For a few minutes, nothing happened. Tommy couldn't see from his vantage point whether Lincoln was the only one in the car, but he wondered why the detective hadn't got out the car. Maybe he was suspicious? He couldn't say why, but perhaps there was something that put him on edge. It could have been the absence of another vehicle at the house, or the fact no-one was standing there to meet him. He didn't know how these things were usually organised, so he couldn't tell what, if anything, had gone wrong.

There was a rustling movement to Tommy's left again, though he didn't dare look round. He presumed it was the rabbit moving away, having got fed up waiting for something to happen. Tommy had to remain focused on the scene below. He could hear the car starting up again and it moved forward slowly, reaching the house and then driving round until it was out of sight.

Tommy sat up slightly. There was no sign of Lincoln's car, which hadn't re-emerged from the other side of the house. He could only presume that it had stopped at the back. Lincoln must have sensed something wasn't right. Why would he have driven round to the back of the house other-wise? It could only be to give himself extra protection against possible attack.

He looked over his shoulder, though it was only more

trees and bushes he could see. He doubted that Jimmy would hear him, even if he shouted as loudly as he could, and there was every chance his voice would carry down the hill and across to the farm house to be heard by Lincoln. If the detective was already on edge, then a sudden cry of 'Jimmy!' would only increase that wariness.

Jimmy was waiting, out of sight, for the sound of a gun shot which would see him spring into action and start up the truck. As long as that sound echoed through the countryside air, then Jimmy would know the job had been done. Tommy hadn't spoken to him about anything else. It wasn't that he didn't trust the other man but . . . he let the thought hang in his mind, knowing that trusting his instincts and keeping quiet had always been the safest course of action.

His plan, risky though it was, felt like the only way he could avoid killing Lincoln. He knew that the cop was coming here expecting a pay-off, but not too many other people did, certainly not the man who killed Kathleen. It hadn't been too difficult to leave a message at the address Joseph had given him. *'Lincoln's going to rat you out for the Delaney girl's murder'*, the scrawled note read, along with the time and place of the meeting Gorevin had set up. Now he had to hope that the bait had been taken.

He was glad at being able to move, even slightly, though he didn't want to kneel or stand up. Even from a distance, he was liable to be spotted if someone glanced in his direction. He lay down again and stared through the sight. He couldn't see the car and there didn't seem to be any movement from within the house either. He moved the rifle slowly from left to right, tracking the front of the house, and then back again. Still there was nothing. He was aware of birds singing in the trees above him, though when he looked up he couldn't spot them. Were they singing to each other, or maybe serenading him? Quietly, he began humming. It wasn't the same tune as the birds, who couldn't hear him, but it sounded nice together, almost melodic, and he kept humming even as he looked through the rifle sight once again.

He could have been on a hunting trip rather than on a mission to kill a man. He pictured himself, lying in wait, still in a thicket of bushes, but his eyes searched out animal prey. A deer, perhaps, or a majestic stag that would strut through the countryside regally, as if it owned all it surveyed. One bullet would cut the impressive beast down. One bullet would guarantee a few full and satisfied stomachs at the end of the trip. The only animal he'd spotted had been the rabbit, however, and while that might have sufficed for a stew, it wouldn't provide the banquet his imaginary stag offered. He could feel his mouth watering at the prospect, and he knew it would do no good to imagine the taste of the succulent meat as it rested on his tongue.

The door of the farm house opened and Lincoln walked out. He was smoking a cigarette. He stood on the porch, blowing clouds of smoke into the air. The detective was smiling. It was a contented expression, and Tommy wondered if there was a bag of money in the house. Maybe that was the money the cops would find when they discovered Lincoln's body?

Tommy adjusted his position on the ground so that he was comfortable. His finger inched closer to the trigger.

He wondered whether he would squeeze it if he had to. What would be his explanation to Dwyer if he didn't? Lincoln took another draw of his cigarette. There was a roar which seemed to fill the whole atmosphere. The singing birds instantly scattered into the air, flying furiously up and up to try and escape the noise. Tommy stared through his sight at the farm house. Lincoln's body was slumped at the door. The detective was dead. He was absolutely sure of that. If he'd been standing over the body, he might have seen a few twitches, but there was no doubt whoever had fired the fatal shot had done their job. Tommy looked up, but he couldn't guess where the shot had come from. The only thing he knew for sure was that it hadn't come from his rifle, and a sudden sense of relief surged through his body. Someone had been desperate to ensure Lincoln remained quiet about Kathleen's killer, and Tommy could guess who that was.

Haunted House

Tommy and Jimmy sat in the church hall. Both men were smoking, watching the door and waiting for Father Mike. The priest had ushered them through to the hall after they'd turned up at the church house. He was surprised to see them standing there but Tommy had decided it would be the best place to hide the gun. He knew it was pushing his friendship with the priest to the limits, but he figured there was much less chance of it being found in the church than in his own house. Not that he should have been too concerned, given the fact he hadn't actually fired the weapon, but it would still require a credible explanation if the cops uncovered it. He expected them to go looking for Lincoln's killer, no matter what Bill had said to the contrary, and at some point they might turn up at his door, if only because the detective had been dealing with Kathleen's murder.

The gun was in a bag which sat at Jimmy's feet. Tommy was anxious to get rid of it, and though he hoped Father Mike would hide it for him, he'd need to return it to Bill at some point. Maybe it had been a test for him, to see if he would go through with it. He didn't know if he'd passed it or not, though the fact he hadn't fired the fatal shot would go against him. He had to hope Bill didn't know that.

'Will he do it?' Jimmy asked. 'Will he hide the gun?'

'I think so.'

'It'll just be for a few days anyway. Once I've got hold of Gorevin, I can come back for it, and he won't have anything more to do with it . . . What will we do if he says no?'

'Who? Gorevin?'

'No. Father Mike. Where will we hide the gun then?'

'He'll be fine.'

'Do you trust him?'

'He's a priest, for God's sake.'

'So?'

'So, of course I trust him. He's a friend too. I know he'll help, even if he's not happy about it.'

He knew Father Mike wouldn't be happy. Part of him was tempted not to tell the priest what was inside the bag, but he wasn't stupid, and Tommy had no doubt he'd look inside the bag anyway after they'd gone. He would tell the truth and, despite misgivings, Father Mike would help.

They both looked up as the church hall door opened, expecting Father Mike to appear. Instead, it was another man who walked in. He stopped, surprised to find Tommy and Jimmy sitting there like a welcoming committee. The man was short, about five foot seven, with light brown, curly hair. He hadn't shaved for a few days, but the growth was light-coloured as well. His shirt was unbuttoned at the neck, and he was still slipping his braces on as he came out.

'How are you doing?' he said.

'Fine,' said Tommy, while Jimmy nodded.

'I think I'm lost. I was trying to get back to the church house.

The accent was unmistakeably Cork, so thick and pure

that Tommy could have cut it with a knife. The face wasn't as instantly recognisable as the voice was, but there was a name flashing in his head and he was sure it was the right one. Des Donnelly. Suddenly Tommy had forgotten about Lincoln's death. Now there were only questions swirling in his brain. What was one of his former IRA comrades doing in New York, and at Holy Cross Church?

Father Mike suddenly appeared at the door as well, brushing past Des and standing between him and Tommy and Jimmy.

'I was wondering where you'd got to there,' the priest said.

'I was just saying to these fellas here that I got lost,' Des said with a laugh.

'Easily done,' Father Mike said. 'Will we head back through? Sean will be wondering where we've got to.'

'Sure . . . Nice to meet you,' Des said, waving at Tommy and Jimmy.

'Same to yourself,' Tommy said.

'Where are you from then?' Des asked.

'Forty-fifth Street. It's not far from here.'

'No, back home,' Des said, with a short laugh.

'Sorry . . . Derry.'

'I would have guessed Donegal,' said Des. 'Near enough, I suppose.'

Tommy nodded.

'Right, let's go,' said Father Mike, moving towards the door. 'I'll be back in a minute, gentlemen.'

'Have we met before?' Des asked.

'I don't think so,' Tommy said, shaking his head.

'Have you been here a while?'

'Years!' Father Mike laughed. 'Pat's a New Yorker now, even with that accent.'

'I thought maybe we'd met back home,' Des said. 'You look familiar . . . I must be getting old. Nice meeting you anyway, Pat.'

'You too,' said Tommy with a nod.

'Maybe we'll meet again,' said Des.

'I'll be back soon,' said Father Mike, closing the door behind him.

'Feck!' Tommy muttered, staring at the door.

He remained on edge until Father Mike came back into the hall, sitting on the edge of his chair, smoking incessantly and staring at the door, anticipating at any moment that Des Donnelly would come bursting through it to confront him. His mind was racing. What was Des doing here? He kept asking himself over and over again. It was like he'd seen a ghost when the figure had appeared. There didn't seem to be any flicker of recognition on his former comrade's face.

Des wouldn't be expecting to see him here. No-one from back home knew where he was. He'd disappeared off the face of the earth as far as anyone who knew him was concerned. Certainly, his comrades in the IRA wouldn't know what had happened to him beyond Glasgow, though Michael Collins knew where he was heading after that. It was the Big Fella who'd sent him to a remote Scottish island to kill a priest who had once betrayed the cause. That the priest was also Tommy's uncle was neither here nor there for the Irish Republican leader, but ultimately, it was what stopped Tommy from pulling the trigger, and it was his uncle who had helped him to escape to New York.

He'd believed that Father Mike was the only one who knew the life that 'Tom Costello' had before arriving in New York, though Bill Dwyer had shown that wasn't the case. Tommy still had to ask Father Mike about that. But if anyone from the IRA had gone hunting for him on that Hebridean island of Benbecula, they would have found him, his name engraved on a tombstone, marking the end of the trail and the end of the story. He was Tommy Delaney now, an Irishman making his way in America, and in a country of immigrants, no-one cared what you'd done or where you'd come from. It was what you were going to do next which was all that mattered.

Now Des Donnelly was in town. Not only that, but he was in the same building, sitting no more than a stone's throw away. Des was a Cork man and fought down south while Tommy had been based up north in Donegal, but their paths had crossed after the uprising in nineteen sixteen, when they'd been in an internment camp in Wales. The Big Fella had been there too, and they had made plans, all the prisoners gathered there by the Brits, for when they were released and sent home, on how to take the war to the enemy. Michael Collins was in charge, of course, and they listened mainly to him, though he would always listen to everyone else's point of view.

Tommy was for Michael Collins. Always. Whether he would have agreed with the Treaty or not, he would still have followed their leader. He didn't know Des Donnelly well enough to be able to say the same of him. He couldn't imagine anyone turning against the Big Fella, though that was evidently the case, since Ireland was at war with itself and Collins was dead, killed by a former comrade. He didn't want to be thinking of such things, being dragged inexorably towards his past, when he had too much to think about in his present.

He was desperate for the priest to return. He had to know why Des was in New York. Five minutes became ten and then twenty, and still there was no sign of the priest. He paced the floor, hoping that at least the physical activity would make the time pass quicker.

'Will you sit down,' Jimmy eventually snapped. 'You're making me bloody nervous.'

'Sorry,' Tommy said, sitting down and lighting a cigarette, but then standing up again after a few moments.

'You're being daft,' said Jimmy. 'I bet he didn't recognise you.'

'I don't know, Jimmy. You heard him asking if we'd met before.'

'But that's just because of the accent. He would have said something if he'd known it was you, even just out of surprise at bumping into you here.'

Tommy frowned but he knew that Jimmy was right. At least, he hoped he was. He sat down again. They heard footsteps approaching, faint at first, but getting louder as they approached along the hall. He was on edge now, and he let out a sigh of relief when Father Mike walked in.

'What the hell is Des Donnelly doing in your house?' Tommy blurted out, even before the priest closed the door behind him. 'Jesus, I nearly bloody died when I saw him.'

'I'm sorry, I should have warned you.'

'Warned me? Christ, Mike, you should have told me right away.'

'But they were here before you.'

'They?'

'Des and Sean Lyons.'

'Sean Lyons is here too? For God's sake, Mike. I need to get out of here.'

'Calm down, Tommy. They don't know you're here.'

'But Des saw me.'

'And he doesn't recognise you. I just told him you're a couple of my parishioners who're going to be painting the hall.'

'See, I told you he didn't recognise you,' said Jimmy.

'They're leaving tomorrow,' said Father Mike.

'Where are they going?'

'A place over in Brooklyn. Someone's arranged it for them. I don't know who. They never told me. I didn't ask.'

The priest came over and sat down beside the two men. Soon all three of them were smoking. Tommy glanced over at the priest, shaking his head every now and then, but no-one spoke.

If Tommy didn't know where Des Donnelly stood after the Treaty was signed, he knew Sean Lyons would oppose it. He was an Eamon De Valera man. De Valera had once been Collins' comrade, but became his enemy, and had led the opposition to the Treaty. Even when De Valera had gone to America back in 1919 to drum up support for the war – many of them thought he should have stayed and fought – Sean Lyons was his eyes and ears in Dublin. Everyone knew that, and so watched what they said as a result. Not that Sean wasn't a brave man. Tommy had heard enough tales of his exploits in fighting the Brits to respect the man, even if he never trusted him. Sean Lyons would have opposed the Treaty. Tommy would have bet his life on it, and if that was indeed the case, it was a good guess that Des Donnelly did too.

'Why are they here?' he asked.

'I don't know.'

'There's a civil war on back home. You know whose side they're on?'

The priest didn't say anything.

'Bloody hell, Mike. They're anti-Treaty.'

'You know them better than me, Tommy.'

Tommy finished his cigarette and stubbed it out in the ashtray that Jimmy held out for him.

'Someone asked me if I could help out for a few days,' the priest said. 'Told me a couple of the boys would be arriving from Ireland and they needed somewhere to stay until something else was sorted out for them. I couldn't very well say no. I never did when I was asked to help you.'

'There are other anti-Treaty men in the city as well?'

'Of course.'

'And in this parish? Who?'

'Tommy, what do you expect? The Treaty's split the country. There's a war on just now so, of course, there are anti-Treaty people here, just as there are some who are pro-Treaty as well.'

'I don't like it,' Tommy said. 'Two IRA men suddenly turn up out of the blue from Ireland. Two anti-Treaty men as well. And with the Big Fella barely cold in his grave.' He blessed himself automatically, and gently squeezed the holy medals round his neck though he didn't hold them like he often did.

'What could I do?' Father Mike said with a shrug and Tommy didn't have an answer to that.

'They'll be away in the morning and you'll never see them again.'

'No-one knows I'm here, apart from you, Mike.' Tommy could feel Jimmy staring at him but he didn't look round.

'The IRA thinks that I'm dead, and even if Des didn't recognise me, I know that Sean Lyons would in a second. I can't afford to be recognised.'

'But you won't be.'

'And they'll know where my loyalties lie. I'm for Michael Collins. Always have been and always will be.'

The priest shook his head, but didn't say anything else.

'You don't think the two things are connected, do you?' Tommy asked.

'What things?'

'Michael Collins' death and now two anti-Treaty men suddenly arriving in New York?'

Father Mike shrugged, while Tommy wiped the sweat from his brow.

'We need to go.'

He stood up and the other two men followed.

'Can we leave this here with you just now?' Jimmy said, picking up the bag.

'Sure. What is it?'

Jimmy glanced at Tommy, who sighed deeply.

'It's a gun. A rifle.'

'You want me to keep a gun here?'

'It's just for a few days,' Tommy said.

'But this is a church, Tommy. The house of God.'

'But you've already got two IRA men here.'

'And that's not by choice. I can't be hiding guns as well.'

'Two days at most,' said Jimmy.

Father Mike shook his head, but snatched the bag out of Jimmy's hand.

'Thanks,' Jimmy said.

Tommy wanted to get away from the Church, and, in particular, away from his two former comrades. That would help him think straight. Sitting in his own kitchen smoking his own cigarettes and drinking coffee from his own cup would give him a reassuring familiarity which might help him try to figure out why the IRA men were here, and once he knew they'd safely moved to Brooklyn, he'd come back to quiz the priest in more detail about his surprise visitors.

Tender Touch

Tommy looked up and saw Theresa standing at the doorway. He hadn't heard her approaching. It seemed like her bump was getting noticeably bigger every time he saw her. He smiled at the thought of the baby soon to arrive, though she smiled back, thinking it had been meant for her. Jimmy instantly made his excuses and headed for the kitchen as Tommy stood up. Instinctively he wanted to rush over and hug her but they still remained tentative and awkward around each other. He stood up.

'Is everything okay? she asked.

'Yes. Why?'

'I just heard you and Jimmy talking and thought that maybe something was wrong.'

'No, everything's fine.'

She nodded, glancing over her shoulder towards the kitchen and then back at Tommy, nodding again.

'I'm glad,' she said, taking a step into the room.

'Did we wake you?'

She shook her head.

'I'm sorry if we were talking too loud.'

'It's fine. I was already awake,' she said softly

Tommy wondered what, if anything, she had heard, though when he searched her face for clues, there was no indication that she had. He took a couple of steps forward and was now standing directly in front of her.

'Theresa,' he whispered, slowly wrapping his arms round her. She buried her head into his chest but her own arms remained at her side. He held her for a few minutes, occasionally letting his lips rest on the top of her head. Neither of them said anything. He could feel her bump pressing against him and he hoped the baby would start kicking now.

Jimmy re-appeared at the doorway, waving a hand to catch Tommy's attention and then gesturing that he was going to go. Tommy nodded, mouthing the word 'Thanks,' though Jimmy was already away down the hall. Eventually, Tommy knew he would have to let Theresa go, though she didn't seem to notice when he did release her from his embrace. She stood on the spot, swaying slightly like a tree on a windy day, and he wasn't sure whether to hold her again, or just stand facing her. Instead, he slowly manoeuvred round her and headed for the kitchen. He filled the kettle with water and set it on the stove, lighting the ring underneath it. He stood watching the kettle as he smoked, hearing the water begin to angrily dance inside it, sending faint smoke signals out through the neck. He thought about Theresa, probably still standing in the middle of the room even though he'd left her, and he realised it was one of the few times they had touched, properly, for months.

The first time he had seen Theresa naked, he told her she was the most beautiful woman in the world. He had sat on the edge of the bed looking at her, his eyes taking in every inch of her trembling body. When she had let her silk slip drop to the floor, she stood nervously before him, her arms not knowing what to do or where to cover. She folded them, covering her breasts, but only for a moment, quickly realising she was left exposed elsewhere. He slowly took her hand which covered the small triangle of hair between her legs, and as she ran her other hand nervously through her hair, he took that one too, looking her up and down as she blushed.

Theresa had shivered as Tommy pulled her towards him. She sat astride him, helping him to remove his vest so that he was naked except for his shorts. She leant in close and their lips met, tongues immediately jostling for space in each other's mouths. His hands cupped her breasts, and she drew a sharp intake of breath as his head moved towards them, his tongue lingering on her nipples. His fingers ran up and down her body, caressing the stretch marks on her skin as she tugged on his hair.

'You're beautiful,' he whispered as they kissed again and she smiled, her face flush with excitement and embarrassment.

They hadn't lain like that for a while now. He wondered if they ever would again. She wore layers of clothes now, whether in bed or if she got up and shuffled about the apartment, which suddenly seemed so big now that it was just the two of them. It was as if all the clothes were an attempt to protect her from the pain, though it was a futile attempt if that was, indeed, the case. He didn't know how she would react if he tried to initiate anything, even just to give her a kiss. He was too scared to try. He made two cups of tea and headed back through to the front room. Theresa wasn't there.

'Theresa! Theresa!'

She re-appeared at the doorway.

'I was just checking on Joseph,' she said, moving into the room and accepting the cup of tea gratefully before sitting down on the couch. Tommy dropped on to the armchair facing her and sighed deeply.

'How is he?'

'Okay, I think,' she said with a shrug. 'He doesn't say much.'

He had wanted to ask the boy about that day . . . Saint Patrick's Day. It seemed so long ago now, yet until there was some settlement of matters, it would always remain at the forefront of his mind. He would still like to ask the boy . . . what? Joseph had been the last one to see Kathleen alive, the last one to hold her, speak to her. He knew who had killed her. That's what the drawing had been trying to tell him, to tell everyone, when he couldn't find the words to say it, but that had all been before he'd been caught and punished. There had been no drawings since.

'I miss Kathleen,' Tommy suddenly blurted out.

Theresa looked at him, startled. She stared and he wasn't sure if she was trying to digest the words or whether her look was of that towards a stranger and she was trying to figure out who he was. Sometimes he felt like a stranger in this house, too often now, and the thought had crossed his mind on more than one occasion that he wouldn't be living here for too much longer. He sensed that his departure would be greeted with relief, if not completely welcomed.

'So do I,' she whispered after a few minutes, looking away from him and staring into her cup like she was studying a picture.

They hadn't really spoken about Kathleen, or how they

felt, since it had happened. They hadn't really spoken about anything, and even now, having elicited a response, Tommy wasn't sure what to say next. He sensed that this was the opportunity to say something, anything, and if he didn't, then it might be closed forever, but at the same time, he knew that the wrong words would have the same effect.

'I dream about her,' he said.

Theresa nodded.

'Sometimes she sings to me. She had a beautiful voice.' The last word almost caught in his throat and he had to cough it out.

Theresa started humming. Tommy stared at her. How did she know that tune? He'd never heard her singing it before. That was his mother's song. *Kate's Song*. Was this just another dream? He glanced round, wondering if Kathleen would suddenly appear and join Theresa in singing.

'That tune?'

'I used to sing it to her when she was a baby,' Theresa said. 'It would always get her off to sleep. It was her favourite.'

She smiled at the memory, and even when she looked up at Tommy, the smile didn't disappear guiltily. Instead, she allowed herself to savour it for a few moments before it slowly faded like a summer sunset. He hadn't been there when Kathleen was a baby, and now he wished he had been. It would have given him more memories to unpack and savour when the need arose.

He never knew who Kathleen's father had been. 'He's dead,' is all Theresa had ever said on the subject, and he had never probed her for more information. It didn't matter to him anyway. That was Theresa's past, and if she wanted to keep it secret, then he wasn't going to try and prise it from her. There were enough secrets that he kept from his own past that he had no intention of ever sharing. It was enough that he was going to be her father – she called him 'daddy,' – and he missed her saying that word more than anything else.

Theresa was humming the song again and Tommy joined in, singing the words in a shaky voice that threatened to disappear completely, though Theresa offered him a smile of encouragement, and so he continued, closing his eyes as he did so. He was thinking of his daughter and also his mother, both of them gone now. He touched his holy medals, hoping that, wherever the two of them were, they were both safe. Perhaps they were together? He was surprised that he remembered all the words, and he completed the song even after Theresa had stopping humming.

'You've got a lovely voice,' she said when he'd finished.

'Thanks.'

He couldn't remember whether she had ever heard him singing before. It wasn't something he did very often, but it had felt nice, just the two of them, sitting here together. He didn't feel the urge to go over and hold her or kiss her. He sensed that the physical contact would break the intimacy which had suddenly and unexpectedly enveloped them. He was scared to do or say anything because he knew it was an intimacy created by the most fragile of bonds that could snap at any moment.

Now Theresa started singing and Tommy sat back in the chair, closing his eyes and letting the voice wash over him. *The Wearing of the Green.* It felt like his whole life was jostling in his head for attention, memories of his childhood in

Donegal, sitting on his mother's knee as she smoked a cigarette and sang him Irish lullabies, or lying in wet fields with a gun pointed towards a deserted road, waiting for a target to appear. The roar of a gun. The scream of a wounded man. Dead eyes that would stare up at him, almost asking, 'Why me?' A rain-soaked city. Glasgow. Where he didn't know who was his friend or his enemy. A red-haired girl, holding him, kissing him, her porcelain flesh only seeming to make her hair burn ever more brightly as they lay together. Waves washing over him as he huddled in a small boat which seemed to defy the laws of nature to make its way from one shore to another. A bigger vessel to carry him here to this city of noise and chaos and concrete. Kathleen skipping down the street, her beaming smile, her brown hair tied up in an emerald green ribbon.

His face was wet now as Theresa finished singing, the tears washing down his cheeks, and he didn't dare open his eyes, though he knew she would have noticed that he was crying. He felt a touch on his face and he opened his eyes as she moved away from him. He knew her lips had gently caressed his cheeks and he smiled as she slowly slipped out of the room.

He was dozing in the chair when he heard the voices. He yawned and opened his eyes. He still held his cup, which was balanced precariously on his chest. It still had some tea in it but thankfully none of it had spilled on to his shirt. He put it down at the side of the chair and stretched. His mouth was dry and he wanted a drink of water and a cigarette. He lit up as he moved towards the door, immediately feeling better after taking a couple of draws.

Theresa stood at the end of the hallway, leaning on the door which was open. Father Mike was standing at the door and he looked beyond Theresa when he saw Tommy appear.

'Are you not coming in?' Tommy shouted, stretching again.

'I'm not staying,' the priest said. 'I just need a word.'

Theresa stepped away from the door as Tommy reached it. Her hand rested briefly on his arm.

He smiled and gently kissed her on the lips. She sighed, giving his arm a tiny squeeze before heading back to the kitchen.

'What's wrong, Mike?' Tommy said.

The priest glanced to his left and Tommy noticed the man standing beside him. He wore a cap and he stood, arms folded and chewing. It might have been gum or maybe tobacco. Tommy nodded towards the man.

'You need to come with us,' the man said.

'I'm sorry, Tommy,' Father Mike said.

'What's going on?' Tommy asked, looking at the priest.

'You need to come with us,' the man said again.

'I heard you the first time,' Tommy said, looking round at the man again, whose hand was now inside his jacket.

'What is this?'

'They want to see you,' the priest said.

'Who?'

'Tom Costello, I'm arresting you on behalf of the Irish Republican Army. You will face a court-martial on charges of treason and desertion.'

'You're joking?' Tommy laughed, looking between Father Mike and the man. Neither of them smiled.

'And who are you?' he asked the man.

'This is . . .' the priest began.

'It doesn't matter who I am. All that matters is that you've to come with me. Now.'

Tommy took a couple of steps back inside the house and the man produced a revolver.

'Now,' he said again.

'Put that gun away, for God's sake,' Father Mike said.

The man lowered the gun but he didn't put it away. He kept looking at Tommy, who sensed that even if he tried to slam the door shut, the man would be through it and putting a bullet in his back before he had a chance to run anywhere. He didn't recognise the man, though it was obvious he'd been sent by Sean Lyons. He knew, as soon as he'd run into Des at the church that he'd been recognised and that his past would inevitably catch up with him.

'Where are we going?'

'You don't need to know.'

'I just need to let Theresa know.'

Tommy took another step back and the man raised the gun again.

'I'll tell her,' Father Mike said, stepping forward and round Tommy.

He continued staring at the man, his mind racing with thoughts of what was going to happen. Desertion and treason, the man had said. His accent was Brooklyn, Tommy thought, though with a hint of Ireland. It was so faint Tommy could never have guessed where. He could understand the desertion charge because that's exactly what he'd done, but treason? That could only be due to his connection with Michael Collins. He couldn't understand any of it, not here. This was New York, thousands of miles away from Ireland, and surely Sean Lyons, Des Donnelly and whoever else would have other pressing matters than dealing with someone who, to all intents and purposes, was dead, and had been for over two years now?

Father Mike returned and Tommy glanced round. Theresa was standing at the kitchen door.

'It's okay,' he said. 'I'll be home soon.'

'I'll cook your favourite for dinner tonight,' she said and he nodded.

The man with the gun coughed and Tommy slowly stepped out of the house, closing the door behind him. The man stood against the far wall and let the other two lead the way, with Tommy at the front. Could he make a run for it when they got outside? The prospect of a bullet in his back remained a distinct one, and what would happen to Theresa if he either disappeared or was shot?

'I'm sorry, Tommy,' Father Mike muttered as they walked down the stairs. 'They made me tell them where you lived.'

'It's fine, Mike,' said Tommy.

'I didn't know what else to do.'

'Don't worry about it. There was nothing else you could do.'

The priest sighed deeply but Tommy didn't glance back at him. He continued down the stairs, still running over the possibility of escape, if not when they stepped out on to the sidewalk, then at some point on their journey. At first he'd presumed they would be heading back to the church house, but he guessed that, even if the priest had been 'encouraged' to lead them to him, he'd still draw the line at anything taking place under his own roof, certainly a court-martial when Tommy's life was at stake.

Father Mike's car was parked directly outside the building and Tommy was ushered into the front seat alongside the priest. The man sat in the back, the gun still resting in his hand, ready to be called upon at a moment's notice. Tommy couldn't see the man behind him, but he knew he wouldn't be able to spin round and surprise the man, nor perhaps managing to disarm him. He could wait until they had stopped at a junction or were driving round the corner and open the door, jumping out and taking his chances. Again, that was a risky move. He might injure himself, or get run over if he fell into oncoming traffic. He could still get shot. He decided to remain where he was.

They were heading towards Brooklyn. The car slowly made its way up on to the Bridge and Tommy glanced out the window, looking out towards the busy sea. He saw the Statue of Liberty, remembering the first time he had set eyes on it. That seemed like such a long time ago now, though it was only three years. He had run away from everything, his old life, his country, the war, and seeing the large green statue welcoming him to this new world and a new life, he realised that he had made the right decision. Now, it seemed to have turned its back on him as they descended into Brooklyn. His old life had finally caught up with him.

Courting Disaster

There was a single wooden chair sitting in the middle of the warehouse. It faced a longer table, and already four men sat behind it; Sean Lyons, Des Donnelly and two men he didn't recognise. There was an empty chair at the end of the table, presumably for the gunman who had brought Tommy here. When he sat down, the panel who would judge him, and no doubt find him guilty, would be complete. The man nudged Tommy in the back with the gun to try and speed him up. It was all for show, of course, to impress his comrades, and it didn't make Tommy move any faster. There had been no hood placed over his head when they were driving here, and Tommy guessed they weren't too bothered whether he recognised the location or not. There would be no return journey home for him.

Father Mike walked alongside him. The priest stared straight ahead, not wanting to catch Tommy's eye. He felt guilty, Tommy realised, though there was no need to. It wasn't his fault. He wanted to tell the priest that, but he didn't want to say anything in front of the rest of them. Father Mike was his friend, and had been from the moment he had stepped off the boat and on to American soil. He had helped him, just as his friend, Tommy's uncle, had asked, and he had always done so without question or complaint. If this was going to end the way Tommy expected it to, then, at the very least, he would say thank-you to the priest.

Their footsteps echoed throughout the large room. It was empty, apart from the furniture set up for the court-martial. Sunlight stretched in from the small windows which ran along the top of either side of the building, and it was bright enough that there was no need for any artificial assistance to shed light on proceedings.

Sean Lyons sat in the middle, flanked by Des on his right-hand side, and the other two men to his left. The spare seat was to Des' right. Sean was obviously in charge. He was the only one who wasn't smoking. He sat, hands placed flat on the table, with several sheets of paper in front of him. He watched as they approached, his eyes immediately seeking out Tommy, who met his gaze and held it.

'This is unacceptable, Sean,' said Father Mike, approaching the table as Tommy was told to stop and sit down on the chair facing the table. Instead of taking his seat with his comrades, the gunman remained standing behind Tommy. Father Mike was now at the table, standing directly in front of Sean.

'This doesn't concern you, Father,' said Sean, staring up at the priest.

'Tommy is my friend and he's done nothing wrong.'

'That's for us to decide.'

'But this isn't Ireland. There is no war here.'

'A traitor's a traitor, no matter what country he tries to hide in.'

'Sounds like you've already made your minds up.'

'Like I said, Father, this doesn't concern you.'

Father Mike glanced round at Tommy and then turned back.

'I can't let this happen,' he said. 'It isn't right, Sean. I've given you sanctuary. I've helped you. You can't do this.'

'It's time for you to go, Father.'

'I'm not going anywhere.'

'This is an official court-martial of the Irish Republican Army, and I am about to open proceedings. Go now, Father. I won't tell you again.'

The two men stared at each other before the priest eventually sighed and turned round to begin the slow walk back towards the door.

'Drive straight home and tell no-one about this,' Sean said.

The priest kept walking, his eyes offering an apology to Tommy as he passed, and Tommy nodded in acknowledgement.

'You shouldn't have brought him here,' Sean snapped towards the gunman behind Tommy as the door had rattled noisily after Father Mike had closed it.

'I couldn't drive and watch him at the same time,' the man said. Sean shook his head but said nothing. He shuffled the papers on the table and then glanced up at Tommy.

'This court-martial is now open and is in session in accordance with the standing orders of the Irish Republican Army as set down by the Supreme Army Council . . . Volunteer Callaghan, read the charges.'

One of the men who was sitting to Sean's left stood up, taking the sheet of paper Sean handed to him. He cleared his throat.

'Volunteer Tom Costello is charged on the following

counts. One, that of treason against the Irish Republic. Two, that of desertion from the army of the Irish Republic.'

'How do you plead, Volunteer Costello?'

Tommy smiled at Sean and shook his head.

'Is that a not guilty plea?'

Tommy was almost tempted to say 'guilty' just to see Sean's face as he stole his thunder, but he didn't want to do the IRA man's job for him, and it would be good to hear all the evidence, whatever that might be. He had no doubt they would deliver a guilty verdict and a sentence of death, but to admit he was guilty now would only hasten the inevitable bullet in the back of his head.

'Your plea, Volunteer Costello?'

Tommy cleared his throat.

'I refuse to recognise the legitimacy of this court,' he said.

'This court is legitimate within the standing orders and regulations of Óglaigh na hÉireann.'

'My loyalty is to Ireland and to the army of the Irish Republic, for which I swore an oath of fidelity. This court has no legitimacy.'

Sean shrugged.

'Not guilty then,' he said to the men either side of him, and Des wrote something down on a sheet of paper.

There was silence in the room, like the few seconds of anticipation before a peel of thunder exploded across the sky. Tommy kept his eyes firmly fixed on Sean, who was obviously preparing in his mind what he wanted to say. Tommy didn't know why they were going through such formalities as an official court-martial. They could easily have just brought him here, pushed him to his knees and held the barrel of a gun to his skull before pressing the trigger.

No-one would have been any the wiser, either here or back in Ireland. He would have just been another dead body to sweep away and bury. The authorities might have looked into who he was or, more importantly, what he was up to, and then decided he was simply one less bad guy to worry about.

No-one would have made any connection to Ireland since no-one really knew who he was or what he had been. These men sitting before him did, however, and he had to be thankful that they were doing everything by the book. In the middle of a war that wasn't always practical, possible or even desirable, so every moment he remained alive was one to savour, and perhaps offer some means of redemption from this situation, unlikely though that seemed.

'So where have you been, Tom?'

Sean's question was quiet, informal, like they were just two old pals catching up after many years apart.

'I've been here.'

'You've been in New York all the time the war was continuing and now . . .'

Sean left the sentence unfinished, though Tommy knew it was only his reluctance to mention the civil war which prevented him from doing so. It was a sad time indeed for everyone, particularly for men who had previously fought shoulder to shoulder against the British.

'So what happened in Glasgow?' Sean asked.

Tommy sighed. That seemed like a lifetime ago, though it had only been three years since he'd gone to the city on Michael Collins' orders, to assassinate a British general. He'd failed in that mission, his last for the republican movement, and he had hoped fleeing across the ocean to America would have put everything behind him.

'You just disappeared. Vanished off the face of the earth . . .'

'And now here I am.'

'Everyone thought you were dead. I don't know how we found out, but someone heard you were buried on a Scottish island.'

'Benbecula.'

'And that was the end of it . . . until we suddenly bump into you in New York.'

'Like a miracle,' Tommy smiled, '. . . risen from the dead.'

'This time we'll make sure,' one of the men to Sean's left muttered. Sean threw him an angry glance and the man didn't say anything else.

'I could ask why you're here,' Tommy said, folding his arms.

'You could, but I'm not the one on trial here, so it's me who'll be asking the questions today.'

Tommy shrugged. He didn't mind sitting here with his former comrades. He was even happy to answer some of their questions since he knew it would make no difference to the eventual verdict or sentence.

'So why did you desert?'

'I was tired.'

'Tired? We were in the middle of a war against the Brits.'

'I'd had enough, Sean . . . enough of the war and enough of the killing. I had to run away because I knew I wouldn't be allowed to leave.'

'So you just abandoned all your comrades – your friends – behind to continue the fight?'

'I'd done my bit.'

Des Donnelly, who was frantically scribbling down notes

on the paper, shook his head. Tommy didn't know why he was writing, unless it was to send home to Ireland as a record of what they'd done to him. The gunman standing behind Tommy snorted.

'You keep doing your 'bit' until we win or you die. That's what you signed up for, Tom. That was the oath you took, the pledge you made. You can't run away from that.'

'But I did.'

'Yes, you did . . . and now you have to answer for that.'

The distance between Tommy and the table was too far for him to reach without being stopped in his tracks, while the man behind him was a few paces away, again for the same reason. He had figured all that out straight away, while he also knew there was only one door in and out of the warehouse, and that was at the far end of the room, impossible to reach without one of them shooting him. For the moment, he knew he was trapped, and there seemed to be nothing he could do to escape. He had to bide his time and hope an opportunity would arise. Either that or before too long he was going to die.

'Bernadette O'Hara.'

Tommy looked up suddenly as Sean said the name.

'You remember Bernie, don't you, Tom?' Sean asked, sitting back in his chair.

Tommy nodded.

'Why did you kill her?'

'What?'

'Was it because she found out you were going to desert?'

'You killed her, Tommy. She was found dead in Glasgow. A bullet through the head. Then you disappeared before you could answer for that murder.'

'But I didn't kill her.'

Sean sat forward, pointing at Tommy.

'She knew your plans and was going to tell us so you killed her.'

'That's . . . that's just crazy.'

'Is it Tom? We know what happened.'

'But I . . . . I loved . . .'

Sean laughed coldly. 'We know about that too. Connor Daly told us everything.'

'Connor?'

'About you and Bernie. How you'd confided in her about your plans to desert, begging her to join you. And when she refused, when she said her loyalty was to the struggle and her love was for her country, you killed her.'

Tommy laughed. It sounded ludicrous as the words poured out of Sean's mouth but no-one else seemed to be amused.

'Connor found her body. He still loved her, you know, even after what you'd done to him . . . what the two of you had done. He was a broken man.'

Tommy wanted to scream that Connor killed Bernie, he was the traitor in the ranks, and he should be on trial instead, but he knew they wouldn't listen or be able to understand, let alone take in what he wanted to tell them.

Tommy thought about Bernie occasionally, though now, images came racing to the front of his mind; her flame red hair, the way she smelt – of strawberry cheesecake – and her smile, which could make his heart soar. He could never have killed her because . . . because . . . because he had loved her.

'So you have to answer for Bernie, too,' Sean said. 'Killing a fellow volunteer is a treasonable offence, Tom.'

'So kill me then. I don't care,' Tommy said, standing up.

'Sit down, Tom,' Sean ordered.

'Put a bullet in my brain. See if I care. I'll thank you for doing it.'

'Sit down!'

Tommy spun round, grabbed the chair and swung it at the gunman who had approached him to get him to sit down. The chair smashed as it connected with the man, sending him sprawling across the floor. Tommy was already on the run now. He hadn't anticipated it being so straightforward to escape, though the element of surprise was working in his favour as the four men behind the table seemed temporarily paralysed.

He raced towards the door as the gunman scrambled about on the floor, looking for his weapon which had been knocked out of his hand. As he reached the door, he heard the roar of the gun and he automatically hit the ground as the bullet slammed into the wall beside him.

'Don't let him escape,' Sean shouted as Tommy fumbled with the handle before getting the door opened and running out.

He stumbled off the kerb, almost falling, head-first, into the path of an oncoming car. The driver braked, thankfully, and the vehicle came to a shuddering halt just in front of Tommy. The driver gripped the steering wheel and glared out through the windscreen. Tommy, still glancing back towards the warehouse, ran round to the driver's door. Seeing him approach, the driver rolled down his window and opened his mouth to speak just as a fist slammed into his face. Tommy opened the door and grabbed the startled man, throwing him out of the car and on to the road.

'Sorry,' he said as he jumped into the car and started driving.

A bullet hit the car, shattering the back window, and Tommy pressed on the accelerator, forcing the pedal to the floor while, at the same time, trying to close the door. The republicans were all out in the street now, and the gunman fired another shot, though this one didn't hit the car. The rest of them seemed to be looking around in search of a vehicle for themselves, while the driver of the car Tommy had commandeered had picked himself up and was staring down the street in disbelief as his car slowly disappeared out of sight.

Tommy turned right at one junction, and then left at the next, barely stopping to check if there was oncoming traffic. He just wanted to get away from the warehouse and put some distance between him and his captors, while also searching for the main road that would take him out of Brooklyn and back in to Manhattan, and home.

He was halfway along the street when he saw the car speeding behind him. In truth, he heard it first, but once he'd spotted it, he knew it was them. They seemed to be going much faster than he was and were gaining on him. He tried pressing the accelerator down again but it couldn't go any further, nor could the car go any faster. If he pressed any harder, he was worried he'd thrust the pedal through the floor. The car raced round the corner and into Fulton Street, and though he gripped the steering wheel, he was going too fast and it began spinning out of control like one of the crazy fairground rides he'd once been persuaded to go on during a day out to Coney Island, though when it came to rest, the vehicle was still facing the right way.

A couple of car horns sounded, which he ignored, though as he moved off again, the Ford appeared behind him, taking the corner with at least the same level of speed as he'd done, though it managed to retain more control and it was quickly gaining on him. Another bullet hit the car, slamming into the side of the vehicle, and Tommy realised that he had no weapon to return fire, even if he had been able to do so while trying to drive at the same time.

Brooklyn Bridge was getting bigger and bigger. He felt if he could get across it, he'd be back on home territory and he'd feel safer, or at least have a chance of escape. The Ford was pulling alongside him, however, and it gave his car a gentle nudge, which was enough to send him veering slightly off course, scraping along the side of all the parked cars, but he kept moving. The chasing car had pulled in behind him again as vehicles raced towards them on the other side of the road, and another shot was fired, this time the bullet hitting the dashboard on the passenger's side. They were getting closer to him.

Still the Bridge got closer. Now the Ford inched closer to him, bumping the back of the car once, twice, three times . . . and it felt like he was no longer in total control of the vehicle himself, but that the other car was dictating his movements.

Suddenly, he veered across the road, in front of oncoming traffic. Horns sounded, brakes screeched, curses were hurled, but no-one hit him. The republicans were temporarily out of sight, though he quickly spotted them again on the other side of the road, and now the two cars raced, parallel to each other, heading towards the Bridge. Tommy tried to avoid any more oncoming traffic, but he did so by making them move out of his way. If someone hit him, it would be all over anyway so he wasn't stopping or moving for anyone.

At some point he knew he'd have to get back on the other side. His luck couldn't hold out for much longer, and he wouldn't get across the Bridge if he continued driving into the traffic. He had to keep watching the road so he couldn't keep his eye on the Ford, though when he pulled the car across the road again, he saw in the mirror that it was directly behind him. It slammed into the back of his car again, jolting the vehicle forward and he nearly hit his head on the windscreen. The contact had created a small gap between the two cars and Tommy tried to speed away from his pursuers.

He glanced in the mirror again just as a car appeared from a side street. It was halfway out when his car slammed into it, sending the other vehicle spinning across the road, while the Ford came to a halt, steam beginning to escape from the bonnet. Tommy could feel himself relax slightly, though he almost immediately he felt something running down his cheek and he gently touched his head. It was bleeding. Pain began to be felt elsewhere, his neck, back, legs, and he groaned, hoping that someone would help him get out of the car because he wasn't sure he'd be able to move himself.

Secret Hopes

There was a shadow in front of him which seemed to bob and weave like a bare-knuckle boxer. He strained his eyes to try and make it stay in one place, though when he did so, he became aware of the throbbing pain that began at the back of his head and then stretched across his skull. He groaned and tried to sink further into the pillow, though even the slightest movement caused a separate but equally agonising pain to shoot up and down his leg. It was as if he was being attacked by two invisible assailants at the same time. It was easiest just to close his eyes, though sleep didn't return. There were murmurs in the background, though he couldn't make out what was being said. In truth, he didn't want to try too hard to listen since the effort of doing so was proving just as painful as trying to focus his eyes.

'Theresa,' he mumbled, though his mouth was dry and he wasn't sure if he actually made any sound.

He felt scared, lonely, and he sensed a few tears mustering in his eyes, which took him by surprise. It was like he was a child again, lying in bed, surrounded by strange people, and he wanted his mother. He didn't think of her very often. The last time he'd seen her, she had been lying on her death bed in Donegal. He had gone to Glasgow after that, and he never saw her again. He hadn't even been able to return to Ireland to visit her graveside. He knew now that he never would. Instinctively, he moved his arm to make the sign of the cross, but the pain as his fingertips touched his forehead was so unbearable that he put his arm back down at his side. It was an exhausting as well as painful gesture and he kept his eyes closed as he breathed heavily.

'It's okay. I'm here.'

He thought he heard a whisper, and he tried to open his eyes again, just to confirm that it was a voice and not just the swoosh of branches in the wind. The effort of doing so was still sore, but he managed enough so that he saw the outline of a body in front of him. It was Theresa, who sat on the side of the bed. She leant over and gently wiped his forehead with a wet cloth, and he closed his eyes again as drops of water ran down his face. It felt like tears even though he knew he wasn't crying.

'Tommy, are you okay?'

He recognised Theresa's voice this time. He moved his head. He wasn't sure if it looked like a nod or a shake, but she remained at the side of the bed, occasionally glancing away like she was looking at someone else. Tommy didn't turn to see who it was. His head was too sore to move. Instead, he stared at her.

'Kathleen,' he whispered.

Theresa glanced away again and then shrugged her shoulders.

'Kathleen's gone, Tommy,' she said slowly.

'I know.'

'Do you want a cigarette?'

It was a voice in the corner, but one that wasn't familiar

to him. It was only when the figure came into view that he recognised Joseph. Between Theresa and the boy, they gently propped the pillow up behind him and managed to position him so that he was almost sitting up, certainly in a better position to smoke. Joseph placed a cigarette in Tommy's mouth, and he held it in place with his lips while Theresa held a match up to the end of the cigarette so that Tommy could feel the tiny heat waves shimmering across his cheeks. He inhaled deeply and closed his eyes, sighing gratefully as his lungs filled up with nicotine, before he released most of it into the air when he breathed out.

'You must have had a bad dream,' Theresa said.

Tommy opened his eyes again and studied his surroundings. There was a statue of Our Lady sitting on top of the chest of drawers facing the bed that he didn't remember ever being there before, and his eyes quickly scanned the room just to confirm he was in his own bedroom. He took another draw of the cigarette. He hadn't spent too much time in here recently, so it wasn't altogether a surprise that things were unfamiliar to him.

'How is your head?'

'Sore,' he said, automatically moving his hand towards it, though his fingers barely touched his flesh. He was scared it would be too sore.

'What happened?'

Tommy looked at Theresa, holding her gaze for a few moments before glancing away as he drew on his cigarette again. He didn't know how to answer that. The more she knew, the more she would become involved, and that might make things more dangerous for her. At the same time, he knew that secrets weren't the best thing to take with you into a marriage and he didn't think she would accept any sort of brush-off from him, not when he was lying injured in their bed.

'Car crash?' he said, offering it more as a question than an explanation.

He wasn't lying to her in that he had been involved in a car crash, but he knew from her expression that he would need to give her more by way of explanation. His free hand stretched across towards her and she gently guided it towards her bump, letting it rest on her and leaving her own hand on top of his. He closed his eyes, just for a moment, but in that tiny fraction of time, it was as if they had gone back to before everything had happened, and he wouldn't have been surprised to see Kathleen bounding into the room to see how he was. When he opened his eyes again, that illusion was gone and it was Joseph who stood at the end of the bed with one hand in a trouser pocket and chewing nervously on his bottom lip.

Tommy wanted to tell Theresa everything. He realised he would have to, certainly about his former comrades, but he wanted to share everything with her. Or was it that he wanted to unburden his own mind? He didn't want to do it with the boy in the room and he tried to signal this with his eyes to Theresa. It took a few minutes, but eventually she seemed to realise. She shook her head.

'Joseph can keep a secret,' she said, patting Tommy's hand that remained on her belly.

The boy stepped forward at that point with a saucer for Tommy to extinguish his cigarette, and it felt like they were both reading his mind at that point. He looked at the boy, who was reluctant to hold his gaze. His left arm still hung at his side and it was enough to make Tommy feel guilty about his own injuries, which seemed minor by comparison. Joseph had become a regular visitor to the apartment since his injury, even before then probably.

Since Kathleen died. Tommy sensed things around him, occasionally glancing over his shoulder and expecting to see someone, hoping it would be his daughter even as his mind told him that was impossible. That was different from Joseph's presence, which was real and visible. He wanted to thank him, but didn't really know how to, or, indeed, how the boy would react.

Tommy needed some fresh air. Theresa wasn't happy about him getting out of bed, never mind wanting to leave the house, and she insisted on going with him, even though, in turn, he wasn't happy about her being out and about either.

'I'm not sick, you know,' she said with a smile when he'd voiced his objections.

'Well, neither am I.'

'Yes, but you've been hurt.'

He shrugged.

'So I'm just coming to keep an eye on you . . . and you can keep an eye on me too.'

She held on to his arm as they slowly walked up Tenth Avenue. He'd suggested they walk towards Central Park, though it was a laborious journey, broken up every time either of them stopped to enquire how the other was doing. He figured that if they did make it all the way to the Park, it would be a nicer setting to sit and think. Once he was on the move, the pain rippling through his body seemed to subside a little, in part because he was more concerned about Theresa. Her bump seemed to lead the way for them and he couldn't help staring at it every few minutes. It was strange to think that there was a baby inside her that was breathing and growing and would one day soon emerge into the world as his son. He remained convinced that it was a boy, just as he remained steadfast in his determination to call him Michael. Theresa would catch him looking at her and smile, giving his arm a squeeze and sometimes running her hand over the bump for a few seconds.

His head was still sore, but the pain was more bearable now. The warm air was helping and he found the gentle breeze which rippled up and down the avenue strangely soothing. Some people who passed them would stare at his head as they did so, the fresh cut on his flesh catching their attention, though just as many would glance at Theresa and offer a silent, almost congratulatory smile at her impending arrival.

Crossing intersections was more difficult than making their way along sidewalks which, thankfully, weren't too cluttered with people. Theresa would stop at shop windows, pretending to be interested in whatever was on display in the window as a way of inducing customers to step inside when he sensed that she was really just wanting a rest. She didn't want to confirm to him that she'd be a burden or that the walk would be too strenuous for her, and while he made sure the pace of their journey was slow, he also didn't say anything at her window shopping stops either.

Eventually, they made it all the way to Central Park. He didn't know how long it had taken them but it had been a slow and exhausting journey. They sought out the nearest empty bench they could find and sat down, grateful to rest their weary legs.

'Maybe we should have just gone to Bryant Park,' he said.

'Now you suggest it,' she said with a smile.

'Are you okay?'

'I'm fine. I told you, I'm not sick.'

'I know, but . . .'

'It's fine,' she said, patting his arm. 'I'm fine. What about you?'

'My head's still sore, but I'm okay.'

'So what happened?'

He sighed. It was a secret he'd never imagined having to tell Theresa. It had crossed his mind on occasion, but he'd never thought it was something she needed to know. Now, with some of his former IRA comrades having turned up in the city, and trying to make him answer for a previous life, it was difficult to keep his past from her. He knew she was watching him as he spoke, studying his face for any sign that he might not be telling her the truth or even just an edited version of it, but having decided to explain what had happened to cause his injuries, he also felt there was no point leaving anything out. Either she knew the whole story or none at all.

Theresa didn't interrupt him at all as he spoke, his mind dredging up the sediment of his past, from his childhood in Donegal right through to his escape to New York, with everything included in between. That meant telling her about Bernie as well. Bernie, who he now knew for sure was dead. He wondered whether he would have tried to find her at some point if he still clung on to the futile hope that she was alive, but he kept that thought to himself. It didn't matter anyway, not now that he knew any such search would be a fruitless and ultimately painful one. He might still harbour hopes of one day standing at his mother's graveside and say goodbye, but he didn't feel the same way about Bernie.

He spoke about the times he fired a gun or used a knife, though he didn't go into graphic detail, or recounted every single incident. It was enough that she knew what he had done. It was more important not to let her know just how much he had done. He mentioned his old friend.

'You knew Michael Collins?' she asked. It was the first time she'd spoke since he began.

'He was my friend. The Big Fella.'

It felt, just there and then, as if just about everyone he'd ever known or loved, was lost to him. He found himself holding Theresa's hand and squeezing it, as much for his own reassurance as hers. At least she was still here. He also realised that, of everyone who was gone, it was Kathleen that he missed the most. He liked the sound of her laughter filling their apartment and wondered how that would have sounded when she was older. He missed her running to the front door to welcome him home, jumping into his outstretched arms with the innocent trust that only a child possesses. He wished that, just one more time, he could carry her sleeping body from the living room to her bedroom, lay her gently down on the bed, pull a cover over her, plant a gentle kiss on her forehead and then stand, almost hypnotised at the door, watching her as she slept and marvelling at the unexpected turn of events which had brought fatherhood into his life.

'I miss Kathleen,' he said out loud.

Theresa linked her arm in his and pressed closer to him.

'What will we call the baby if it's a girl?' she asked.

'It's going to be a boy.'

'But what if it's a girl?'

Tommy shook his head. 'It won't be.'

'Don't be so sure, mister,' she said, caressing the bump as if she already knew.

He would take them to Ireland with him one day, he decided there and then. Theresa and their son. They would take the long boat journey back home to Donegal, and he would lay flowers at the grave of his mother, remembering, too, the little girl who just happened to share her name and who should have been there with them. He didn't know who would remember him, or just when it would be safe to return, but the thought of never seeing Ireland again was an impossible one to contemplate. They could even go down to Monaghan, where Theresa's family were originally from, if she knew their home village or parish.

'What are you so happy about?' Theresa asked.

'Nothing . . . I'm not. I was just thinking of Ireland.'

'And what about the men who wanted to kill you?'

'I think they still do.'

'So what are you going to do?'

'I don't know . . . Ask for help, I suppose.'

'Help from who?'

He shrugged, suddenly reluctant to mention Bill Dwyer's name. He'd wanted to tell her everything, but another secret had just been created. She would know who he was.

Everyone in Hell's Kitchen knew of Big Bill, and she wouldn't be happy if she knew of his involvement with the gang boss. Tommy lit a cigarette and offered the packet to Theresa, who shook her head.

'What are you going to do?' It was as if Theresa could read his mind.

'I don't know.'

'Don't do anything stupid.'

'I have to do something.'

'I've already lost a daughter, Tommy . . .'

'You won't lose me. I promise.'

He kissed her cheek and was relieved that she didn't pull away from him. They sat for a long time in silence, watching people go by, until they both felt rested enough to make the return journey home. It had been nice to be out together, though there was a nagging sense of guilt gnawing at his conscience that he hadn't told Theresa everything that was happening. Sometimes it was better not to know – safer – he told himself, though without conviction.

Revelations

They drove in silence, Jimmy behind the wheel and Tommy alongside him. Joseph sat in the back, staring straight ahead between their shoulders and out the windscreen. The view was of Sixth Avenue, stretching far off into the distance, lined on either side by buildings of all shapes and sizes, some of them seeming to stretch all the way up to the clear, blue sky, while others, dwarfed by these concrete giants, looked small enough that they would be the same size as a grown man. Of course, standing in front of even these 'small' buildings, any man would feel tiny and insignificant.

Jimmy occasionally glanced to his right, sometimes frowning, sometimes shaking his head like he had no idea who this stranger was sitting beside him. The silence which enveloped the car had been their constant companion from the moment they'd left the church house.

Tommy leant his head against the cold glass of the car window and stared out at the city, which always seemed to be on the move. Shops selling all types of household goods were jostling for custom with cafés and corner shops. Clothes shops offering the latest styles at knockdown prices. Two for a dollar. He didn't even notice what was being sold. Street vendors had set up stalls at random pitches along the sidewalks, selling fruit and pastry and cheap goods that had obviously been acquired by less than legitimate means. Each of them had someone watching out for any approaching cops, when everything would be hastily packed away and they'd vanish until the coast was clear again. American flags hung from several buildings, usually hotels or larger department stores, attached to poles fastened on to the brickwork. The flags barely fluttered in the stillness of the day.

Tommy had given Jimmy the address. It was the one that Joseph had told him and the boy nodded in agreement when he said it. They'd had to pick up the rifle first, and while Father Mike was relieved to hand the bag over, he held on to it for a few seconds as Tommy tried to take it.

'Take it easy, Tommy,' the priest eventually said, having wrestled with the right words to offer and not really sure, even after saying them, that they were.

Tommy nodded as the car horn sounded impatiently. His former IRA comrades had lost the sanctuary of the church house. They wouldn't have been surprised after the court-martial, though they would still want somewhere to lie low and avoid any attention that might come their way following his escape. Father Mike knew they were in Brooklyn, but beyond that he had no idea. It remained a problem for Tommy, but it could wait for another day. The priest remained at the front door of the church house as the car pulled away, not offering any gesture by way of farewell, though Tommy was hoping that a prayer would be said at least for their safe return.

When they were still a couple of blocks away, Tommy told Jimmy to park the car, pointing out the best place for him to pull in.

'Stay here,' he said to them as he got out the car. 'I'll be five minutes.'

'Where are you going?' said Jimmy.

'Don't worry. I'm only going to have a look.'

He returned to the car within a few minutes, but now took his place in the back seat alongside Joseph, who sat, mesmerised, as Tommy loaded the rifle. He knelt up on the seat and rested the rifle on the window ledge, allowing the barrel to press against the back window. He was tempted to break the glass, but there was no point and it would only annoy Jimmy

'Sit back,' he muttered to Joseph, who pressed himself against the door as he stared at Tommy.

Now it was a case of waiting. It might be five minutes or it could be five hours. He hadn't told Jimmy that, but they were going nowhere 'till he'd finished what he'd come here for. He touched his holy medals instinctively glanced to his right now. It was Joseph who looked back at him now, and the boy smiled, a smile that was a mixture of nerves, excitement and fear. Tommy winked at Joseph and his grin got even wider.

The sight was trained on the front door of the building. It was like he was back in Ireland, though he was aware, however, that this wasn't an open field but a busy street, and he didn't want the gun protruding out the window in case it attracted unwanted attention.

'I need a coffee,' Jimmy muttered, starting to open his door.

'You can't go,' Tommy said.

'You've got to be kidding.'

'I need you to get me out of here as soon as it's done.'

'We could be here for hours. I'll only be five minutes. There's a place just round the corner.'

'What happens if you're not here?'

'Jesus, Tommy. You're really trying my patience.'

'I'll get it for you,' said Joseph.

Jimmy looked at Tommy, who glanced at the boy and then nodded.

'But don't be long,' he said as Joseph took the dollar bill from Jimmy.

'Get yourself a soda,' Jimmy said and Joseph smiled, gratefully, before heading off to find a cafe.

Tommy resumed his vigil, aware that Jimmy had lit a cigarette and was filling the car up with smoke.

'Roll your window down, Jimmy,' he snapped.

'Are you wanting one?'

'Not now,' said Tommy.

The door of the tenement building opened and a woman appeared. Tommy tensed, his focus suddenly intensified, the grip on the rifle tightened, his finger caressing the trigger. He didn't recognise her, but every movement at the front of the building was making him more alert and on edge. It was an automatic gesture, and one that Jimmy, who'd also turned round to stare towards the building, would have expected.

Two men walked out the building and down the stairs, stopping on the sidewalk beside the woman. One of them took off his hat and wiped his brow. It was the man from Joseph's drawing. Angelo. Almost in the same moment, his companion stepped forward, blocking Tommy's view. He remained poised and ready . . . Patience was a virtue. He gritted his teeth and realised his finger was twitching anxiously at the trigger, eager to press it and kill the man who had done the same to his daughter. He was fighting a strong urge to do it, but that wasn't part of the plan. He had to stay focused. The man blocking his view now took his own hat off and turned round, looking up the street towards where they were parked. Tommy jumped back, pulling the rifle into the car.

'Jesus!'

'What is it?' Jimmy asked.

'It's Gorevin.'

'Where?'

'Up there. Standing outside the building.'

Jimmy leant forward and peered through the window.

'Jesus!' he blurted out, like a delayed echo of Tommy. 'What the hell is he doing there?'

Tommy shrugged, almost in the same instant that the street seemed to fill up with cars racing in both directions towards the building where Gorevin and Angelo stood.

'What the hell is going on?' Jimmy asked.

'I don't know. It looks like cops.'

It was cops. Lots of them. Twenty or thirty at least. They were pouring out of their cars, guns drawn, shouting orders that merged into one cloud of noise that floated down the street towards Tommy and Jimmy. Angelo suddenly disappeared from view, felled by the swinging arm of one officer, while Gorevin stepped towards the kerb. The cops ignored him, instead congregating on the sidewalk above Angelo's body.

'Go! Go!'

'What about the boy?'

'Just go, Jimmy. Get the hell out of here.'

The car pulled out from the kerb, its wheels screeching as rubber burned on the hard surface of the road. Tommy slumped down in his seat, hiding from the curious stares of people who'd stopped at the sudden burst of noise and who watched the Ford weave through traffic until it disappeared from sight. He hadn't fired the rifle, again. That had never been his intention, though he hadn't told Jimmy that. He'd been expecting the cops to arrive. One anonymous phone call revealing where Detective Lincoln's killer could be found brought them rushing to the address. It was Gorevin's presence, standing beside Kathleen's killer, which unnerved him. Like Jimmy, the one question he wanted answered was, what the hell was Gorevin doing there?

Joseph stood on the sidewalk holding a cup of coffee and staring at the space where the car had been. He looked up and down the street but there was no sign of it. He'd taken longer than he should have because he'd waited to drink the soda in the store. He didn't think he'd be able to carry both the coffee and the bottle back, and if he didn't return the empty bottle to the store, then he'd lose the two-nickel deposit. Not that it was really his money, of course, since Jimmy had given him the dollar bill, but he guessed the man wouldn't be looking for any of it back, so those two nickels were his. Even after getting the drinks, he still had enough for a bar of candy, while he also ate in the store. It was a Baby Ruth bar. It was chewy, with peanuts mixed through it, and covered in chocolate. When he'd finished it, Joseph stuffed the wrapper in his pocket and ran his tongue along his lips to try and mop up any tell-tale signs that he'd eaten it.

Now, as he remained on the sidewalk, not knowing what to do next, he wished he'd bought another bar. He put the cup of coffee down at the side of the kerb and took out the coins he still had in his pocket. He could go back to the store and buy another bar, but he had to get home now and he knew he needed the money for a train ticket. He couldn't understand why they'd left him here. Surely they couldn't have forgotten about him?

Joseph realised that, no matter how long or how hard he stared at the space in front of him, the car wasn't going to reappear. He needed to get home now, back to his own neighbourhood. He looked along the street towards the house that he'd told Tommy about. It looked to him like a million cops were swarming about on the sidewalk and on the road, preventing any traffic from moving. He turned and began walking towards the station. He'd only been here once before but he remembered the route and his pace quickened as he got nearer and could hear the trains rattling by on the line. Soon, he would be home again, though he wanted to go straight to Theresa's apartment. Hopefully, Tommy would be there to offer an explanation as to why he'd been abandoned, and in 'enemy' territory.

They both stood leaning against the car, looking out towards the river, smoking in silence. The sun seemed to have caught them in its spotlight and Tommy had taken off his jacket and thrown it into the car. Beads of sweat ran down his spine which he could do nothing about, though he was able to wipe his forehead with his shirt sleeve every few minutes. It was only now, in the stillness of the September day that he felt calm again. His heart had stopped thumping and his breathing was regular. He could feel the beginning of a headache taking shape in his skull but he hoped the cigarette might help. There was background noise, of ships and boats and barges announcing their arrival or bidding farewell. The rumble of the city, of traffic and people mingling together, seemed to rise up from the built-up areas nearby like shimmering heat on a summer's day.

They had stopped at the piece of waste ground down near 24th Street. He hoped Joseph wouldn't be too annoyed that they had left him behind. He was sure that, when the boy returned with the coffee to find the car gone, he'd quickly leave the scene. He'd apologise later, even if he didn't offer a proper explanation. His mind remained in a state of flux, unable to figure out why Gorevin had been there.

'Do you remember when you came here?' Tommy asked, flicking his cigarette on to the ground.

'What? To this place here?'

'No . . . to America . . . New York.'

'Of course I do. You never forget something like that.'

'Do you think you'll ever go home?'

'To Ireland?'

Tommy nodded.

'This is my home now. Eighteen ninety-two I came here . . . That seems like a lifetime ago now. I just had the clothes on my back and a bit of paper with an address of a cousin who gave me a bed for a few weeks until I started working wherever they'd give a shovel.'

'I was born in ninety-two.'

'Jesus, you're just a boy.'

'I'd like to go back one day.'

'What for? The place is a bloody mess.'

'Maybe when I'm old and grey, I'll go home to Donegal.'

'I won't.'

Most of the time, Tommy never thought about going back to Ireland. He might only have been here for two years as opposed to Jimmy's thirty, but he felt like it was his city now. Yet, Ireland was still in his blood and always would be. He wanted to stand at his mother's graveside in Donegal and say goodbye. Even if he was old and grey, that would still be his wish.

'So why was Gorevin there?' Tommy had asked Jimmy the same question over and over again to the point he was only receiving an exasperated sigh in reply. Neither of them knew the answer but it had given Tommy a shock when he'd seen Bill Dwyer's right-hand man standing beside the man who had killed his daughter. The cops had taken Angelo, just as he'd hoped they would, and Bill Dwyer was none the wiser as to what had happened, either to Angelo or Lincoln.

Now that he had some time to collect his thoughts, he was even more curious as to why Gorevin had been there. He'd been in the room when Bill had been talking about the chess game. He'd been the one who had given Tommy his instructions on killing Lincoln, which was being done with the aim of provoking Reina and flushing out Kathleen's killer. Now, here he was, standing in the middle of the street with the person that Tommy had told Bill he wanted to kill.

'It doesn't make any sense,' he said.

'I know,' said Jimmy. 'So you keep saying.'

'So why was Gorevin there?'

'For God's sake, Tommy. Will you give it a rest?'

'Do you not think it's strange?'

Jimmy flicked his cigarette end away and stretched.

'There's only one man who's got the answers, Tommy. You'll need to ask him.'

Tommy nodded. He knew Jimmy was right. He would have to ask Bill Dwyer why Gorevin was with Kathleen's killer, and he had to hope that there would be a proper explanation. Tommy wasn't in the mood for any more chess games.

Checkmate

The hallway was cool and dark, and Tommy leant against the wall, smoking a cigarette. He had been standing there for at least fifteen minutes. The man who'd brought him here had disappeared behind the door he was standing at, closing it behind him. Tommy had pressed his ears to the wood, trying to hear anything behind it, but there was only silence. The man had told him to wait there and he didn't look a person used to being disobeyed. Tommy had asked Jimmy to set up another meeting with Bill Dwyer, but it was the gang boss who had summoned him to one of his warehouses in Lower Manhattan. A car waiting outside his apartment had driven him here. Tommy was glad at least of the opportunity to speak to Bill. His head was swirling with questions and he needed answers.

He hadn't told Theresa where he was going. More secrets, he thought, but as he looked at her, sleeping in bed, he didn't want to disturb her. She was tired now most of the time, but he could understand that, given she was carrying an increasingly heavy burden. Not for much longer, though, and it was why he didn't like leaving her on her own. He'd knocked on Alice Payne's door on the way out, asking her to look in on Theresa later. It gave him some sort of reassurance.

Even if he hadn't completely confessed his past, and it seemed like he was keeping other things from her to balance up what he did reveal, it had helped them. More than any of what he told her, however, was the fact that Kathleen's name was now being uttered between them and that allowed memories – happy ones – to float through the house. They now mingled with the sadness, and the tears that still flowed were for a mixture of emotions.

He heard footsteps and looked down the hallway. A silhouette appeared at the far end and stopped. Tommy pushed himself off the wall, dropping his cigarette on to the ground and crushing it with his foot. Slowly, the figure approached. Tommy recognised the footsteps. It was Gorevin. As he got closer, the blond hair seemed to glow in the gloom. He stopped a few feet away and lit a cigarette, which illuminated his face briefly, and Tommy could make out his crooked nose. He was sure Gorevin smiled as well, just for a moment, but it still looked like a joyless expression.

'So you're waiting for Big Bill?' he asked.

Tommy nodded.

'A few things to discuss, I imagine?'

'One or two things.'

'I'm sure Bill has a few things to say to you too.'

Tommy lit another cigarette, and it seemed like they were swapping balls of smoke, firing them at each other until it felt like they were standing in the middle of early-morning mist. He preferred the fact that Gorevin's face was blurred, because his expression unnerved him. It always looked so calm and controlled, yet he knew, behind that façade lurked naked evil. He felt a slight chill shimmer down his spine.

'We've got a few things to talk about too,' Gorevin said.

'Have we?'

'You know we do.'

Had Gorevin seen him after all when he'd looked up the street towards the car? He thought he'd been quick enough to duck down, but it might have been when the car screeched away. He could have recognised the car, and then guessed who was in it.

'Jimmy told me.'

'Jimmy?'

'He knows where his loyalties lie. Do you?'

'What's that supposed to mean?'

'You think you saw me standing with someone you wanted to kill, someone who is part of a rival organisation.'

'I know what I saw.'

'You say that, but I'm not sure that you did. You saw the man who killed your daughter, and it made you angry and confused. You thought someone else was there too, but it was just a case of mistaken identity.'

'I know what I saw.'

'Happy are those who believe but who do not see.'

'What's that supposed to mean?'

'I think you know.'

'You'll have to spell it out for me . . . Francis.' Tommy almost spat Gorevin's name out at him. He didn't know why he did it. He knew it sounded insolent, aggressive even, and that wasn't the best attitude to adopt in dealing with Gorevin, but there was something in the other man's tone which irritated. It was like the old Tom Costello had re-surfaced, the one who never backed down, and who was afraid of nobody. Gorevin didn't look like he was annoyed, however. Indeed, he laughed. It wasn't one of his characteristic short, sharp, cold laughs, but a loud noise that seemed to come all the way from the pit of his stomach and fill the hallway.

'Saint Francis of Assisi saved my life,' he said. 'When I was a baby, just a couple of months old, I was very ill. They thought I was going to die. The priest had even been called to give me the last rites. There was no hope for me. But my mother never gave up. She had faith. She prayed to Saint Francis. Every morning and every night, she prayed to him, and he heard her prayers. I got better . . . as you can see now. And from then on, I was called Francis. I was named for my father, but I'm called after the saint who saved me . . . So I'm very proud of my name.'

Tommy shrugged as Gorevin stepped closer to him.

'You want me to spell it out for you, Tom?' Now it was Gorevin's turn to spit out Tommy's name – he called him 'Tom', of course, and he did it contemptuously, like he was clearing his throat. 'I can do that for you, if that's what you really want.'

'I know what I saw,' Tommy said.

'When you go into that room, you'll say nothing to Bill about what you think you saw.'

'I'm not scared of you.'

Gorevin laughed again, though it was a short sound this time.

'There is a man sitting in a car outside your apartment right now,' said Gorevin. 'He is waiting for me to arrive. If I'm not there by three o'clock, then he will get out of the car, walk across the street and up into your building. He'll take the stairs up to the third floor and knock on the door of your apartment. When Theresa answers it, he'll push his way inside, close the door, take out the knife from his jacket pocket and cut her throat, letting her fall to the floor and bleed to death which will also kill the baby she's carrying . . .'

Tommy could have challenged Gorevin to prove he was telling the truth, but he knew, in his heart and in his guts which were now churning, that Gorevin wasn't bluffing. The other man lit up a cigarette, and he blew some smoke into Tommy's face, which stung his eyes and made him cough.

'So did that spell it out for you okay?'

Tommy nodded, just as the door opened and the man who'd told him to wait in the hallway, popped his head out.

'It's time,' he said.

Gorevin brushed past Tommy without another word or even a warning look aimed in his direction. Tommy sighed deeply, slowly turning round and walking towards the door.

Bill Dwyer was sitting on a large armchair, his legs crossed. He smiled as Tommy came into the room, and he put down the glass he was holding on to the table at his side. Tommy presumed it contained rum. He stood up and walked towards him, holding out his hand.

'It's good to see you, Tom,' he said.

Tommy took his hand, offering a weak handshake in return and an even weaker smile.

'You look as though you need a drink,' Bill said, giving his back a heavy pat. 'Sit down, rest those weary legs . . . Vinnie, a scotch for our friend here,' he said to the man who'd shown him in.

Tommy sat on the chair Bill guided him to, though he remained balanced on the edge of it. Gorevin stood in the shadows, just out of his eye-line, but Tommy was aware of his presence, and conscious of his threat. Vinnie handed him a glass, which he took without reply, immediately taking a sip of the liquor, which offered no comfort. Bill remained standing in the middle of the room.

'You might recognise this man, Tom, but let me introduce you,' said Bill, and Tommy glanced at the figure sitting in a chair opposite.

'This is Mister Reina . . . Can we call you Gaetano?'

'Sure, Bill,' Reina said.

'Gaetano, meet Tom Costello.'

Tommy stared at Reina, who offered a small nod by way of greeting. He held a smouldering cigar in his right hand, which he now placed at his lips, sucking on it and blowing smoke out into the room. Tommy could smell the aroma and automatically breathed in to capture some of it. It was the smell of wealth.

'Mister Reina was very keen to meet you,' Bill said, sitting back down.

He was smoking too, though it was a pack of *Luckies*. You could take the man out of Hell's Kitchen, thought Tommy, watching as Bill lit up . . . he offered the packet to Tommy, who put his glass on the floor at his feet and took one. Vinnie was still hovering nearby and instinctively offered a light to both of them.

'Where do we start, Tom?' said Bill.

Tommy shrugged, glancing at Reina first through the cloud of cigar smoke, and then back at Bill. He shrugged again. Bill gestured towards Reina, who cleared his throat and stretched across to the table, placing his cigar in the ashtray where it continued to release small spirals of smoke into the air.

'One of my men is in jail right now,' said Reina. 'And he's heading for the electric chair. Do you know why?'

Tommy shook his head.

'The cops say he killed Detective Lincoln. Can you believe that?'

Tommy glanced at Dwyer, and then round at Gorevin who stood, arms folded, staring impassively at him. Tommy wished there was a clock in the room so that he knew how long it would be before Gorevin slipped out and headed to his house. Until then, his mind remained cluttered with the worry of what might happen to Theresa.

'Sometimes you don't always get what you ask for in life,' Bill said, and Tommy looked at him. 'You came to me for help, Tom, and I said I would do what I could. A man can do no more than that, but there is a bigger picture here, and that's important too.'

'I'm not sure I understand, Bill,' Tommy said slowly.

'Angelo is one of my most trusted lieutenants,' said Reina, as Dwyer continued staring at Tommy. 'And he's not a man I want to lose.'

'It turns out that someone else did the little task I set you, Tommy,' said Dwyer, sitting forward. 'Now why wouldn't you have told me that you didn't shoot Detective Lincoln?'

'I don't know, Bill. I panicked. I couldn't believe someone else was there and I didn't know what to do.'

'I don't know what Angelo was thinking about,' said Reina. 'I still don't understand why he killed Lincoln. He worked for us. Angelo knew that.'

Reina puffed on the cigar he'd picked up again. A feeling of nervousness washed over Tommy. There was nowhere to go and nothing he could do. When he left this room, there would be no gun to pick up and aim, no cause to fight, and possibly die for, and no-one in the city to help him. He was alone, apart from Theresa, and he could feel what strength he still possessed begin to drain out of him.

'Your other problem has been dealt with,' Bill said.

'What problem?'

'Francis told me,' Bill said, pointing at Gorevin. 'A bit of bother that arrived from Ireland.'

'I can handle that myself,' Tommy said.

'There's nothing to handle,' Bill said. 'Francis sorted it. They won't bother you again. They'll be focused on their own fight from now on.'

Tommy didn't know what to say. Some sort of thank-you would normally be appropriate in the circumstances, but he couldn't bring himself to speak to Gorevin – it still chilled him whenever he looked at the man – while Bill had helped him in ways he hadn't asked for.

'Sometimes you don't always get what you ask for in life,' Dwyer repeated, almost as if he read Tommy's mind. 'Mister Reina and I have no wish to fall out over this. What's done is done. Lincoln is dead. And now I'm going to help him. There are things we'd like to do together, things that involve the hand of friendship. I am sorry, Tom, but this is the world we live in and this is how it works.'

Tommy had finished his cigarette, which Vinnie noticed, attentively holding out an ashtray for him to stub it out before taking a step back into the shadows. He folded his arms and looked between the two gang bosses.

'Mister Reina's man will not take a seat in that electric chair. Vinnie here will swear that he was with Angelo the day Lincoln was killed. They were sitting in a speakeasy in Hell's Kitchen, playing cards and drinking scotch. Is that not right, Vinnie?'

'Yes, Bill. That's what happened. Angelo was with me all day.'

Dwyer nodded and Reina smiled gratefully. Tommy felt drained now, too weak to stand up. It was over now and he had failed. Angelo wasn't going to the electric chair. He was going to walk free. Tommy had failed Theresa and, more importantly, he had failed Kathleen. The green ribbon which he still carried in his pocket suddenly felt like it was on fire and burning his flesh as a punishment for his failure.

'Francis will drive you home,' said Bill. 'Go back to your wife, Tom . . .'

Tommy started to speak.

'. . . Well, make an honest woman of her, then,' Bill added with a smile. 'Raise your family, Tom, and let go of the things you can't control.'

Gorevin stepped forward but Tommy wouldn't look at him.

'I only wanted to find who killed Kathleen,' he said.

Reina cleared his throat.

'We are not heartless men, Mister Costello,' he said. 'I am a father, too. So is Bill. We know how difficult this has been. To lose you daughter . . .' he shook his head, while Bill nodded in agreement.

'And I can understand your reaction, your need for revenge. That won't bring your daughter back, Mister Costello. That is the truth of the matter.'

Tommy didn't know what else to say.

'I am sorry, Mister Costello,' said Reina. 'I truly am.'

'We are just tiny figures in a bigger picture,' Bill said, standing up. Reina followed suit.

'Just pawns in the game,' Tommy muttered and Bill laughed.

'Very good, Tom. I see you're learning about the game.'

Gorevin had released his grip of Tommy's shoulder and took a step back. Bill and Reina walked out, Bill patting his shoulder gently as he passed. It was time for Tommy to go home too, though what would he tell Theresa? Nothing, he realised. There was nothing he could say. It was just one more secret that he'd have to keep from her.

Family Man

They held hands as they stood nervously at the wrought-iron gate as if they weren't sure whether to go on or not, staring straight ahead beyond the gates and up the gravel path that snaked through the graveyard. Occasional bursts of traffic drifted by them on the road behind, but it wasn't enough to draw their attention away from what was in front of them. There seemed to be endless lines of graves, some of them marked with simple wooden crosses, while others had headstones of varying shapes and sizes. The more ostentatious ones stood out, large marble structures with statues of saints or Our Lady keeping watch over the dead.

Slowly, they moved forward and through the gates, beginning to walk up the gravel path. Tommy hadn't visited this place very often but Theresa knew where she was going. She retraced the steps they'd made on the day of the funeral, and ones that she'd followed many times since. If she closed her eyes she could still find her way to the right place.

The graveyard was quiet. Occasional movements caught their eye. There were a few random souls moving between the gravestones, laying fresh flowers, throwing old ones away, mumbling prayers whose words had long ago been ingrained in their minds, or muttering as if in conversation with an invisible companion.

She stopped again at the brow of the hill to regain her breath. He stood beside her. She leant on the handle of the pram and smiled.

'Is she still sleeping?' he asked, trying to peer over Theresa's shoulder for a glimpse of their daughter.

'Babies always look like they're having the best sleep in the world,' she said, idly fixing the cover, pulling out one of the corners and tucking it back in again. 'She looks just like her big sister when she was sleeping.'

'She's beautiful.' He let his hand rest on hers, which still clasped the handle of the pram. 'Just like her mother.'

They stepped on to the grass, Tommy welcoming the softer surface underfoot, though it was more difficult to push the pram and he took over from Theresa. They walked slowly past the rows of graves that seemed to form a guard of honour on ether side of them. He caught snatches of names, dates of birth or death, causes of death or who had been a husband, wife, daughter or son. None of this information he kept in his head. About three-quarters of the way along, they came to a small, white marble headstone. Stepping up to the side of it, Theresa slowly knelt down on the damp ground. Her fingertips gently caressed the name at the top of the headstone.

'KATHLEEN DELANEY

Her eyes closed as her head rocked back and forth like she was praying, or maybe just remembering. He knelt down beside her and looked at the headstone as well. She was only five-years-old. That's what he was reminded of. He stared down at the small grass mound and tried to comprehend that she was under there. Kathleen. It was a strange thought. He pictured her face, closing his eyes to get a better image, but it was starting to fray round the edges, and he was worried that, one day, he wouldn't remember anything. He looked again at the words on the headstone, and hoped that wouldn't be the case.

At first, after their daughter had been born, he didn't think it was a good idea to bring her here.

'A graveyard is no place for a baby,' he'd said.

'I want to introduce her to her sister.'

'But a graveyard, Theresa? It doesn't seem right.'

'You don't have to come if you don't want to,' she said, 'but Mary-Kate and I are going.'

He knew that he wouldn't able to persuade her to change her mind, and though he hadn't gone too often before, now he could hardly bear to let the two of them out his sight. He knew Theresa occasionally visited when he was out at work but he sensed that she preferred it too when they all came together, as a family. He had a proper job now, working with a firm of road builders who were based in Lower Manhattan, but whose trucks and workers spread out across the island and beyond. It was hard, and there were occasions when he thought about doing something else for an easier life, but he'd made a conscious decision to leave all that behind him, and he had to stick by that.

He also knew Theresa was much happier that he'd turned his back on his previous life. He had to try and make her happy. He'd resolved to do that, and he now had Mary-Kate to consider as well. He wasn't bothered for even a second when the midwife had come into the kitchen to tell him that it was a girl. It was his baby. Their baby. That's all that mattered.

There was a knock on the door. Theresa looked up and then over at Tommy. It was a sound that was still synonymous with sadness or danger. He stood up, smiling, and handed Mary-Kate to her. The baby was sleeping, and she barely stirred when transferred from father to mother. He kissed the top of her head gently, and then did the same with Theresa.

'It's fine. It's someone to see me. I'll just be a minute.'

'You said that before.'

'I promise.'

He kissed her again, this time on the lips, smiling as he sensed Joseph's eyes watching him. He ruffled the boy's hair as he walked past him and headed out to into the hall as Theresa sat back down with a sigh, and he could hear her talking softly to their daughter as he reached the door. When he opened it, there was no-one there and he stepped out on to the landing, automatically glancing to his right. Just like before, there was a man lurking in the shadows. It must offer a natural protection and instinctively these men sought it out.

'Mister Delaney?' the man said, stepping forward and walking up the stairs until they stood face to face.

'Do you know what it is I want?' Tommy asked.

'Yes.'

'And can you do it?'

'That's why I'm here.'

Tommy nodded. He slipped his hand into his shirt and

pulled out the bag of money that had been lying under the mattress for so long now. It was Paolo Monti who had given it to him all those months ago, nearly a year now, in fact, and he was glad to be rid of it. The man took the money and immediately slipped it into his jacket pocket.

'Are you not going to count it?'

'I know it's all there, Mister Delaney.'

Tommy took out a sheet of paper from his pocket and unfolded it. He handed it over as well. It was a pencil drawing, one of the pictures Joseph had done of Angelo. It was the only one the boy had kept.

'That's him,' he said. 'That's the man you've to . . .' He let the sentence hang in the air. They both knew what was being agreed. There was no need to spell it out. Jimmy would have explained it to the man beforehand. Tommy knew Jimmy still felt guilty about what had happened with Gorevin. He had agreed to help. More than that, he had offered, and this was one secret Jimmy wasn't going to share with anyone. Angelo had been released, just as Dywer had predicted, but Bill still never knew that Tommy had Angelo's address. Information is power, the gang boss had once told him. He was right, Tommy thought with a smile.

'The address is on the back,' Tommy said.

The man studied the image. The address was the one that Joseph had given.

'You need to destroy that,' he said, nodding towards the drawing.

The man took out a lighter and held the flame to the paper. It instantly caught fire, and the flame raced across the sheet, which quickly turned black and shrivelled up. The man let it go, and the ashes floated to the ground. He tapped the side of his head and Tommy nodded. The man turned and walked down the stairs. Tommy stared at the fragments of paper for a few seconds before kicking at them, scattering them once more. He stepped back inside and closed the door. Theresa would start to worry if he was away for too long. He heard a cry. Mary-Kate was awake. The sound made him smile. It always made him smile.